CYBER
WARRIOR

Also by M. G. Harris

The Joshua Files series

Invisible City .

Ice Shock

Zero Moment

Dark Parallel

Apocalypse Moon

The Descendant Code

The Mind Game: Volume One

The Mind Game

False Flag

CYBER
WARRIOR

M. G. HARRIS

First published in 2025 by Darkwater Books

An imprint of Harris Oxford Limited.
6-7 Citibase, New Barclay House, 234 Botley Road,
Oxford, England, OX2 0HP

ISBN 978-1-909072-67-1

www.themgharris.com

To my husband David, with love and grateful thanks for so many wonderful years together.

ONE

VACATION

We needed a vacation.

It'd been over a month since me and Kenzie zipped off to Mexico on an unauthorized search for our missing school buddy from way back when. Kenzie's moms, Bobbie and Zara, had managed to remain relatively chill, at first. But then things escalated.

When I say 'things,' I'm referring to some *light* geopolitical dabbling, or put another way, 'espionage.' Parents don't generally have to stand by while their kids get recruited-slash-blackmailed into doing shenanigans for the intelligence services. Bobbie and Zara took it roughly as well as could be expected, given what happened in Alaska, where Kenzie and I came close to drowning in a sinking yacht. About that, they were not 'chill.'

The Alaska operation happened shortly after we'd been living for weeks under the eye of CIA, moving from a bucolic safe house in the country, where my late guardian, Olga, had sent us via posthumous instructions, to another place in Bethesda. The second move wasn't on Olga's advice, posthumous or otherwise, but on the orders of CIA 'Targeting Officer' Margo Daniels.

My little investigative podcast, *What Happened to the Santiagos*? had propelled me, my best friend-slash-adoptive brother Kenzie and then by default, also his two moms, into a shadow world of spies and geopolitical machinations. Six weeks ago, we'd been blissfully ignorant.

I can't claim that any of us were particularly thrilled with this development. It simply wouldn't be true. On the other hand, something was beginning to happen to me that would take me a while longer to understand. I might not have loved our new, secret lives for us, but I'd already begun to get used to it. 'Used to it' being a euphemism for 'addicted to,' obviously.

There is no adrenaline rush I know of that's on a par with coming close to your own death and escaping.

People with superior physical coordination than mine probably learn this younger than I did – they might go skiing or snowboarding, climbing or even one of the more extreme sports. I'd never tried any of those. Partly because my parents – two staid accountants, or so I thought – weren't the type to do any of those fun activities. Their idea of a vacation was to drive to a national park, camp in a tent and hike through nature, with a few days in a city on the way home, days spent exploring museums, coffee shops and 'antiquing.'

Kenzie was significantly luckier: his moms lived for adrenaline. Zara was raised on a cattle ranch in Chile, loved horseback riding and hunting. Bobbie grew up in Denver, Colorado and spent winter weekends on the slopes. The winter before I blew up our lives by searching for Maxim Santiago, they'd taken me skiing for the first time. From the first day, I'd seen how little my upbringing had prepared me for integrating into such a sporty family. Kenzie took his ability to ride horses and ski for granted, until he saw what a klutz like me had to go through each time we did those things. I didn't like to hold them back, that's the truth, but it couldn't be helped.

When Bobbie proposed something entirely different for our vacation, I guessed she had in mind a memory of my bruised pride and exhaustion during previous vacations, when they'd tried in vain to get me up to speed with their favorite sports. She could already predict my reaction. *Yeah, no.*

"It has to be a real vacation," she said, with a careful glance at me. "I don't care if the CIA want to follow us. Nothing we can do about it, anyway. But we're not staying in the city for the whole summer. There's simply no way."

Scuba diving was my idea. Zara and Bobbie were a little miffed about not being able to go overseas, but they soon enough warmed to my suggestion. My thinking was – none of us had ever tried it, so we'd be on the same level. We'd take a course over the two weeks prior to leaving, getting ourselves the basic certification in a local swimming pool. Then we'd meander over to Pennsylvania passing through a couple of well-loved watering holes and ending up at 'Lake Hydra.' All three were springwater-filled quarries that'd been turned into scuba diving destinations complete with submerged cars, bicycles and even an old school bus to give divers something to explore. An activity-packed vacation with minimal driving, maximum variety, no airports: perfect.

Even Margo Daniels gave us an 'official' blessing, although I thought I'd detected the faintest hint of a sharp intake of breath at the mention of Pennsylvania. It wasn't too long before I figured out why. That wily lady spy was already one step ahead of me and I didn't even know it.

Why scuba diving? It's possible that subconsciously, I longed once again to dally on the thin line between life and death in water. I didn't examine it all that closely at the time, it just felt like something cool we could all try that wouldn't put me at a giant disadvantage compared to Kenzie and his moms. Other than that, there was nature and all. Outdoor cookin' and campfire songs, just like my own folks used to enjoy before they got themselves banged up in maximum security prison after laundering money for international cartels and whatnot.

Just kidding. Neither of my parents was serving their time in a maximum-security prison. If I'd ever visited them, maybe this image wouldn't have persisted in my thoughts. But I really hadn't been able to get myself there. *Mama* and *Papa* were arrested two years ago. All their rich clients had scrambled, the instant that word got out they were turning state witnesses, leaving no-one to pay my parents' bail. Even had just *one* of those clients been the generous type, which they were not. My folks had been in federal prison, ever since. My mom was in Martha Stewart's 'alma mater,' Federal Prison Camp Alderson down in West Virginia, my dad was in Allenwood Low, Pennsylvania.

Which, almost certainly, is what gave pause to Margo Daniels, when she heard me mention our planned trip to Pennsylvania, because Allenwood is a little over two hours' drive from Lake Hydra. Anywho, I'm giving Daniels credit for extrapolating my thoughts, because when I first suggested the scuba thing, almost nothing was farther from my mind than dropping in on Papa. Yet, by the time we set off, I'd persuaded Bobbie and Zara to take a significant detour on our way back from the flooded quarry, where we became kind of *actually good* at scuba diving.

It's undeniable that the four of, me, Kenzie and his moms, had suffered a major disruption to our lives, when we became the focus of unwanted attention from Third Russian Empire foreign intelligence operatives known as Chekists. It's why CIA moved us to their safe house in a nearby state Bethesda, Maryland, banned us from our old haunts around D.C. and put a tail on us wherever we went. I got it – they knew we could any minute be approached by Chekists. The official line was that CIA were watching out for us. But given the way our Alaska operation ended, I have a sneaky feeling it had more to do with Margo Daniels being worried that we'd flip or get flipped, and end up working against CIA.

Bobbie was enjoying a long summer vacation from teaching and Zara generally worked from home, giving online therapy to clients all over the US. They could handle a few weeks or even months in another location than their home. For me and Kenzie however, the longer this went on, the more our entire futures were on hold.

"College is out for this year," Daniels had rather imperiously informed us, during our de-briefing after the Alaska fiasco. She basically ordered us to defer the places we'd accepted, mine at Georgetown and his at Carnegie-Mellon. "Maybe next year," she'd conceded. And then promptly refused to discuss specifics.

All this to say that from the start of July, Kenzie and I had no fixed plans for the following twelve months. It was a strange sensation, the first time in my life that I'd had nothing to do and no firm idea of when I'd be needed to be anywhere or do anything in particular.

Kenzie barely missed a beat, he dived back into

cyber-space. It was where he'd planned on spending his college years, anyway, studying cyber security. "Maybe I'll wear a 'black hat' awhile," he'd quipped. "Try my hand at being a freelance 'cyber warrior.'"

I figured it was all talk. "Cyber warrior, you? Good luck with that, right under CIA's nose."

Officer Daniels probably wouldn't even stop him. If he erred, all the more *kompromat* to use against Kenzie for the future. When it came to giving us enough rope to hang ourselves, she was very much pro.

We knew this, she knew that we knew, yet even so, Kenzie thought about risking it. The lad was turning out to be even more reckless than I'd have guessed.

But then, maybe we both were.

TAPACHULA DEMANDS TIME

There'd been a lot for Kenzie and me to discuss, after we'd returned from Cuba, where we'd helped our old pal, Maxim Santiago, to liberate twenty-some kids and teenagers from a remote camp owned by the Krylov Foundation. After an exciting kerfuffle, spiriting me and Kenzie's family out of the Falls Church house and into Olga's safe house, he and I had enjoyed lazy days in the country, some of which time he'd deigned to spend with me and not on his computer. Since that Cuban adventure, we'd talked it over; what we thought about Maxim, whether he'd changed since our childhood days and if so, how; about Atlanta Camaguey, the lithe, friendly and subtly charismatic, non-binary 16-year-old who'd joined Maxim in Mexico.

But returning from the 'false flag' operation in Alaska, that was different. We'd come close to dying, watched teenagers around us disappear into the ocean depths and finally, seen the aftermath of a darker side of our telepathic friend, the so-called 'unicorns' or 'two-dubs.' Oh yeah, we'd witnessed up close, the deadly powers of a Generation 6 telepath.

"We first saw it when Maxim made those helo pilots crash, in Cuba," Kenzie reminded me. "We just didn't know it at the time."

When Maxim's younger brother, Sacha Montecristo,

had used the advanced telepathic powers that first appeared in the sixth generation of telepaths, it'd been more obvious to us. No way to deny it to ourselves, after that. Death had been the result; violent, self-inflicted death and derangement. For Sacha, whose mind had unleashed the chaos, there'd been damage, too. For all I knew, the boy would never recover.

There was a hard edge to Maxim, a determined ruthlessness. When he'd made those pilots crash into each other, crash and burn, I'd seen little sign of remorse. Towards the end of our brief time with Maxim, I came to recognize this about him, but also to understand that it'd been there from the start.

I wouldn't have guessed the same might be true for Sacha. He'd struck me as a gentle person, someone used to *not* getting his way and living with it, somehow. Maybe I'd gotten him all wrong, but the despair in his entire body, when he saw what his power had done to two Chekists, had seemed genuine.

It's easy to reduce the two brothers to 'Cain' and 'Abel.' We tried to resist the draw of the obvious. But as our conversations progressed in the days that followed, Kenzie and I settled somewhere on that continuum. Maxim was a natural leader with the ability to rally people to his cause and no sign of reluctance to go all the way. Sacha, however, was something else. A reluctant leader, perhaps. But maybe just as capable as his brother.

With Atlanta, we were on even less solid ground. The Atlas group had rescued Atlanta from Cuba, were paying for their education. Atlanta claimed to have been faking any support for Maxim, argued convincingly that their presence and action in the Cuba operation were part of their undercover role on behalf of Atlas.

"I don't buy it," I admitted to Kenzie. "I think Atlanta's closer to Maxim than they let on."

"But they're so convincing," he mused.

"In both roles, though. As Maxim's friend *and* as Sacha's."

Atlanta was a puzzle, we concluded, and left it there, for now.

Despite hours of conversation covering Maxim and Sacha, however, we'd not yet touched on the sordid topic of any feelings I might have for Maxim, nor on the confession Kenzie had made when he'd believed himself on the point of death, when he'd told me he 'loved' me.

Do confessions *in extremis* count? Some might say it's easier to believe people when they think they're uttering some final words. Me? I wasn't so sure. Those hours on a sinking yacht and then clinging onto a life raft with cold death just inches away, had changed something fundamental about my brain. My thoughts seemed literally to flow differently, now. Everything seemed to be routed via the person who'd been on that raft, like I was seeking her opinion on everything.

Would this be how you'd have chosen to spend your future, if you'd have been given the option then?

If the same thing had happened to the boy who'd said all those things to me, on an upturned raft in a storm, in the middle of the Bering Sea, then maybe the Kenzie who was here today, let's call him 'Marc,' maybe *Marc* didn't feel the same way?

Days went by with Marc not saying anything about those feelings or anything close to the topic, making zero reference to what he'd said, not even when we talked about Maxim, who he'd accused me of wanting instead of him. The more time went by, the more I wondered. Had Marc Mackenzie left behind those feelings, along with our almost-deaths, off the coast of Siberia?

As for my own thoughts on the matter? Difficult to say, at this point. Nothing was firm in my mind. Even something as concrete as my life goal of being an investigative journalist or something similar, maybe going pro with the podcast, was all up in the air. Everything about my future had been derailed. I existed in a state of uncertainty, like Schrodinger's cat, or do I mean Heisenberg's particle?

And it wasn't just me. While the Czar's 'Mind Game' waged behind the scenes, flipping governments and democracies around the world, a darker future was growing ever more likely. I wanted to believe that Maxim, Sacha and the other telepaths could help us fight against all of that, but sometimes it felt like I'd seen enough to wonder – maybe the telepaths were the greater danger?

Exploring the clear blue depths of those water parks, Guppy Gulch, Hyde's Quarry and Lake Hydra, I found a way to push all the existential angst into the background. From my very first dive, I sensed the terror of the watery depths receding, replaced by stillness of aquatic life. Plump koi carp and other fish had little fear of the divers, swimming alongside us as we floated above abandoned buses, wrecked mining equipment and piles of slate. There was serenity and peace. It seemed miles removed from the horrors of the Bering Sea, cold and yawning, ready to swallow Kenzie, me and all those others, whole.

In between longer diving sessions each day we cooked sausages, chicken breasts and tuna steaks on the barbecue, ate potato chips and ice cream by the kilo and occasionally waved discretely to whoever we'd identified as our CIA shadow, usually some conspicuously inactive visitor who did little more than hang around in the parking lot or by the water's edge, pretending to watch birds through binoculars. Each day, I felt my thoughts and feelings, my hopes and fears, untangle just a little more.

After a week of this, I was ready to talk to Kenzie honestly about him, me and Maxim. But then I made the mistake of checking Telegram, hashtag 'tapachula,' and my curiosity kicked in, again.

The day we'd left Alaska, I'd seen a new comment on my podcast. It seemed to be from Maxim.

This looks interesting. I may have something for you. The Dream Thief.

Ever since, I'd been checking a few Telegram channels that I guessed he might be posting on. There'd been nothing, but then again, I wasn't exactly sure what to expect.

On the seventh day of our scuba-diving trip, I saw a message in the 'mythic mexico' group that gave off Jaguar-vibes. It wasn't signed 'The Dream Thief' exactly, but the initials were there, as well as #tapachula.

`Find yourself at #Tapachula. It is seriously underrated. Sometimes you have to visit with family. Even if it's been a while, even when they've wronged you. You only get one mom, one dad. It's time to make that visit. Tapachula Demands Time!`

THREE

IGNORE THE BRAT

Kenzie was skeptical at first. "Tapachula Demands Time?"

"TDT. The Dream Thief."

His eyebrows lifted by a squinch. "You think? Max doesn't do 'subtle.' When he wants you to do something, he makes it pretty clear. Remember how he'd text us about all those extra rehearsals, back when we were kids? It wasn't exactly 'might be an idea to practice a bit today,' was it? More like, 'get your ass to rehearsal right now, or imma gonna call you every five minutes until you do.'"

I had to give Kenzie that. Maxim's summons to the practice room had been as blunt as they were frequent. There wasn't much sign he'd changed in the intervening years, either. Anyhow, I stuck to my guns.

"TDT in any form *at all,* together with hashtag 'tapachula,' that's a message. Maxim knew we were being watched. He had to assume our phones might be hacked, too."

Kenzie gave a grudging shrug. "Your phone already was hacked. But not by Chekists."

"CIA, Cheka; Maxim didn't want either to know what he said to me. Posting a comment on the podcast, that's public. He knows that. So, he can't send anything sensitive there – but he did tell me to expect something soon. I've been watching all the Mexico channels. There's been exactly four mentions of #tapachula. This is the only one that's not about tourism."

"*Find yourself at hashtag Tapachula. It is seriously underrated.*" Sounds pretty touristy."

"The rest of the message, though."

Kenzie scanned it once more. "Visit with family? You don't have family there."

I shook my head. "It's not about seeing them in Mexico. It's about visiting my mom and dad. At least, I think it is. Look, it's a dumb message. Makes no sense to anyone but me."

"It's dumb," he agreed. "Not gonna argue with that. Question is, why would Maxim want you to visit your mom or dad?"

Slowly, I nodded. "That is the question. Do you think your moms would be willing to take the long way home? The long way, via Allenwood Low?"

Blinking a couple of times, Kenzie cottoned on. "Your dad is in Allenwood Low. Wouldn't you rather see your mom?"

"I dunno, maybe? But she's not as nearby."

An air of suspicion crept over him as Kenzie considered this. "So, when you suggested this trip, did you already have this all planned out?"

"What? No!"

His eyes narrowed. "You sure? Seems like something you'd do."

"Says the guy who hid his involvement in a scheme to blow up a pipeline from us all, for months."

There was a brief silence, then he nodded. "Well, you got me there."

"Maybe I don't mind the accusation," I said, a tad mollified. "For what it's worth, I think something like it might have occurred to Madge."

"'Madge,' is it, now?" He stroked his chin, approvingly. "I like that, for us. Less scary than 'Targeting Officer Daniels,' that's for sure. Not that we should ever stop being afraid of her. She's *objectively* scary."

"Margo Daniels? She's just your regular, middle-aged auntie."

He arched an eyebrow. "If my auntie worked for CIA, I'd expect better treatment. Like, less blackmail, cooler assignments and way, way better training."

From here, Kenzie and I segued into yet another iteration of a conversation we'd begun to have almost daily, namely, how cracked it was that we'd been expected to do so much for CIA, on so little training. Sacha and Atlanta hadn't seemed to find the expectations all that demanding. But then again, they'd been trained in some kind of tradecraft by the people who ran the Atlas group, telepaths descended from those who'd never been enslaved first by the Soviet Union's Kremlin and then by General Krylov.

The Atlas group had helped a tiny handful of 'unicorns' from the Krylov Foundation to escape Cuba, including Sacha and Atlanta. In return, I had the impression that Sacha and Atlanta now worked for them. The 'work' consisted, so far as I'd seen, in some form of spying. They'd been destined to be sold into slavery, controlled by intelligence services in despotic regimes around the world. It struck me as ironic and also a little sad that they'd ended up doing the same kind of work, even if it was for Aleks Rubenovich Atlas, the group's leader.

Kenzie's sidebar didn't last too long, however. Worry furrowed his brow the instant our conversation lulled. It was like I could visually register his thoughts returning to the possibility that Maxim had reached out to me in code. While I arranged our picnic table at the waterside, he did nothing but watch, shoulders and fingers tensing up more with every passing minute. Finally, once I'd set out plates of tuna sandwiches, tortilla chips and tomato salad, he looked about ready to launch.

I pretended not to notice, picked up a sandwich and took a bite, all the while gazing into the middle of the lake. Two hours earlier, we'd dived down to meander among the sunken, rusted school bus that lay on the bottom of the old shale pit, or whatever was here before they flooded it to make a lake. Something about his growing indignation warned me that the peace we'd found in that silent palace of clear blue water was about to head off into the sunset.

"Why are you so set on seeing that guy again?" Kenzie began, belligerent from the outset. "You heard what Sacha said about his own brother. And Atlanta dropped a couple salty words about 'Jaguar,' too."

He waited for me to reply, eyebrows knitting together as he watched me compose my thoughts. I took my time with it, too. There were just so many different ways I could have responded. The ways that would hurt him, the ways that would console him and everything in between.

Instead, I went with another question. "What do *you* think we should do about Maxim? Ignore him?"

Emphatically, Kenzie nodded. He picked up a sandwich and took a giant bite. "Uh huh," he managed to reply between gulps of tuna and bread. "Sounds like a *tremendous* plan. Ignore the brat. What's he gonna do, think bad thoughts at us?"

I could feel my jaw loosening as I watched righteous indignation work its way through him. "Wow," I said, my voice low. "You sure changed your tune. When we were out there in Cuba, you were just about falling over yourself trying to prove how useful you could be to him. *Me, Maxim, me! Let me do the EMP thing.*" I narrowed my eyes, only semi-serious. "Such a little pick-me boy. And you're mad at *me* for showing just a little bit of interest in a message telling me to visit my g-d parents in literal prison?"

The indignation vanished, replaced at once with the hard flash of genuine anger. He tossed some chips and tomatoes on his plate, added two sandwiches and then rose to his feet. For a second there, it seemed like he was maybe going to call be the 'b' word or even worse, but whatever insult or curse he was brewing, it stayed inside. With a baleful glare, he turned and left.

I watched him walk away. He'd seemed about to perch on a table not far away, but thought better of it and kept going until he'd put the ice-cream hut between us.

On a table nearby, his two moms had been watching with evident interest. I turned slightly to them, wondering if they'd use the moment to try to lecture me. But all they did was to simper, perfectly poised on the fence between sympathy and accusation, then return to their own private conversation.

All right. So Kenzie didn't like the idea of me being in contact with Maxim. Which made sense, if what he'd told me just weeks ago, about being in love with me, was true. I stared at the tomato slices, studied their intricate structure and the plump, juicy coating of each seed.

What did it say about me that I couldn't stop myself from wanting it to be a message from Maxim, that more than anything else right now, I wanted to respond?

PRISON VISIT

Bobbie and Zara were fully on-board with driving the extra few hours so that I could visit my dad in prison. They wanted me to go even further: *why only him, why not hang out with your mom, too?* It was like a dam breaking, when they began to talk. Evidently they'd been in touch with Cristabel and Rogelio, who were both 'heartbroken' that I'd not been to see them even though they 'understood.'

Well, I could handle sympathy from Kenzie's moms on behalf of my parents. Bobbie and Zara were parents too, it made sense they'd at least partly identify with them. What was harder to take was their rationale, delivered with flinty-eyed directness by Bobbie and doe-eyed compassion by Zara.

"After all, they're not the only ones who've been happy to cooperate with drug dealers, are they?"

Not to get picky, but my parents had laundered money for businesses that turned out to be owned by Russian oligarchs, none of whom were particularly known to be drug dealers, even though one or two were being investigated for connections to international crime cartels. They'd been additionally threatened with charges under the Espionage Act, none of which had been proven, and offered a plea deal. Eight years was on the steep side for money laundering, but they took it anyway. Now people acted like they'd been found guilty of treachery, but they had not.

Frankly, it was disappointing to hear Bobbie and Zara repeat some of the even worse, unproven allegations. Their implication was obvious and frankly, I didn't care for it. By helping Maxim to rescue children and teenagers from a remote prison camp where they were being prepared to be sold into slavery, I was indirectly 'co-operating' with a 'drug dealer,' just like my parents.

Obviously, I pushed back. "Maxim isn't a drug dealer; he was just house-sitting for one."

"If you believe that then I'm worried for you," Zara said.

"Be smarter," Bobbie added. "You've got great instincts for taking care of people. Maxim may have used that to take advantage of you and Marc."

I flashed a glance towards Kenzie, who lurked beside the water's edge, just within earshot. He wouldn't meet my eye.

Zara pressed me further. "Is it so hard to believe Maxim's done more than house-sitting for this Carillo family? They've helped him out quite a bit, isn't that what you told us? For instance, where did all those kids go in Cuba, after you'd gotten them out of the camp? Didn't the Carillos help out there?"

"Atlanta told us something like that," I admitted. "It wasn't part of his plan, but we had a bunch of Cuban military helicopters on our tail, so he changed things up. And so what if the Carillos helped? Why shouldn't they? Cuba is full of people who hate Czar Ilyin. Most of the population, I'd guess. Almost anyone who isn't pro-Kremlin should be glad to help the K-Foundation kids stay out of the Czar's oily hands."

Bobbie shook her head, disappointed. "Tell me

you're not that naïve, Roni, please. The Carillo family are drug dealers, that's their business. All their assets are likely to be part of it. Maxim mightn't be directly involved but he's benefiting from their business, one way or another."

From over by the lake, Kenzie called out, mildly, "Robin Hood stole from the rich to help the poor. Cocaine is a rich-people drug and the only product the Carillos sling is pure Colombian blow. Just saying."

That quip earned him a wry grin from me. Mostly, I resented Bobbie's assumption that I'd not thought of this. Of course I had. Yes, dealing with the Carillos was sketchy as heck. Maxim and the other two-way telepaths, or 'two-dubs,' were struggling to survive in a hostile environment. If a drug dealer threw them a life-line, how was that in any way analogous to my college-educated parents agreeing to launder money for Russian oligarchs, in return for cold hard cash?

"If you go visit your parents, maybe they'd have an answer to that question," Zara suggested, gently. "Either way, you should see them, Roni. It's been too long."

I raised my eyes to Bobbie and Zara in turn. This felt a bit rich, given their previous statements about 'drug dealers.' If my parents hadn't taken the plea deal, maybe they could have avoided this kind of misinformation? At this point, any hope that Kenzie's moms might adopt me one day were looking optimistic, at best.

Anyway, two mornings later Bobbie drove us all to Allenwood, where my dad, Rogelio, was a 'guest' at the low security men's prison. The reality of what I'd been avoiding these past two years crept up on me, even before we'd turned into the parking lot.

"Mister CIA is still with us," commented Kenzie,

watching the white Toyota Camry via the passenger seat mirror. It had been a hundred yards behind us all the way from Lake Hydra. Not very subtle. As I stepped out of Bobbie's car I gave the driver, an African American man with a clean-shaven head who looked to be in his forties, a cheeky wave. He stared right back at me and after a second, tipped his head, a grudging acknowledgement.

"Least he can't follow me inside," I said. He wouldn't be able to get his listening equipment close enough to snoop on me with my dad, either. "Privacy at last!"

Weeks ago, when we'd discovered that our phones had been hacked, Kenzie and I had devised a super-sophisticated method of secure communication – we'd write notes to each other on paper, taking turns with the pencil, then we'd destroy the paper. Sacha had begun to teach me a private sign language, but events had overtaken us. It was still a great idea, but Kenzie and I hadn't gotten around to learning more than a dozen words, yet. That was a mistake, on our part.

As I stepped out of the car, the acrid scent of concrete and disinfectant assaulted my senses. If despair has a smell, if putting your life on hold while you wither away stinks of anything, that's its scent. The towering walls of the prison loomed overhead, casting a shadow over everything within its grasp. Even the air around the prison seemed tainted with the weight of regret.

The buildings were bleak, gray structures devoid of any semblance of life or warmth. They seemed to suck the color out of everything around them, as if an evil wizard had waved a wand and turned everything in sight into a lifeless landscape. A place of irrelevant dreams, where hope came to die.

I fought to hold back the wave of dread that washed over me as I made my way towards the entrance. Guilt gnawed at my insides, a steady reminder of my failure to visit sooner. All those moments lost, those conversations we'd never had, because of my anger. And yet still, I balked at the imminent meeting with my father.

As I approached the security checkpoint, carefully I watched the faces of the other visitors, each one wearing the same expression of resignation and sadness. We were all prisoners in our own way, trapped by circumstances and bound by duty. Maybe none of us truly belonged here.

The guard at the checkpoint eyed me with suspicion as I handed over my ID, his gaze lingering a moment longer than necessary. Bobbie had volunteered to be the designated adult who accompanied me, and I knew things were bad when she suddenly took my hand in hers, squeezing warmth into our connection until I looked at her. I resisted the urge to roll my eyes and instead opted for a tight-lipped smile. Bobbie saw right through it. "It's okay, I'm here," she whispered.

Finally, we were granted entry and made our way through the maze of corridors towards the visiting area. With each step, I felt a little heavier, a tad guiltier. Anyhow, I pulled free of Bobbie and pushed forward, driven by a sense of obligation that could no longer be ignored.

Leaving her several paces behind, I entered the visiting room. I couldn't help but feel a pang of sadness at the sight of Papa sitting alone at a table in the corner. His eyes lit up when he saw me. I saw at once that for him joy was something long forgotten. The look on his face, the blend of sorrow and euphoria at seeing me for the first time in two years, tugged deep inside me at a place I'd believed unreachable. My throat clenched around a sob.

FIVE

REUNION, PART 1

When you see prison visits on TV and the guards yell 'no touching?' Yeah, that's nonsense. Maybe in higher security places, anyway, not in the kind of place where they put away accountants who cook the books. My dad didn't let go of my hand the entire time we were talking, and his eyes never stopped shining with tears.

Perched on the edge of his chair, my father, Rogelio, appeared smaller than his six-foot frame suggested, his slim frame disappearing within the ill-fitting prison uniform. Familiar, black-rimmed glasses perched on his nose, but the frames looked greasy. Despite such a diminished appearance, there was dignity in the way he carried himself, a reminder that even within the confines of the prison walls, his mind remained free. Yet, beneath the facade of composure, lingered a melancholy that seemed to seep into every fiber of his being, a silent testament to the toll that incarceration had taken on his spirit.

"Thank God you came, thank God," he kept saying, gently massaging my hand with his. He raised it to his lips and planted a kiss, murmuring a prayer. "*Que bendición*" – 'what a blessing.' Then leaning forward he whispered, "They cannot listen in, here. Keep your voice very quiet and we can talk, really talk."

I pulled back a little, confused as I looked into his eyes. "They...?"

"*Sia*," he whispered, barely audible. "*La agencia.*"
The Agency.

When he saw that I'd understood, he nodded. "*He* told us. Your old friend. The one you..." Swiftly, his eyes scanned the area behind me. Then, apparently reassured, he continued, "The pianist."

It took me a couple of seconds to catch on. Hearing Maxim referred to as 'the pianist'" was pretty much the last thing I'd expected him to say.

I found my voice. "He...? You've been in contact with him...?"

My dad nodded. When he spoke again his voice was almost inaudible and from this point on, he only spoke in Spanish. "A mutual contact in Venezuela." The barest hint of a grin touched the edges of his mouth. "From what I heard you had quite the adventure. My girl! You make me very proud."

That did it, the tears began to flow. So did the guilt. Why did I stay away from him for so long?

"Shh, shh," he said, soothingly. "It's okay, we understand. You were mad with us. Totally understandable."

I stared at him, unable to talk as tears streamed down my cheeks and the sniffles hit me.

"It's okay. All good now, my girl, all good. We did a lot of things wrong. There's a lot for me to apologize for and I will. But not right now. Right now, apart from seeing you and *this*..." Here he once again brought my hand to his lips and pressed another kiss. "I have a message for you. The pianist wants to see you. Shh, don't react. Laugh. Go on, laugh like I told a hilarious joke."

I forced a laugh, and he grinned widely. "That's it, keep going."

Dialing the laughter down into a chuckle, I leaned closer to listen.

"I'll give you his message, but when I'm done, I need you to say to me, all the things you've been holding back." He met my gaze with silence, then a nod. "Yes. *Those* things. Things your new friends will expect you to say to me. And when you say them, no need to do it quietly."

"Papa," I began, imploringly.

Seeing him again, hearing his voice and witnessing what time and regret had wreaked on his body, in that moment I didn't care why he and my mom had taken the plea deal, why they hadn't put up a fight, why they'd allowed even the worst stories to circulate about them. Even if the most dreadful things turned out to be true, and they'd knowingly abetted agents of the Third Russian Empire, they were *still* my parents. I'd been close to death now; I understood how short life could be: too short not to reconcile with the people who'd cared for me the first fifteen years of my life.

"You'll say all those things," he repeated, steadily. "And I'll deserve to hear them. But first, listen. The pianist is waiting for you." Then he lowered his voice and spoke through gritted teeth, lips hardly moving. "Mocambo." On the table, with his left index finger he spelled out the word so that he didn't need to repeat it. Then he drew a six and whispered, "Tomorrow. Now, get ready to snatch your hand away and get angry. In *English*."

With one final close stare, he slowly leaned back into his chair, loosening his grip on my fingers before with a subtle gesture, barely a nod, he gave the go-ahead.

I slowly withdrew my hand, then raised and landed both fists on the table. Swallowing, I launched into a rant that to be brutally honest, I'd been dreaming about, ever since the shock of my parents' arrest. All the ways they'd lied to me, about working late, about who they knew, about what their clients did, even about the plea deal, an *estupidez* they'd insisted was all about getting a shorter sentence, maybe four years and which had made the final decision – eight years – such a bitter pill to gulp down. It had landed so hard on me; I thought I'd been sucker punched. Never letting me get to know Olga, who they'd chosen to be my guardian. Secrecy and lies that had so badly damaged my ability to trust them, I wasn't even sure if I wanted them to be my parents any longer. I confessed my thoughts about being adopted by Kenzie's moms and felt a rush of adrenaline watching my dad flinch, even though he must have braced himself, even though he'd been the one to encourage the tirade.

"You must never say any of this to your mother," he managed to say in English, chin trembling. "Promise me you never will. She wouldn't be able to take it. She'd never speak to you again."

Blood rushed into my cheeks, and I choked up. Sardonically, I replied in a voice so tight, it was almost a squeak. "Oh, I know that much. With mom, it's all about her. Why do you think I haven't been to see her? I'd say something honest and she'd probably disown me."

To my slight astonishment, Papa didn't correct me. Instead, he shook his head, sadly. "Where d'you think you get that righteous anger, Roni? When you see your mother – and I hope you soon will – you take care what you say to her. Some things can never be taken back."

He tipped his head towards the door and with

unmoving lips murmured, "As good a time to go as any, *no te parece?*"

Papa was right – it struck me as a good idea, too. The guards were studiously avoiding eye contact with us but not good at masking the curiosity I'd piqued in them, by raising my voice to him. I stood up, clumsily pushing back the chair.

"Take some time, *mija*," he said in a normal voice, with a swift sideways glance that confirmed to me that this was yet more play-acting. "I know you're angry. And that's okay. But the truth is that it's been too long. Even if it's to listen to you shouting, I want to see you."

"Not my mother, though, am I right?" I couldn't help but twist the knife a little. Yes, I was kind of a B. Hindsight is everything.

Papa squirmed a little before admitting, "No, not your mother. Better wait until you're calmer than today."

Under the table, I could see his hands making the 'push off' gesture, wafting me in the direction of the door. I pulled back my shoulders and tossed my head – I love a good head toss, when the moment calls for it. "We'll see," I said.

At the sight of his expression then, pride and sorrow in equal amounts, a rush of empathy swept through me and for a second or two, I thought I'd be overwhelmed. But I didn't let him see, I masked the emotion with a curt nod and then head down, I strode toward the exit, pushing past Bobbie as I headed out.

She caught up with me about two minutes later. I didn't ask what she and my dad talked about, but to my mild surprise, I realized that I wasn't worried about any tea-spillage from her. Bobbie knew what was up, she could be trusted to keep her mouth shut when the situation called for it.

Whatever my dad and I had said to each other, only

two pieces of information mattered, two fragments of a message from Maxim that my dad had breathed to me and written with his left hand, not his usual hand for writing, presumably to confuse any snooping cameras.

Mocambo, at six.

SIX

REUNION, PART 2

Mocambo was the name of a Dominican restaurant in Harrisburg, PA. It was the nearest place with that name to the prison and too conveniently on our way back to Bethesda for it not to have been part of someone's plan – that someone being Maxim, I supposed.

Maybe I was too paranoid, but our friendly neighborhood CIA guy wasn't tailing us for the good of his health – we had to assume he was listening in on our conversations. Certainly he rarely let us out of his sight, and with a line of sight you've got the conditions for a parabolic audio snooping. But about thirty minutes after leaving the Allenwood penitentiary, we had a stroke of luck: it began to rain hard. Parabolic microphones are almost useless in rain. So, I took the opportunity to tell Kenzie and his moms the message my dad had conveyed from Maxim aka 'the pianist.'

There were a bunch of questions about how I could know for sure my dad had been referring to Maxim, mostly from Bobbie and Kenzie. Zara had grown reflective and after a few minutes said, "Your parents probably do know the major money laundering operators in Venezuela. I know they took at least two business trips to Caracas, Roni. Your mother mentioned it to me once. So, if Rogelio is citing a contact in Venezuela, that's probably something he knows about."

The question was, why was Maxim dealing with money launderers in Venezuela? I guessed that Bobbie's take on that was similar to mine – it pointed to more crime. Given what my parents were in prison for, I couldn't exactly get uppity about Maxim doing the same thing. Yet, it was an instant, sharp reminder that having anything to do with Max was likely to be dangerous and possibly lead to jail if not worse.

Steadying the wheel, Bobbie listened to us all on the subject before saying, "This place is in Harrisburg?"

"Looks like a café," I confirmed, checking Bobbie's phone. "Caribbean food, bachata and salsa nights, the usual. We could maybe get a hotel room, go do something touristy for Mister CIA's benefit, then go to Mocambo for early dinner. All very normal."

Harrisburg is the Pennsylvania state capital and even though it's a small town, it has some cute bed-and-breakfast-style hotels for the tourists who favor visits to nearby Gettysburg or Pennsylvania Dutch Country. Kenzie's moms, however, picked the Quality Inn. It was nice enough, right next to the river. After a week of scuba diving, I'd have traded either for an afternoon just mooching around in small-town America, but we needed a stronger cover story. So, for the third time in our lives, we went to Gettysburg.

For Bobbie, the roadside pie stands made it worthwhile. When Mr. CIA stopped too, we didn't even bother to pretend not to notice him. If the man wanted to eat an entire peach pie on his own, you better believe we'd be watching him do it. Quietly but firmly, I insisted that we took our pies 'to go' – it had to be believable that we'd be eating dinner around six.

By five-forty we were parking in the lot of

Mocambo. Stepping inside felt like a vibrant escape to the streets of Santo Domingo. Rustic wooden tables and chairs, reminiscent of beachside cafes, adorned the tiled floor, while colorful red-and-blue flags of the Dominican Republic fluttered from the ceiling. The walls were adorned with photographs of iconic Dominican landscapes — from the azure beaches of Punta Cana to the lush greenery of the countryside. The air was alive with the infectious rhythms of merengue and bachata, courtesy of the legendary Juan Luis Guerra. Aromas of savory *mofongo* and zesty *tostones* filled the air.

We took a table with a view of the door, and I positioned myself to watch it. It felt unreal. Was it possible that he'd actually show up here? My heart was pounding a steady drumbeat, and my skin glowed with a light sweat.

I thought: *This is what it does to me, anticipating seeing Max again.*

It took most of my energy to put on an act with Kenzie and his moms, forcing my mouth into casual grins, when I felt nothing like smiling, but instead nodding and making eye contact with whoever was speaking to make it look like I might be remotely interested in anything they were saying. All I heard was 'yadda, yadda, yadda.'

From behind me, a server fanned out four menus and reached in front of me, placing them within reach of my hand. As my index finger and thumb closed around the nearest menu, I heard him whisper close to my ear, "Go to the ladies room."

Instantly, I froze. It was Maxim's voice.

Kenzie hadn't yet glanced up and at that precise moment, Maxim disappeared from view, dodging behind another server who passed by our table right then, carrying a tray of heaped plates. By the time I'd glanced over my shoulder, Maxim was nowhere in sight.

I turned to the others and cleared my throat, uncertainly. "Can you order me a Diet Coke? I'm going to the restroom."

Kenzie and his moms traded friendly smiles, too busy studying their menus to notice anything odd. As I rose to my feet, the door of the café swung open, and Mr. CIA walked in. Before he could catch sight of me, I ducked behind a potted palm and slunk away, past the decorative bar, where a neon green outline of a coconut palm cast its glow onto a flag of the D.R. I found the restrooms and was about to push open the door to the ladies, when I felt a hand grip my forearm and lead me firmly through the door.

This time, I heard his voice in my head. *Keep going, don't turn around, don't look at me. Your shadow is taking a stroll around the restaurant – we both need to get out of sight.*

Two hands pushed me into the middle of three stalls, closed the door on me. I pushed back onto the door, cracking it open enough to see the back of the guy who'd grabbed my arm. He was heading toward the stall nearest to the window. The brief glimpse I caught was enough to identify him – Maxim.

He looked different than how he'd been in Mexico; the shaggy, sun-bleached hair had been buzzed down to a tidy half-inch of light brown hair. It changed his appearance dramatically, made his eyes appear larger and his face more open, innocent and at least two years younger than Maxim's 19 years. Dressed in the Mocambo's signature blue polo, black pants and narrow white apron, from a brief glance not even I would have clocked him as Maxim.

Then I heard his voice inside my head.
Hola Padi! Sit down, try to breathe easy.

I took a few deep steadying breaths.

If you're picking up on any of this, tap lightly three times on the wall nearest to me. Ta-ta, space, ta. like that.

I did as he asked. Just then, the door to the ladies opened.

Make some noise, hum a tune, or something.

Tentatively, I hummed the chorus of the Juan Luis Guerra song that had been playing in the main restaurant.

So – my little brother taught you how to receive a broadcast? Remind me to thank him when we finally catch up.

In his thought, I sensed Maxim's amusement. Mere inches away from the stall doors, Mr. CIA's footsteps padded the restroom for a minute, before turning and exiting.

Let's stay put awhile. Better you don't speak at all. CIA may have planted a bug.

An exasperated groan escaped me, and he chuckled.

Yeah. Sucks that CIA have plastered themselves all over you and Kenzie's family. But if they can keep the Chekists off your back it's probably worth it.

As it dawned on me that I wouldn't be able to get any answers to my many questions, I sighed deeply. Not for the first time, I longed to have two-way telepathy. Being a 'one-dub' was mostly super-frustrating.

To my right, I heard the scrape of something hard sliding on the floor, then spotted a small black phone – a cheap Nokia. My pulse sped up a notch as I picked it up and tried not to factor in the *ick* of touching something that had touched the restroom floor.

A new burner for you. My number is in it. Text only. When you can be sure you're not overheard, let me know. Then I'll call. He paused for a moment. *It's so good to see you again, amiga. Can't wait to be able to hug you.*

I pressed my lips together hard, and trembling, pushed down my overwhelming desire to reply.

SEVEN

BURNER

Maxim's texts began pouring into my burner phone. We told him where we were staying, he caught us up some on his recent movements. He'd been in the USA for eight days, smuggled in by a *coyote* and carrying a fake passport that he couldn't risk using in an airport, in case he was photographed. He'd gotten himself a job bussing tables at Café Mocambo, based on a letter of recommendation from Beto Carillo. He'd gotten messages to my father in prison via the relative of another prisoner – both associates of Carillo. You had to admire the tradecraft – avoiding surveillance was second nature to him.

I don't plan on staying long in USA. CANNOT be seen with you. The only thing I have going for me is that US authorities don't have my face on file. Will leave as soon as we've talked. Meet tomorrow? I'll text details early tomorrow. Sweet dreams.

"All this to meet up with you," marveled Kenzie later that evening, as we settled down to sleep in neighboring beds.

"Hush," I said.

Mr. CIA had long ago ditched the subtlety – now that he'd seen us watching him watching us, he'd become brazen, checking into the same Quality Inn, while we were still in the lobby. It was never about knowing where to find us. When you have the full force of the state behind you, traffic cameras and facial recognition and whatnot, you can locate almost anyone.

Maxim's theory was that Daniels was trying to keep us safe from the Chekists. I had a different theory, though; Daniels wanted eyes on me specifically – in case any of the telepaths tried to reach out.

CIA struck me as pretty dumb, just the same. Obviously we'd figure out other ways to communicate with Maxim. But having Mr. CIA tacked on certainly made it harder. The discipline it took to make *not a single mistake* was a *lot*. From the minute I walked out of the restroom after Maxim, I'd felt a weight of pressure at the base of my throat; words and even thoughts choked back behind a dread of discovery.

We turned out the lights, Kenzie put in Bluetooth earbuds and rolled away from me. I switched my phone to silent and was sliding it under my pillow, when the screen lit up. Another text from Maxim.

Are you alone?
Yes.
You've probably already guessed that I need a favor from you and Kenzie. You do one thing for me, am I right? And now I can't leave you be. (^‿^)
Old style emoji? Nerd. What do you want?
I'm guessing your shadow will be down early to breakfast – he can't risk you getting there first. Can you meet me now?
Now? Already in bed.
I'm outside. There's a side exit. Pretend you're going for a soda. Come right away.
Give me five minutes. Kenzie might be awake.
Okay.

I edged out of the bed and landed both feet silently on the carpeted floor. When I was sure that Kenzie hadn't stirred, I stood up and paced cautiously over to the easy chair beside the window, where I'd discarded joggers and a hoodie. In another minute I'd changed out of my light cotton PJs and into the clothes I'd worn before. I dropped the burner phone into the back pocket of my joggers, pausing when Kenzie's breathing changed slightly. He turned over in bed. Every muscle stilled as for a few seconds, I waited for him to settle, then picked up my sneakers and headed for the door. Very carefully, I opened the door to our hotel room and stepped out. The door closed behind me, pulled back on a spring. Too late, I realized that I'd come out without my key card.

Oh well. Good excuse to stay out awhile.

I headed for the stairwell and hurried downstairs. The fire exit was clearly signposted as being on the floor below the lobby and breakfast room. I kept going all the way until I reached the fire exit. The exit didn't seem to be alarmed, just a regular fire door that locked from the outside. My breathing became rapid, shallow and ragged, my chest trembled from the anticipation of seeing Maxim again. I stopped to take a few more slow breaths. What was going on? I couldn't understand why my body was reacting this way, when I was at best merely curious to see Maxim and find out what was going on.

It's the fear of being discovered. If they catch me with him they'll know it's Maxim, they'll have his image and he'll never be safe in the USA.

Yes, that was probably the reason, I told myself. One more deep breath and I pushed open the door to the outside, cringing momentarily, half-expecting to hear an alarm. But nothing. Relieved, I slipped out of the corridor, onto the sidewalk around the block from the B&B's main entrance.

In my head, I heard his voice. *There you are! I'm in the car.*

A few yards farther along the street, the passenger door of a car swung open. I approached and leaned down to look at the driver. With one hand still on the wheel, Maxim gave me a little wave. Blue lights from the dashboard lit up his face just enough for me to see his grin. I climbed into the car and closed the door. For a moment we just peered at each other in the dim light. As my eyes adjusted, I saw that his chin was now covered with grainy stubble. Without another word, he stretched out both arms and drew me into a hug.

Thank you. Thank you for this.

I pulled back to look into his eyes, but he'd already begun to turn back to the steering wheel. It was disconcerting – I'd forgotten how easily he was able to turn the charm on and off. Now he switched on the car – a small hatchback, probably a rental, judging by the clean-car smell. The car began to move away.

"We're going somewhere?"

"Back to Mocambo." He glanced at me. "The music is louder now, and there's dancing. Harder to listen in on us, if your CIA fella manages to follow."

I pointed at his face. "But they'll see me with Stubble Boy?"

He blinked, steadily. "If they even recognize you, they'll see you with a long-haired guy with a *beard* and a different nose."

I peered at his nose, then prodded it. "Yep, that's quite the schnozz. This what you call 'tradecraft?'"

But he wasn't taking my bait, played it totally straight. "I brought clothes for you too, and a wig. Is that okay? And a fake ID, because it's over twenty-one only, at night."

I withdrew into the car seat, sensing my doubts grow. "You think I can pass for twenty-one?"

Now that he'd found a way to tease me back, he finally grinned. "In the outfit I brought? For sure."

For a few seconds, I just watched him. This felt suddenly a little dangerous, maybe even a thrilling adventure, the intoxicating mixture I'd experienced at the start of our Alaskan operation.

Abruptly, I asked, "What was your brother's camp name?"

Maxim startled, making a left turn. "He never told you?"

"For some reason, no. It didn't come up. What was it?"

"'Blackbird.' Don't ask me why because I have no clue."

"Did you ever see Sacha, as a baby?"

"No. He was born after Masha left with me. Different birth mother than me, obviously."

I hesitated, thinking. "Do you think Sacha was a replacement for you? Another shot at getting a Generation Six kid?"

Maxim was quiet for a moment, concentrating on the traffic, of which there was a surprising amount. We'd hit what passed for the night-life zone of Harrisburg and cars were crawling, searching for street parking near the five or six loud bars in the neighborhood. Mocambo lay a little farther beyond.

"Well, look at you," he murmured, the bare hint of menace in his reply. "All interested in the two-dub breeding program."

"Obviously I'm interested," I snapped back. "I live with a target on my back these days, thanks to the fact I know you, and now Sacha, too.

He gave a heavy sigh, as if disappointed that our

catch-up and his charm offensive had been cut short. "A Generation Six replacement? Could be. They never gave up hope of finding my mother and me, but if they could make Sacha then they probably had more embryos from Masha and our father."

I chuckled, dryly. "Every time I get mixed up with 'Blackbird' or 'Jaguar,' things get crazy."

"I could say the same thing. You and Sacha – vortices of drama."

"Me? I'm just along for the ride."

He chuckled. "Sure, if that's what you need to tell yourself."

"I mean it."

He pulled into a parking place, the neon lights of Mocambo now visible, half a block away. Reaching into the backseat, he lifted a duffel bag and handed it to me, pausing for a second or two before he said, "So... I listened to your podcast. 'La Chica Curiosa'? That's why you're here, that's why this is happening: curiosity. Insatiable curiosity."

I unzipped the duffel and pulled out a garment that had a satiny feel. If it was a dress, it was a short one. With one eyebrow arched, I reached in deeper until I found a pair of high-heeled strappy sandals. Holding up both, I said accusingly, "Really? We're going for 'slutty?'"

"We're going for 'twenty-one,'" he reminded me. "And you can still say 'no.'"

I clutched the dress and heels to my chest. "Turn down an invitation to go dancing in a bar? Now that wouldn't be very curious of me, would it?"

EIGHT

A FAVOR

Whilst I changed my outfit in the back seat of the rental car, Maxim completed his own disguise with a long-haired wig and baseball cap. Scraping myself out of the car, I glanced down at legs I hadn't seen this unclothed since Halloween two years ago, when I'd gone along with a crew that went out as slutty cat-girls. No judging, now – people do all kinds of silly when they're fifteen.

I rearranged my stance the way you have to when you wear high heels. Maxim averted his gaze, pretending to study the parking sign. It was awkward. I thought about making some snarky comment. He'd probably see right through it. Then again, that would have meant a degree of interest in what I was thinking, which would be unlike him. Was I conflating Max with his brother Sacha, who had never quite convinced me of his inability to read minds? Sacha had struck me as a lot more empathetic – enough to sometimes give the impression he could read my thoughts, at least.

More likely, Maxim's thoughts were elsewhere – already moving toward whatever it was he wanted to accomplish tonight. *A favor from me and Kenzie*, I reminded myself. But there was something else, too. He could have asked for a favor inside the car and let me get back to my bed without risking any suspicion.

Watching him tuck a tight-fitting, plain black T-shirt into his black jeans, before checking his wig and baseball cap in the rearview mirror, I sensed nervousness. Whatever his experience of life in Cuba and Mexico, this was the USA, entirely new territory for him. Even Maxim could be out of his depth.

He locked the car with the flick of a remote, then offered me a hand. I took it, grateful for the help to balance those idiotic heels. Frankly, we probably looked ridiculous.

"Can you even dance" I muttered, as strains of loud bachata music reached us. Dancing wasn't my thing, although Zara and Bobbie were obsessed by it and had taught Kenzie and me the basics of most tropical dances. We could go through the motions and not a lot more, let's leave it at that.

Maxim's grip on my hand tightened. "I'm Cuban," he replied, archly, speaking Spanish. "Of course I can dance."

He could, too. No sooner than we were inside the Mocambo – café by day, nightclub by night – he was swinging me around into a gentle hold, his right hand resting lightly at the base of my spine, his left arm firm as he led me into a couple of turns. The tension between us lifted away immediately, both of us smiling widely and making eye contact. If I'd been more relaxed, I know I'd have enjoyed the sensation of being in his arms. Annoyingly though, all I remember is an over-riding urge not to act like a klutz.

Very nice, he said, telepathically. *You go dancing with Kenzie?*

I laughed. "With Kenzie? Only at his moms' parties."

The music changed; a driving beat emerged as the

music switched to reggaeton. Abruptly, he released me, stopped dancing. *We need to talk.*

"You seem to be doing just fine."

A look of frustration crossed his face, and it struck me that he probably couldn't hear me over the music. We'd only be able to talk if we could dance closely and he didn't seem to want to do that to reggaeton. I glanced at some of the other couples, some dancing apart, some grinding close. Yeah, maybe not.

He led me by the hand through a throng of sweaty dancers and to the bar, where he paid in cash for two *Cuba libres* – rum with Coke and lime – and then began hunting for somewhere to sit. We found a booth whose occupants had vacated, leaving jackets, drinks and a single Latino guy as placeholders. In that tough Cuban slang, I'd occasionally heard from Maxim, he asked the guy if we could perch for a few minutes, until his friends returned. After a slow blink, the man replied with a guarded nod.

We perched, still holding hands. Maxim took a long sip from his cocktail and then added his second hand and looked into my eyes.

I need you and Kenzie to get someone for me. His nickname was Trogon, he's another two-dub. Six months ago, he was taken by his controller in DPRK – what you call North Korea. Before I escaped, we talked about getting out together. He didn't make it. But he's going to be in the USA. I need you and Kenzie to make contact, offer him a way out. Get him to defect.

I'd heard enough. Pulling my hands away, I stared. "This is the favor?" Whatever I might have imagined he was about to ask, getting involved with another spy agency wasn't it. I scoffed, "No. I don't know much, but I know people don't easily escape from North Korea. The entire country is a prison, even if you can't always see the bars. Your buddy will be guarded night and day."

Eyes imploring, Maxim gave an impatient shake of his head. *You're wrong. People escape it all the time. They wait until they're abroad and they walk away. Trogon didn't want to go to DPRK – he was dreading it. I promised I'd help him.*

I could feel anger settling in. The dancing, the music, the cocktail, it had all been to soften me up. Buying time to calm down, I drank some of the rum and Coke. Delicious. The alcohol buzzed on my tongue, but I couldn't relax.

"*You're* here, why don't you do it?"

He shook his head, irritated. *I can't risk being photographed, and I can't stay. Trogon will be in San Francisco four days from now, at an international math competition. All the competitors will be staying in the same hotel – the Westin Saint Francis on Union Square. You need to meet him and get him away from his minders. That's all. Everything else is already set up. Get him to a safe house and my plan kicks in.*

Sullenly, I took another drink. "More wackadoodle."

Will you do it?

I faced him squarely. "Don't see how I possibly could."

His eyes narrowed. *Please. I need Trogon. I need him very badly. If I don't pay the Carillos back for everything they've done for me, I have to hand over two of the two-dubs.*

"Figures," I said, a little harshly. "If you deal with those guys, don't be surprised if they demand payment. I guess cleaning house for Beto didn't quite cut it?"

Between gritted teeth, Maxim breathed, "I won't lose any of them. Not one." Reverting back to telepathy he continued, *If I trade even one, I'm no better than Krylov.*

"That wouldn't be very 'liberator' of you," I agreed. "Why is this guy so important?"

Aside from the Gen Six two-dubs, he's the most valuable of us. Trogon is a math genius. The Kims of DPRK have been involved in breeding his line, from a Korean father they picked out thirty years ago. Only Trogon seems to have inherited the math skills. He's been training in cyber warfare since he was fifteen.

I thought of the undercover North Korean two-dub operative we'd encountered in Alaska. So – she wasn't the only one.

Trogon's birth name is Jang Saero-yi. He's part of an elite, cyber warrior unit. North Korea's hacker groups are very, very dangerous. They hack defense systems, water and electricity supplies, even hospitals. They once shut down the whole of the British health system for hours. Cyber warriors are major players in the 'Mind Game.'

The name 'Jang' set off an alarm – the North Korean agent we'd met in Alaska was named 'Susie Jang.' I told Maxim.

I don't remember a 'Susie,' he admitted. *Then again, we went by camp names. There are only a few Korean surnames. It's not impossible that they're related.*

"Getting your buddy away from the North Koreans won't stop the 'Mind Game' though, will it? They'd just replace him."

In a tight voice he insisted aloud, "I *need* him." He threw a furtive glance over his right shoulder towards the restrooms, where a tanned, thin black woman in her early thirties stood alone. She had on gray joggers and a lemon-colored cropped top that showed off a lean, toned belly and appeared to be peering at a point slightly to the right of us.

Maxim fell back onto telepathy and continued, surveying the surroundings. *I have to get Trogon, Padi. Without him, I'm in a lot of trouble. So please, just listen. Don't reply. That woman near the washrooms, she's watching us. Drink now, turn your face away.*

I turned away but before I did, from the corner of my eye I glimpsed the woman now openly staring at us, a total Nosy Nellie. I lifted the glass of rum and coke and sipped slowly. Maxim heaved a sigh, turned back to me and very gently, took ahold of my chin, staring deeply into my eyes. I froze, staring right back.

I'm sorry Roni, I think you've been made. They must have left an agent in the café in case you came back to rendezvous with someone. This just got a lot harder. We can't risk leaving together. I'm going to give you cash for a taxi. I have to stay here, dance with some more girls, keep up my cover. They're going to be waiting for you back at your hotel. Now, we need to make it look like I'm some random who's been hitting on you. Then you need to send me away. I'm going to lean in for a kiss. And you hit me, okay?

Before I could even think of a response, Maxim's face was right there, his lips were on mine. I didn't have to pretend – instinctively I recoiled. For a split second we stared at each other.

I said, 'hit me.'

I landed a stinging slap to his left cheek. He rose to his feet and backed away, rubbing his face.

Urgh. Good. Now, stay close. This conversation isn't over.

NINE

Round Midnight

Maxim made a show of being upset at the humiliation of getting slapped. His little outrage act went on just long enough to use as an excuse to whine to two nearby Latinas. They'd seen it happen and were snickering from behind their drinks. He led both to the bar and loudly ordered them each a *Cuba libre* before turning back to me with an aw-shucks shrug and pointing at the nearest of the two girls.

"Your loss, baby," he called to me, loud enough for anyone close to hear, presumably for anyone using fancy listening equipment, too.

I threw him a fierce scowl, took another drink from my glass and on a reflex, reached for the burner phone.

Instantly, Maxim slid off his bar stool and crashed to the ground, right in front of me. The girls he'd joined gasped and burst into laughter. He got up, dusted himself off, making a big deal of his bad luck. Then I heard his voice in my head again.

Don't let the woman see the phone. Go to the restroom right now, break it up, toss the phone in the garbage and flush the SIM. Do it now, while I've got you covered.

I glanced up then, realized he was blocking the woman's view of me. Stumbling slightly on the stupid high heels, I stood up and transferred the phone into my left hand. The phone was just small enough to fit into my palm, so taking care to saunter past Nosy Nellie with my left side facing away from her, I made my way into the restroom.

Inside the same stall as earlier, I sat down. With shaking hands, I disassembled the phone on my lap, removed the SIM card. It skated off the dress onto the floor. As I bent down to grab it, I heard the door to the restroom fling open. I managed to grab the tiny SIM card before anyone could peek under the door to see me down there. I lifted the toilet seat, tossed the SIM and flushed. The rest of the phone was still in my hands. Would Nosy Nellie dare to search me right here, right now, the instant I left the stall?

The only place I could stash the empty phone was the feminine hygiene bin. I lifted the lid and stuffed the burner inside. Then I took a breath, preparing to confront the woman. As I exited the stall, I spotted her at the right-hand side of the trough-like sink, washing her hands. I didn't allow myself more than a single blink in her direction, sweeping my gaze across the length of the mirror as I approached. Taking my time, I soaped both hands, then rinsed. In the meantime, my watcher paced over to the sole dryer, drying her hands thoroughly.

I dried my palms on the seat of my dress and turned my back on her. The instant I stepped back into the bar, I spotted Maxim. He'd moved onto the dance floor with one of the two girls. They seemed to be having a good time together, enjoying a slinky bachata. Was I jealous? Obviously, *no*. I was alert, senses prickling, hyped and a little scared. This had gotten way too exciting, too fast. I wasn't ready.

Did you do it? Put your right hand on the bar if you did.

I did as he asked, heaving a sigh. Sacha was so right – we needed to practice a secret sign language.

We'll have to continue this another way. I'm sorry this didn't work out. Will you do it, will you at least meet with Trogon? He'll be at the International Math Olympiad. San Francisco. Four days from now.

I shook my head and bowed a little deeper, my eyes fixed on the ground.

Please. Just meet him. Jang Saero-yi, remember his name. I'll find another way to contact you.

For a long moment I remained still, head down. Nosey Nellie passed by close enough for her elbow to knock against my shoulder.

"You okay, hun?" she murmured. "Need any help?"

I forced my expression into a neutral smile, then stood up straight, looked her right in the eye. Her face was a mask of concern. "I'm okay. Thanks."

Horrifyingly, she stepped closer, feigning friendliness. "You waiting for someone?"

I swallowed, then decided to stick as close to the truth as possible. "Honestly? I kind of sneaked away from my family. It's... it's my first time in a bar. We were here earlier and I thought it seemed cool, so..."

Nellie's eyes had narrowed, were watching me closely now. I saw doubt cross her face, as though she could scarcely believe she'd wasted her time on a kid playing hooky.

I drew my lips into a weak-tea smile. "I guess I wasn't ready."

Her gaze had become stern, positively school-marm-ish, nothing at all like the good-time-girl vibe of her outfit and hair. "You're under-age? Good thing for you I'm off-duty, else I'd arrest you."

I gaped. "You're a *cop*?!"

Her lips thinned; her eyes filled with undisguised contempt. "Get on home, girl. Right now."

Get on home with what money, exactly? I thought.

Walking all the way back to the riverside Quality Inn in these shoes was going to be murder – assuming I didn't get actual-murdered on the way.

But as I neared the door, one of the servers finished taking an order and then made a beeline for me. As she pushed past me, she cursed in Spanish and grabbed my left hand from behind her waist. Before I could object, she'd passed me something hard and compact. I stopped myself from turning to watch her go, put my head down and continued to the door. When I got outside, I passed the item to my right hand and still walking, glanced down at the item she'd passed on. It was a roll of dollar bills.

I kept walking, hurried when I saw a taxi drawing up at the sidewalk. Two Latino men in black-and-white dress shirts and smelling of sandalwood cologne stepped out of the car. I shouted at them to hold the taxi for me. One of them stayed by the car, held the door open for me and waited until I'd stepped inside. All very courteous, I must say. It was my first time being treated like that – what a difference a short dress and heels make, right? On the other hand, I was tense the whole time, hoping they wouldn't hit on me. That's the problem, right there. You just can't tell if it's going to go that way, so it's not easy to enjoy.

I'd taken the safe seat – on the diagonal behind the driver. This meant that I could keep one eye on him, but also the converse. It wasn't safe to unroll the bills and count them. However, I was pretty confident they were fifties, at least. A fifty would pay for the journey back to the hotel. If they were hundreds, the roll of bills might even pay for two flights to San Francisco.

I halted my train of thoughts with a sharp inhale. *Already thinking of doing what Maxim wants!*

Grimly, I pulled my focus to the taxi's navigation

screen. It showed details of buildings and parks as the car made its way through Harrisburg. We'd be at the hotel soon. Maxim had warned me to expect our CIA shadow to show up, all butt-hurt about my sneaking out. I thought about discarding the wig. How would I explain the change of clothes? Or why I no longer had my own, from before? For a couple long minutes I stared vacantly while my brain tried to crunch through all possible reasons for that. No plausible explanations came to mind. I decided to go with – '*what* change of clothes'? There was a chance Mr. CIA hadn't seen me leave the hotel with his own eyes.

Was Maxim right about them leaving an agent in case I returned? Or had they tracked me down to Mocambo and *then* sent an agent over? Maybe I'd been spotted by a street camera?

Aw, crap. They have facial recognition, and they have street cameras.

Throwing myself back into the rear passenger seat, I closed my eyes and let out a low, despondent growl.

Was there no escaping these people?

TEN

TAXI DRIVER

I'd practically resigned myself to getting caught by Mr. CIA when an idea hit me. I leaned forward, thrust my face between the taxi's two front seats.

"Hey mister, any chance you can drop me around the back? Like, approach from a side road or whatever?"

The driver eyed me cautiously. He was a balding, white man, perhaps in his fifties. He glanced down at his navigation screen and then nodded, curtly. "I can drop you in a street behind." A few minutes later he'd pulled into a little side road next to a kindergarten. I climbed out onto a sidewalk flanked by a short row of three-story weatherboarded houses. I peeled a bill from the roll, relieved to see it was a hundred, and poked my head through the open passenger window.

"I got no change for a hundy," the driver said, not touching the cash in my outstretched hand.

Our eyes met for a second. I don't even know why I hesitated – it wasn't my money, and I wasn't exactly in a great position to negotiate. Yet somehow I found myself saying, "On a twenty-eight-dollar fare? C'mon, mister!"

"No credit card? Huh. You're out awful late. Now you want to be dropped outta sight? Seems like you should be glad if I keep my mouth shut."

"You got any spare clothes?"

"Do I carry any girl's clothes in my taxicab?" He gave a calm blink. "No miss, I do not. Now, would you mind getting away from my window?"

"Could you maybe take me to an all-night store to buy some?"

For a few seconds, he merely gazed at me, levelly. I half thought he was going to pull away, dragging me along until I squirmed out of the open window. Then he simply shrugged his shoulders. "All right. There's one not far from here. Custom T-shirt place."

I got back into the car and we drove for another couple minutes. I checked the meter – the fare was now $35.

"Wait here while I grab something, then drive me back and you can keep the whole hundred? Deal?"

The driver gave a resigned nod. "Obviously, I'm not gonna leave a little girl out here all alone in the middle of the night."

Little girl? I suppressed the urge to glare, reminding myself that this guy had no idea of the kind of things I'd been doing over the past two months. I headed to the store, rang the bell to attract the night attendant, then selected a baseball cap, T-shirt and joggers from the sample stock. Back in the taxi, I paid the driver, then pulled the T-shirt and joggers over the dress, removed the wig, putting both in the thin plastic bag in which I'd been handed the new clothes. Finally, I bunched up my hair and crammed it into the baseball cap. In the rearview mirror, I caught the driver looking at me.

"It's good," he admitted. "You look pretty different. Which I'm guessing is the aim?"

He drove me back to the hotel, this time around the front. I was about to push open the taxi door with the high heel of my sandal when I remembered Maxim's advice to me and Kenzie about footwear. In Mexico, back when we'd been planning to disguise ourselves to pass through the airport unnoticed, he'd shared some pointers.

Be sure to change your shoes, too. That's the most common mistake people make, not changing their shoes.

Well, I'd blown it – no spare footwear. Annoyed with myself, I undid the straps on the sandals and dropped them into the bag, along with the wig. As the taxi drove off, I let my shoulders fall into a slouch, swinging the bag around my hand as I swaggered, stoner-like, towards the lobby of the hotel. To my giant relief, the doors weren't locked.

There was no sign of Mr. CIA, though. He might have been watching from his car, or his window. Or maybe he was waiting for me in the corridor outside our room? My stomach knotted. I wasn't out of the woods just yet.

Mr. CIA could watch either the elevators or the stairs, not both. I took my chances with the stairs. As I reached the level just below ours and watched the doors to the stairwell push open, my whole body tensed. When Kenzie's face emerged, gingerly, I felt my shoulders drop with relief.

"Dude!"

He glanced up the nearby stairs and then approached grabbing my hand and pulling me through the doorway. He then led me or rather dragged me along the corridor. After a second or two I realized what he was doing. We headed for the fire exit stairs. It was a good plan, switching to a different stairwell at the last minute.

"They have someone watching the elevator, the stairs and I'm guessing, the door to our room," Kenzie whispered as we progressed down the corridor.

"Then where are we going?"

Abruptly, he stopped. We were outside a room on the floor below ours. I watched him push open the door, which was on the latch. He grinned and held open the door. "It's okay. It's empty. I sneaked inside when one of the chambermaids was cleaning on the night shift."

Obviously, I was impressed.

The room was in darkness, but there was enough outside light streaming through the open blinds for me to make out the outline of his face. He was grinning widely.

"I woke up and found you gone. Figured you'd sneaked out to meet Maxim. So, I sneaked out, too. I was on my way back when I saw Mr. CIA snooping around. I couldn't risk going back to the room, so I walked the corridors a while, until I found someone cleaning. It was easy! We can stay here until breakfast."

I gave him a gentle push to the chest. "You big dummy. The minute we show up, they'll grab me. How will we explain being in this room? My only chance to get out of being questioned is to walk out of our room, all wide-eyed. As things are right now, I just about have plausible deniability. They can't prove I was anywhere but my own room."

He fell silent for a couple of minutes and then said brightly, "So we'll climb out onto the balcony. Go up to the next floor and sidle across until we get to our room. This room is one-twelve, ours is two-eighteen. We go up one level and across by three."

I hesitated. Had either of us touched the balcony door of our room? There was a good chance it would be locked from the inside. But it was a start. We could figure something out once we got there. We stepped out onto the balcony of room 112 and studied the climb to the floor above. Standing on the edge of the balcony, Kenzie was tall enough to reach the lowest rung of the one directly above. I gave him a boost and in another two seconds, he was up. Then he reached an arm down to pull me up until I was able to grab the lowest run of the balcony above. In less than five minutes we'd made it to our room's balcony – if Kenzie's calculations were right. He tried the door. It was locked. Before I could vent any frustration, that genius boy pulled out his phone, holding it to his ear.

"Mama? Can you come to our room, right now? Yeah. Real quick. It's like Palm Beach, again. Yeah. Please hurry."

"How will she get in?"

Kenzie chuckled. "Are you kidding? Ma always gets an extra key for the room I'm in. Ever since I locked myself on a balcony in Palm Beach."

Sure enough, a few minutes later Zara was sliding open the balcony door, tsking with disapproval yet also a little smug that her tactic had finally paid off after who-knows-how-many years.

Once I was inside, she took one look at my outfit and frowned.

"'Don't make me use my Mexican Mom voice?'"

I glanced down at the baggy white T-shirt emblazoned with that slogan in red and green letters. "Oh, yeah. It... it was my mom's.," I said, lamely. A reach, but it was all I could summon in the moment. "She bought it for a joke."

Zara recoiled, instantly wary. With good reason – it wasn't the kind of thing my mom did at all, but I guess it was too much of a reach just then, to imagine that I'd sneaked out to an all-night custom T-shirt shop. I hated to lie to Zara, but Kenzie and I were still minors for a few more months. Zara and Bobbie would face consequences for anything illegal we might inadvertently get dragged into. Until I saw a little more of how this played out, I couldn't risk involving her.

"Honestly, you two," she said. "Didn't expect you to still be playing the fools, not after what you've been through."

The corners of Kenzie's mouth turned down; he bowed his head. "Yeah. We weren't thinking."

She glanced at the handle of the balcony. "Wait, but it locks from the inside... so how did you get stuck?"

Kenzie was already walking her out of the room. "It must have jammed. I'm really sorry we woke you. Can you tell Bobbie we're sorry?"

He closed the door after her. "You'd better talk fast, Padilla."

I sat on my bed. "That was pretty good teamwork."

Kenzie strode across the room and sat opposite me on his bed. He glared. "Don't change the subject. Why'd you meet Maxim? And why alone?"

"If you'd have been there, would have been harder to get back without getting caught. Trust me, you were exactly where I needed you to be."

"Well now, *that* hits different." His nostrils flared and again, he fell back on silence, waiting expectantly.

After another moment, I began to speak. "Maxim wants us to recruit someone for him. Another two-dub, one that was farmed out before we got into the camp. His name is Jang Sero-ee, or something. Korean, anyhow. Max calls him 'Trogon,' which I guess is his Krylov camp name. He's working for North Korea."

Kenzie inhaled, sharply. "Any relation to Susie Jang?"

"Yeah, I wondered about that, too. Maxim said this 'Trogon' is a 'cyber warrior.' He said he 'needs him.' He was pretty insistent. Like, very."

At the mention of 'cyber warrior,' Kenzie became noticeably more alert. "A North Korean cyber warrior, he actually said that?"

"Called North Korea 'DPRK' but otherwise, yeah."

He paused, reflecting. "North Korean cyber warriors are hard core. If Max needs someone that good, it's because he's planning something big."

"Like I said, he seems set on us getting Jang."

"Meaning what for us, exactly?"

"Jang will be at a math competition in San Francisco. Maxim wants us to help him get away from his handlers."

"Oh yeah? He wants us to turn a North Korean spy? That's hilarious. Did he give you any pointers?"

I took off the baseball cap, shook out my hair. "Nope. We ran out of time. There was some janky woman in the bar, watching me."

"And 'janky' just screamed 'CIA,' did it?"

"No clue who she worked for. Maxim spotted her. She had eyes on me, no doubt."

"How'd they find you so fast?"

I replied slowly, "I don't think we were followed from the hotel. My guess is that she was already at the Mocambo, waiting to see if we came back."

"Good call, if so. Then Maxim's been made?"

I quirked my lips. "He had on a disguise. Me too. You should have seen us. *El Guapo y La Fea.*"

"*Fea*, you?" Grinning, he shook his head. "Not in a million years. You're beautiful."

The word fell between us like a feather floating down on a pocket of air as we watched its progress. It was his first tenderness since Alaska, when he'd told me he loved me. My first reaction was relief – so I hadn't imagined the whole thing, at least. Watching me, after a shy, uncertain start his gaze grew steady and confident.

I broke the tension by emptying out the bag I'd been carrying since the taxi. The dark-blonde wig and heeled sandals fell onto the bed next to me. "Not really my drip, though."

In silence, he picked up the shoes and glanced down at my bare feet. "You remembered what Max told us about changing shoes. Nice."

"You know me, I'm all about paying attention in class."

Kenzie's tone became thoughtful as he twisted the sandal strap of one shoe around his index finger. "You know where to find 'Jang Sero-ee?'"

"Maxim said he's with all the other math contestants. I have money for airplane tickets, too."

Our eyes met. "It'd be cool to go to San Francisco," he began, "I've never been."

"Me either."

He paused, uncertain again for a brief moment. Then he dived in. "It'd be especially cool to go there with you." And there was that steady gaze, again. Hopeful, not caring that I saw his hope. His confidence was a little unnerving, reminded me of Maxim.

"Question is," he continued, "Do we tell my moms?"

A good point and a huge question.

ELEVEN

THAT'S THE DEAL

We couldn't use our phones to book flights or even to search for information about the math competition, because it was more or less a given that CIA had found a way to hack our phones. Even within the confines of our hotel room, Kenzie and I didn't feel safe discussing the possibility of getting Jang. The previous night, he'd tracked Mr. CIA to a room on the floor above, more than ten doors along from ours. There were a lot of walls to hear through, but we'd been out of the room for thirty minutes during breakfast. Probably long enough for either him, or an asset on the hotel staff to plant a bug.

Grabbing some time away from our shadow was our first goal. I figured the river was a good bet. The Susquehanna flowed directly in front of the hotel and a few minutes' drive away was a place that rented boats and kayaks. Kenzie's moms were happy to drop us off at the river, while they got on with their own stuff. They might have felt differently had they known what'd gone down the night before. But so far, so good. Not even Mr. CIA seemed to know for certain that I'd gone back to Mocambo. Maybe he believed it was a case of mistaken identity, maybe he knew there was no way to prove it, anyhow, so it was a waste of energy. All he could do was to continue to track us. Well, he was welcome to try it.

The river was pretty, dark green water flowing between banks of picturesque hotels and pubs as well as foliage. The harbor was busy and raucous, with many speedboats and a river cruiser boarding. Sharing a two-person kayak, Kenzie and I were close together, could speak quietly. We pretty quickly got a solid lead on our shadow, who didn't seem to know how to kayak and wasted the first few minutes trying to get into the seat. Meantime, we were paddling hard upstream, not talking, using all our energy to get farther away. After ten minutes or so, I looked over my shoulder. Mr. CIA was nowhere to be seen. We slowed our pace and began to plan.

First we had to buy plane tickets. Since we'd be paying with the cash Maxim had gotten to me, that meant finding a travel agent. The night before, we'd concluded that this was how his moms could help us.

"We have to tell them either way," Kenzie had insisted. "I'm not lying to them about taking a flight, not again. They'd never trust me. They can buy the flights for us. It's the only way."

I don't know when he persuaded them or how. All I know is that something had changed for his parents, ever since Margo Daniels blackmailed us into going on an operation for CIA. Now, it felt like Bobbie and Zara were likely to be on board *especially* for anything that might tick off Daniels. Not that they weren't patriotic or that they weren't scared for us, but I guess that's what happens when you put someone's back to the wall.

While Kenzie and I were leading Mr. CIA up the Susquehanna River and towards the outskirts of Harrisburg, Bobbie and Zara were organizing our trip to San Francisco. When we reconvened three hours later at a riverfront restaurant, Bobbie handed us an envelope containing tickets and the intel.

"We're not thrilled at the idea of you getting into something new, obviously," Zara told us, her large brown eyes wide and serious. She sighed. "But we've discussed it. You're not kids anymore, only in the most technical sense and in a few months, not even that."

Bobbie nodded. "What we can't do, is to let you do everything alone. Which is why it's a mistake to fly."

Kenzie tapped the envelope. "The tickets?"

"Bus," Bobbie said, very firm. "Flight manifests aren't secret enough, not when the CIA are tracking you. You don't need a passport for the bus. We got you tickets in our names – Bobbie and Zara Mackenzie."

It was a smart idea. Once Mr. CIA realized that he'd lost track of us, he'd search the car rentals, bus and flight manifests. Almost certainly, he'd search for our names, not Bobbie and Zara's. Before you start thinking that Kenzie's moms were actually letting us off the leash, treating us like the adults they claimed to see in us, their plan entailed following us to San Francisco and checking into a hotel not far from the Westin, where the 8th International Math Olympiad was scheduled to begin next week. They'd paid for our bus tickets with their own cash and given us another thousand. Added to the roll of bills I'd been handed at the Mocambo, we had enough to stay for two weeks at a budget motel in San Francisco.

"And you're certain that *all* you need to do is talk to Jang Saero-yi?" Zara asked, fixing us in turn with a critical stare.

They'd found his name on the list of entrants for the Math Olympiad and prepared a dossier about Jang. It was all of two sentences long: 'Jang Saero-yi, 18 years old, born Pyongyang. Hobbies include playing the piano and pachinko.' At least half of this had to be a lie – he wasn't born in Pyongyang, but in the Krylov Foundation camp in Cuba, and from what we knew of the camp, he probably didn't play piano, either. No photo, nothing that'd help us to recognize him.

"Talk to him," I confirmed, "pass on messages from Maxim, help him get away from his handlers and to a safe house."

"None of which is illegal," Kenzie added. "They're on US soil."

Zara said, "Just the same, we'd like to be on hand. You might need backup."

I thought about the pistol she'd bought, back in the small town, where I'd first been accosted by Officer Margo Daniels. There'd been no sign of it since that day, yet I knew that Zara had been one hundred percent serious about buying it. Maybe this was what she meant by 'backup.'

I objected. "The minute you two show up in San Francisco, they'll be onto us."

Bobbie replied with a wan smile. "Perhaps. But that's the deal. Take it or leave it."

Obviously, we took the deal. How could I resist another mystery associated with Maxim? Sacha's warnings about 'Jaguar,' Atlanta's too, I ignored them, or at least, I put them aside. There was bad blood between the brothers, I got that. But Maxim had never done anything to harm me. He hadn't gone looking for me – the opposite, in fact. Discovering that I was a one-way telepath, a one-dub, was a revelation whose shockwaves were reverberating through me. Changing who I was, changing what I wanted out of life. I was still in that process, hadn't yet landed.

Kenzie had a simpler reason, however.

"It's not like we have anything else," he said. We'd

been paddling a steady rhythm upstream, working hard to keep out of range of our CIA shadow. Cool water streaming down my arm as I lifted the paddle, I paused to wipe my brow. He stopped, too. We began to float back downstream, but by then, it didn't matter. Our job had been to lead him onto the river and leave Bobbie and Zara alone. Soon, he'd catch up enough distance to get us in range of his audio equipment. Maybe we were, even now. My advice – don't become a target for the intelligence agencies – you rarely get more than a minute's peace.

"My climate activism – that's over," continued Kenzie. "Can't do much now, not with them watching me. Can't go to college either, thanks a bunch, Madge."

I watched Kenzie drain his water bottle, then fill it from the river and empty it over his head. Another hot day, they all were. Hot and slow and until yesterday, when I'd visited my father in prison, aimless. A vacation, perhaps. But Kenzie made a great point – a vacation from what? Margo Daniels had ruled out college for us. Instead, this was to be our 'gap year' – a European idea that was almost universally adopted by graduates of DC International. Some lined up a college place deferred for the following year; others left their application for a gap year. Others of us, Kenzie and me included, had different plans.

"I could still do my podcast."

Kenzie shucked his shoulders and with a wry grin, said, "You could try. Maybe she'd let you."

"She?"

"Madge, obviously. Targeting Officer Daniels. Maybe she'd allow that."

I picked up the paddle from where I'd left it resting on my lap. A quick check behind us revealed what we'd been expecting – Mr. CIA, a bucket hat protecting his shiny bald head from the sun, was only thirty yards behind us. It was time to turn around.

I wasn't' sure whether it was some as-yet-unexpressed will of Officer Daniels that was keeping me from returning to my podcast and my ambition to become an investigative journalist, or my own inability to switch off from what we'd begun to uncover about the world.

There existed a network of telepaths operating on behalf of intelligence agencies around the world, most of them working to undermine the USA and its allies as part of Ilyin's 'Mind Game.' Sacha and the Atlas Group hadn't yet joined any side, from what I could tell. Maxim was building his own group. He couldn't be for the Russian dictator, Ilyin, or else he'd have let Ilyin keep all the kids at the Krylov Foundation. But other than that, where his loyalty lay was a mystery.

Like it or not, I had to accept that I was in a unique position. I was a one-dub – not as spectacularly rare as a two-way telepath, but still unusual. I knew and had telepathically bonded with both Maxim and Sacha. Maybe I had a part to play in helping them to use their powers to help protect our society's respect for democracy, rule of law, equality and human rights?

TWELVE

RECRUITMENT

Getting onto the San Francisco bus without Mr. CIA tracking us there, was a thing of beauty. In Harrisburg, all four of us boarded a bus to Gettysburg. He followed in his car. In Gettysburg we wandered around for a while then waited for a chance to slip away. Kenzie and I boarded a return bus – but a return to York, not Harrisburg. Bobbie and Zara led him around the museum for another ten minutes until he figured out that Kenzie and I had ditched. It would have been obvious which bus we'd taken – only the York bus had departed in the time window. But by the time he caught up to it, we'd already admitted our 'mistake' to the driver, had been put off the bus and were waiting by the side of the road, crouching behind a billboard until we saw Mr. CIA's car whizzing past. Then we walked back to Gettysburg in time to catch the Harrisburg bus. And by the time we boarded a Greyhound to St. Louis, our faces hidden with caps and medical face masks, he'd lost our trail.

Three days and seven hours later, we arrived in San Francisco. We'd just had time in Harrisburg to buy some spare undies, toiletries and snacks to keep us going on the journey. Kenzie's moms made the same trip, different route, meandering across the country over five days. We laughed a lot, imagining that useless CIA guy reporting on the daily to Madge, trying to guess where we'd gone.

We were planning to stay at a budget hotel a block from the Westin on Union Square, but first Kenzie and I went on another shopping trip, this time for clothes. 'Pretty Woman' it wasn't, but when we dropped stuffed store bags onto the bench at a Shake Shack and scarfed down some chicken sandwiches, it felt kind of awesome, anyway. I was in the coolest city in the nation with my best friend and I hadn't stopped buzzing since getting that first message from Maxim, via my dad.

Yes, we were feeling pretty clever. So, it was a shock and somewhat of a deflation, when a middle-aged, slightly chubby African American woman with a pleasant, smiling face slid a tray loaded with burger, fries and a milkshake onto our table, asking sweetly, "All right if I scooch up with y'all, sugar pie?" Such a shock that for at least two seconds, my brain didn't register the identity of the woman who'd parked her butt next to mine.

In horrified, silent awe, Kenzie and I watched Targeting Officer Daniels unwrap her burger and take a modest bite. Her shoulder-length hair was loose and frizzy, not straightened and tied back as usual and she'd swapped her usual tailored suit for black flared stretch pants and a navy-blue knitted cardigan over a scoop-necked white T-shirt.

The CIA officer gave us a friendly grin. "Now, don't tell me you kids seriously believed ol' Dashiell was the only tail I had on you?"

"What do you want?" I asked, my throat muscles tight as a drum.

"I been watching you. For people with zero training, y'all didn't do too bad with the dry-cleaning," she said, referring to the way we'd successfully shaken off Mr.

CIA. "Someone less careful than me might have trusted Dashiell to do the job properly. But I know you two kids have access to something I don't. Anyhow, I decided not to take any chances."

"Answer the question," demanded Kenzie.

"What do I want? No small talk, hey? I can respect that." Carefully, she placed her burger within its crinkly wrapper. "Isn't it obvious?" She fixed me with a piercing stare. "I want to recruit you."

Kenzie said, "Us?"

Daniels's eyes flicked over to me. "Just her."

A beat passed. Finally, I dared to ask. "Why?"

She held up both hands, resigned. "Because you have influential friends, Roni. And also, you're a telepath. Kinda."

For several seconds, I didn't reply, struggling to keep my breathing steady. How could she know? Mentally, I rifled through the possible explanations. Had Sacha or Atlanta said something to Training Officer Lyle Prince? It seemed unlikely – from what I'd seen, Sacha and also the Atlas Group had done what they could to stay out of the reach of any US government agency. I couldn't see why that would change, now. Maxim, too, was doing what he could to stay under the radar. The leak, I realized with a slow and sickening feeling, was way more likely to have come from me or Kenzie. We must have badly underestimated the effectiveness of their audio surveillance.

Looked like there was no getting rid of this woman. "Recruit me to what?"

"Also, why not me?" added Kenzie.

Daniels was setting up a new unit within CIA. "The idea is to put together a team of assets including telepaths from the regular community, like you, with people like Sacha and Maxim."

By 'Sacha and Maxim' it turned out that she meant, actually them, because there were, in fact, zero people 'like' them, unless you counted the other three members of Generation 6 who were all aged under seven years old at the time. Did she seriously intend to recruit Sacha and Maxim to her team? Did she actually believe that I'd help her to persuade them?

I reminded her that I'd already tried to recruit Sacha to assist the CIA, yet he remained as elusive as ever.

"I didn't foresee what happened in Alaska," she admitted. "That's on me. But I don't see it as a failure, more a near miss. Sacha and Atlanta agreed to help us carry out one operation. Far as I'm concerned, they're already one-time assets. They might be willing to do it again."

"That's what we are to you? Assets?"

With a confident nod she agreed, "That's right."

"So why don't you want to recruit me?" Kenzie asked again.

She turned to him with a surprisingly gentle look. "I'm sorry, kid. You got a scooch too close to committing an act of outright terrorism. You're lucky to have stayed out of prison. There's a good chance you'll never be trusted in the security services."

I took a moment to think through what she'd just said, then chuckled. "A guy who literally encouraged a violent attack on the Capitol and an insurrection is allowed to run for president, but a teenager who didn't even enact a bit of light climate activism can't join CIA? Sounds pretty hinky to me. Anyhow, if Kenzie is seen as a security risk, why are you asking me this in front of him?"

Mildly, she added, "Well, there's also the small matter of his thwarting the entire purpose of a CIA operation..."

A defiant Kenzie thrust out his chin. "By keeping the peace, d'you mean?" Under his breath and barely audible he added, "Crazy warmonger."

With a knowing smile, she shook her head. "I'm a black woman serving in the CIA. You don't need to tell *me* that our justice system has loopholes for rich white folks. And as for asking you in front of Kenzie... This isn't a secret y'all can keep from each other. If you agree, Roni, it needs to be understood between you that afterwards, there will be things you can't share.

Kenzie frowned, muttering, "I'm allowed to *know*, but not to help?"

"We need you to stay squeaky-clean, young man. Keep your record clean for five years, no hacking, no activism. Then maybe we'll talk."

I glared at him. He was acting like I'd be on board for any of this.

Margo Daniels continued her pitch. "Now, let's get down to business. Y'all are here because of the math contest, presumably? One of the competitors is a unicorn, yes?"

I replied, coldly, "They don't like that term."

"Potay-toh, potah-toh," she intoned, dismissively. "Are you recruiting this person on behalf of your buddies in the Atlas Group?"

It took effort to keep my expression neutral but inwardly I was rejoicing. Her guess was a good one and logical, given the timing and location of our arrival in San Francisco. Yet it appeared that Daniels didn't know as much as I'd feared. CIA hadn't overheard our conversation at the riverfront restaurant with Bobbie and Zara, where we'd discussed the plan to get Jang Saero-yi. Most importantly, they didn't seem to know about Maxim. The asset they'd placed at Mocambo had gotten very close, but it looked like Maxim's quick thinking had saved him.

Kenzie also said nothing, watching me for a cue. I cleared my throat, which was a little scratchy from nervousness. "Actually, yeah, that's pretty much it. We haven't yet been told who to contact, or how."

Daniels replied so quickly and naturally, it seemed like she believed me. "We've figured it's one of three possibilities. A kid from Iran, one from the Third Russian Empire and another from North Korea." Now she peered at me with a mixture of hope and determined resolve. "Either way, we can help you. Whichever of those boys you're hoping to get away from their minders, we're ready to help. We can get him to a safe house. We can help him to defect."

Uncertainly, I nodded. Her sudden earnestness was quite the swerve, I wasn't sure how to react.

"We're all on the same side, here," Daniels said. "I hope you'll see that?"

"What about Alaska?" I asked. "You're not angry?"

"About how things went down on that operation?" She shrugged. "You're not responsible for anyone in the Atlas Group, I know that. You're just an asset, Roni, you're not trained, like a case officer. Maybe one day, if that's something you'd like to consider." Once again, she fixed me with that penetrating gaze. "I see a great deal of promise in you. You're smart, resourceful, resilient, you're good under pressure, you're brave. Loyal to your friends."

"And most importantly, she's friends with the two people you most want to recruit to your agency," Kenzie said, his voice tinged with cynicism. "So ultimately, you're counting on Padi *betraying* her friends."

THIRTEEN

You're Already Involved

You have to hand it to Margo Daniels – her approach this time was completely new. The wheedling that turned into coercion, the thinly veiled threats of blackmail, those were gone. She'd simply looked at me blandly and laid it on the table, straight: she saw a genuine risk that either the Atlas Group or Maxim's new group might join forces with those aligned against 'the West.'

"You care about democracy, free elections, human rights? The rule of law?" She barked a short, bitter laugh. "Maybe you're too young to appreciate what you take for granted. The majority of the human population lives under the rule of tyrants like Ilyin. His 'Mind Game' is all about removing trust in democracy so that people give up and let dictators take over *everywhere*. It's about ending the United States as it was conceived, about destroying the European Union, South Korea, Japan and the parts of Global South that don't already have a Kremlin or Beijing-controlled puppet government."

"We don't have 'democracy' here either, we don't have 'human rights,'" Kenzie countered, angrily. "Our consent is manufactured by a media that lies to us about climate change and anything else they want to hide; we have a state that protects billionaires from the consequences of their destruction of the planet."

"See, this is why we can't recruit you," Daniels said,

turning to him with a weary shrug. "You haven't learned to distinguish the bad from the terrible. Even if you think things are bad, there's always something worse."

He glared. "You actually think I'd work for the Central Intelligence Agency? After the things you people have done?! Even without the assassinations and the attempted coups in foreign countries, I won't defend a system that lies about climate change."

"Those coup attempts were a long time ago," she replied, sounding sad but also defensive. "We don't do that stuff now. We defend our own freedoms, yes, the very freedoms that allow you to sound off about us, to criticize the government and not wind up getting tortured, left to rot in some godforsaken hole in the ground."

Kenzie fired right back: "When the climate blows up it won't matter if we're allowed to disagree with the president or whatever. We'll all wind up in the same 'godforsaken' hole."

A note of exasperation entered her voice. "It's sad that you believe that, honestly. But you *personally* probably won't be the first in line, when the authoritarians come for people. Your two moms, they might be higher up on the list. The Czar and all his dictator buddies, they're not fans of equal marriage."

"We're not little kids," I interrupted. "Obviously we realize that a lot of governments are worse than ours. But *we* are no fans of CIA, either. And we haven't forgotten how you basically blackmailed us into going to Alaska, where we almost died."

"And I'm truly sorry that things went south the way they did. Sorry that I have to ask this of you. Believe me, I don't want to be trying to recruit a newly-minted, high school graduate. You deserve more time, you deserve to go to college, grow up some more, fall in love, y'know, all that normal stuff." Here Daniels paused and let out a sigh, a sigh that hinted at regret for something she herself had lost or perhaps, missed out on. "You deserve to take your time to think about whether you even want to get into the fight. But not everyone gets to choose whether to play the 'Mind Game.' Like it or not, Roni, you're already involved. And that's on you, no-one else made you go looking for Maxim Santiago."

She stopped, abruptly. To my astonishment, she seemed to have become overcome with some emotion that she now struggled to contain. Could have been frustration at two dumb, idealistic kids, could have been she was having second thoughts about the whole thing. After a few seconds, however, she appeared to snap out of it and returned calmly to taking dainty bites out of her burger, while Kenzie and I looked on in growing bemusement. A little mustard leaked onto the corner of her mouth, but after she'd done eating the burger she dabbed her face with a napkin and then began working on the fries, taking intermittent sips from her milkshake. When it became clear that this pause wasn't going to be brief, I picked up my half-eaten chicken sandwich and got on with finishing it.

Kenzie had already eaten everything in front of him, so he stood up to refill his soda. The instant he left, Daniels began to speak rapidly, one eye on Kenzie's departing back.

"I know you care for him, Roni. But you're allowed to have your own views. Marc is an idealist, and that's great. I wish him all the luck in the world. Me and people like me, it's up to us to make sure he gets to live in a world where he doesn't automatically get beaten up, imprisoned and even outright killed for taking action on those kinds of belief."

I had to laugh. "You literally threatened him with prison."

"I did no such thing. Just pointed out that if he'd carried out his original plan re the pipeline, that would have most likely been the consequence. We have to have laws, Roni. We have to enforce them."

"Laws to protect the rich and powerful," I objected.

"Laws to protect everyone," she said, evenly. "Listen hon, you can't lay all the problems with our legal system at my door. I'm just a CIA operative, not a senator or congressperson. I'm another cog in the wheel. But I do believe in our country, for the best version of what we stand for, for the rest of the free world. And I'm telling you now, woman to woman, that if Ilyin wins the 'Mind Game,' things will get a lot worse for billions of regular people. Not just in this country, but all over the world. Ilyin and his ilk, they believe that the vast majority, literally almost everyone on the planet, exists only to further the power and ego of a handful of men like them. Everyone else? We're nothing more than objects in their field of vision. If we help them, good. Maybe they don't kill or persecute us. Get in their way?" She flicked her index finger against my right hand, snapping it hard enough to make me flinch. "Objects. In their field of vision. Nothing more than a bug."

I closed my eyes and began to rub where she'd flicked my hand. "All right, all right. Just tell me what you want me to do."

Kenzie returned and sat down again, rattling the ice in his soda. "What'd I miss?"

Daniels popped a mayonnaise-covered fry into her mouth and chewed slowly before resuming. "It's a real shame your telepath buddies refuse to talk to us directly," she told us, with a sorrowful shake of her head. "Unless and until they do, we have no way to assess them, which means we continue to view them as a threat. The Alaska operation proved to us that Atlas has active assets in Russia. And Maxim, well, you know him better than me. What I know is this: he's powerful and he's not declared for our side. That alone is enough to classify him and his people as adversaries."

I told her that reasoning struck me as too black-and-white. That I reacted this way didn't surprise her, but it didn't make her back down.

"When it comes to the 'Mind Game,' there are no shades of gray."

The restaurant was starting to thin out as the lunch crowd left. Tables either side of ours were now empty, one still strewn with the debris of a meal it'd taken a woman and three ten-year old boys only a few minutes to demolish. A few minutes ago, the general background din of the restaurant would have provided cover but now, anything we said might be overheard.

Leaning both elbows on the table, I rested my chin in cupped hands and gave Margo Daniels a sickly-sweet smile. "You've said your piece, Officer Daniels. I've heard enough. You want to recruit me. When? And to do what, exactly?"

Daniels's face lit up, beaming with surprise and delight. It wasn't at all the response I'd expected from my attempt at a mean-girl power move. On the contrary, it was as though I'd finally done something she actually admired.

"Oh, I like this version of Veronica, I do. I got all kinds of plans for *this* lady. But you can tuck her back in your purse for now, sugar. There's no such thing as a free lunch; I am *well* aware of that particular disappointment. And anyways, I'm pretty sure you're done handing out freebies, not so?" An eerie grin began to twitch at the corners of her mouth. "That's why I come bearing gifts."

I squinted. "What 'gifts?'"

"Whatever you're planning on doing here in San Francisco, we want to help. To be candid, it's in all of our interests to get a unicorn away from their controller, if that controller works for one of our adversaries. Better with Atlas or Maxim Santiago than with any friend of the Czar's." She nodded slowly as I stared, slack-jawed and trying to bend my mind around the fact that the CIA wanted to help *me*. "And I mean it – no strings. Just me doing a solid for someone that I'd very much like to become a colleague. Because, Roni, I'm not exactly saying that 'only you can save the world.' But as it happens, you do find yourself in a unique and potentially critical position."

I leaned back in my chair and began to laugh.

Only you can save the world.

Yeah, right.

FOURTEEN

FIRST NAME TERMS

It wasn't strictly true what Margo Daniels said about there being no-one to blame but myself, for searching for Maxim Santiago. Okay, right up until I was about to travel to Mexico with my legal guardian, Olga, it'd all been me. But the morning she was poisoned by a Chekist, Sacha Montecristo had *incepted* me to keep that flame of desire alive. Even after I'd learned that Olga was dead, he'd telepathically induced a dream in me – a dream that planted an insatiable desire to find Maxim.

Without Sacha's intervention, would I have stayed the course? I'd probably never know for sure. But I doubted it.

Obviously I was chary about the whole CIA recruitment idea. Joining any kind of secret service might have been fortieth on my list of dream jobs. All the same, Daniels came through for us right away, with a couple of passes to the International Math Olympiad and an upgrade in our accommodation. Now we were registered as reporters for *The Bottom Line* – the newspaper of a tiny public university in Maryland, Frostburg State. When we told her we'd never heard of it, Daniels just nodded.

"Kinda the point. Not likely to bump into another student from there who might question your cred."

Other than that, we were in the dark. Maxim had

given me no more guidance than to make first contact with Jang Saero-yi. Yet when we checked into the Westin on the booking Daniels had made for us, there was an envelope waiting for me at reception. I opened it, expecting more instructions from her. Inside the envelope was another cheap phone. I waited until we were inside our room and then called, expecting to hear her voice. When instead of that I heard Maxim's smooth yet sullen voice, I jolted.

"Are you working for CIA now, Padi?"

"Max! Where are you?"

His voice dropped lower, now tinged with regret. "I should have known."

"I'm not working for them. You don't get it, do you? They've been stuck to us like a band-aid for weeks. Wherever I go, there they are."

"What do they want?"

"For us to help you get Jang."

There was a long silence. "They know about him?"

"They figured out this is about one of the mathletes, they've narrowed it down to Jang and two others. They want to help you get him out. Better with you than with an ally of Ilyin's, according to Daniels."

"What's in it for them?"

I hesitated. Even I wasn't sure of the answer to that question. "My good will?"

"They want to recruit you." Maxim sighed. "It was probably inevitable. What will they do if you refuse? Kill you?"

He said this so calmly, I felt a tingle at the base of my spine. That thought hadn't even crossed my mind. Faintly, I asked, "They'd do that?"

"It depends. I don't know that organization, how it works. The Krylov didn't train any of us to serve in

Western secret services. But the Cheka would absolutely kill you if you refused them."

Kill me? When I thought about it, it made a kind of implacable sense. If I was dead I'd be no threat to their ambitions. Then again, nor would I be, if I simply returned to my life as an investigative podcaster.

Meantime, Maxim kept rolling on. "I need time to think about this."

"You wanna call it off?"

There was another tense silence, broken when he finally snapped, "*I can't.* I already told you, I need Trogon. Nothing works for me without him. And all those kids we got out of the camp? Same goes for them. Without Trogon, our choices become extremely limited."

"What's he going to do for you?"

Maxim heaved a jagged sigh. He sounded deeply weary. "I owe the Carillos money. A *lot* of money. They funded the break-out, now I have to pay them back. Trogon can make cash appear from thin air. I need that cash. And that's it."

I couldn't have hidden my skepticism, even if I'd tried. "Cash from thin air?"

"Yes. For all intents and purposes. We need a few people to collect it – I'm working on that. But most of all, we need Trogon. So – dangerous as it is to get close to CIA, we may need to go ahead."

"What if I don't want to 'get close to CIA?'"

"Then you shouldn't have gone to Alaska," Maxim deadpanned, ending the call.

For a while neither of us said anything. I crossed the room to the window and for a minute or two, gazed out over Union Square. An incredible view. We'd never stayed somewhere this expensive and definitely not in the center of a major city. Skyscrapers surrounded us, classic majestic stone towers from the early twentieth century and a little farther out, gleaming glass, steel and concrete. I watched people down on the square crossing its broad white stripes, a few of them meandering from umbrella to umbrella, most others striding with purpose. Was Maxim watching us from there? Was 'Dashiell,' the spy formerly known as 'Mr. CIA?' I turned back to survey the room. It was a fancy hotel, top-end business fare.

Kenzie kicked off his sneakers and flopped wearily onto one of the beds. A sour smell rose from his sweaty socks. We probably both stank, after three days on a bus. I was on my way to the bathroom to take a shower and scrub some clothes in the sink, when there was a knock on the door. A delivery – a large paper bag containing two New Balance shoe boxes and other stuff beneath. The delivery girl handed me another envelope. It was sealed, with nothing but our room number written on the front.

I fished inside my jeans pocket for a tip, found a crumpled five and handed it over, making a mental note to get more change. The rest of our money was all hundreds. Placing the package on the bed, I opened it. The boxes contained sneakers, obviously. Tan-and-white for me, black-and-blue for Kenzie. Underneath the boxes were two pairs of chinos, tan and gray and four polo shirts, two powder-blue, two navy. I checked the sizes, then tossed one box of sneakers plus gray chinos and navy polos over to Kenzie.

I sat on the bed and opened the envelope. This one *was* from Officer Daniels – a notecard with a to-do list jotted with what looked like a Sharpie, and two Frostburg State university student ID cards, one in each of our names.

1. Learn about Frostburg State, decide your majors and minors.

2. Check website of The Bottom Line.

3. Go to the Grand Ballroom and register for the event.

My phone dinged – the regular, CIA-bugged phone, not the burner from Maxim. I showed the text to Kenzie. "It's from Madge. 'Call me if you need anything else. Margo.' Well, how'd you like that! We're finally on first name terms with a CIA operative."

Kenzie smirked. "What could possibly go wrong?"

FIFTEEN

THE KIM PINS

It felt good to have a new mission. Maybe that's the secret to happiness – to have a purpose. Three long days on the coach with only one book to read was more than enough for me to start getting antsy. Kenzie and I had worked a bit on developing our own sign language but after a dozen signs or so, we'd run out of steam.

That had left plenty of time to reflect; about how I'd ignored my parents these past two years, about why I'd been so angry with them, how betrayed I'd felt. At the time people, including Kenzie's moms, had urged me to get therapy. They were sure Olga would agree to release funds to pay for that.

I refused because I didn't *want* to feel better about it. My anger came from shame and betrayal. Shame and betrayal struck me as the normal response to finding out that your parents committed treasonous crimes, for which they would now be imprisoned for the rest of your young adulthood. They wouldn't be around to see me fall in love, get married, maybe even to see their first grandchild, all the things I'd planned for my mid-to-late twenties.

(Yes, I wanted all of that before I hit thirty, don't judge me. Being an only child wasn't something I wanted to impose on my own kid, so I had to start early enough to fit in a second kiddie, while earning enough to look after the first.)

Seeing my dad again, though, had brought back a rush of feeling for him, something I'd forgotten. Inside the prison, I'd felt emotionally blocked, as though all my feelings were underwater and I could see them through deep water, like the sunken bus and crumbled buildings we'd scuba-ed around in the diving lakes. Each day since then, however, those feelings, childhood memories of my mom and dad had slowly returned to me. This time, I hadn't pushed them away, I'd allowed myself to sit with them, even though it hurt.

After I'd taken a shower, brushed my teeth and put on the bland 'tech-bro' uniform that Margo Daniels had picked out for us, I pocketed the ID card, placed all our cash in the small backpack I'd been carrying since Harrisburg, a sense of contentment settled over me. Sad memories of my parents were once again pressed safely to the recesses of my mind. Only what was directly in front of me mattered. We had to get Jang Saero-yi. The rest, I'd figure out later.

In eleventh grade, Kenzie and I had attended a model United Nations event, the only time I'd done anything remotely similar to registering for the International Math Olympiad. We enrolled as student reporters and were immediately offered a list of contestants in case we wanted to interview anyone. Walking away, I scanned the list. The North Korean team wasn't listed. I went back to the registration desk and asked for a full list.

The staffer seemed surprised at the omission. I guess it was below his pay grade to know why the team's names were missing. "Oh well, they're definitely here. I registered them myself. You can't miss them, they're all wearing really bright red polo shirts with pin badges of their leader, the 'Kim.'"

We joined the mixer in the side-room of the main ballroom, which was filling up with team members, all wearing matching polo shirts, and a handful of others – presumably spectators like us. Almost everyone looked to be aged less than twenty, most looked like high school seniors, around 17 or 18. This was very different than the model UN event – mainly because almost all the participants were male. Looking around, I gave a low whistle. "Testosterone levels are *dangerously* high. There are probably fewer than ten girls in the whole room, including me."

Kenzie eyed me, warily. "Not gonna say a word on that."

"Oh, you think girls can't math?"

Diplomatically, he replied, "I think you choose not to."

We plunged into the heaving throng of mathletes. I relayed the staffer's description of the North Korean team to Kenzie, who headed to the other end of the room in pursuit. Meantime, I examined the faces of those around the entrance. A few minutes later he was back. He'd found them huddled in a corner with three members of the Chinese team.

"Were they wearing their lanyards with badges?"

Kenzie nodded. "All four of them. We'll go over. I'll get them talking. You follow me and take photos. Then we can look at the name badges."

I had a better idea. Jang Saero-yi had grown up in the Krylov camp, where the main language was English. He'd probably be the only one who'd speak English, definitely the only one who'd do it fluently, without any accent.

We approached them together. Three were chatting,

one of the Chinese boys and two Koreans. All wore red polos, but the North Koreans wore a different shade of red and of course, the Kim pins. Since I don't know either Mandarin or Korean, I don't know what language they were speaking but at least those three all understood it. The others stood by in silence, not really engaged, just sipping from paper cups of juice.

I went straight for the guy from China's team, who'd done most of the talking. He was boy-band cute, with thick, floofy bangs and grinned widely showing perfect, white teeth unlike any of the North Koreans, who all had boring buzz cuts and didn't smile.

Making a show of looking at his name badge, I flashed him a flirtatious grin. "Hao Li? Are you the captain of your team? My name is Roni Padilla and this is Marc Mackenzie. We're from Frostburg State, we'd love to interview you for our student paper, *The Bottom Line*."

Hao Li smiled, very friendly. "I don't speak so much English," he said. His accent was thick, so I guessed he was telling the truth.

I noticed that all the other boys in my field of vision were immediately quiet, their expressions suggesting instant suspicion. Ignoring this wasn't easy but I brazened it out. "Oh, that's too bad, do any of you speak English? We'd love to interview someone from Korea, I'm such a huge fan of K-pop."

This time, I carefully watched the impact of my words. Hao Li creased up with laughter, while one Chinese boy and one North Korean looked instantly guarded, the only one of his team-mates who seemed to have understood what I'd said. I risked a quick glance at his name badge, but annoyingly the lanyard was twisted and the badge reversed.

I turned my back on the North Korean boy, just

enough so that I could face Kenzie. We'd practiced a few more hand signs on the long journey down, so when I signaled to him with my right hand 'Behind me,' he knew at once who I meant.

In the meantime, Hao Li stopped laughing long enough to explain his outburst. "K-pop is from South Korea. *These* guys are DPRK. North! You need to talk to *those* guys over there." He pointed a little way across the room to a cluster of maybe ten boys, four of them Asian and wearing white polos. Two were chatting in loud, strident English, all four a lot more animated than the North Koreans and frankly, with better haircuts.

Can you hear me?

I froze.

You're not imagining this. I am broadcasting to you.

Someone in the room was telepathically broadcasting to me! Jang Saero-yi? For the hundredth time at least, I wished that my telepathy was two-way. But unless the broadcaster revealed themselves, I had no way to communicate with them.

The voice in my head was so jarring, I couldn't stop myself frowning. There was something uniquely weird about the voice, but I couldn't figure out what. Hao Li happened to be facing me at the time. When the smile dropped off my face, his friendly demeanor vanished.

Ah, so you can. I heard a rumor, seems like it's true.

This time, I knew what was strange – the voice in my head was *my own*. It was like hearing my own internal narrative except totally disconnected from my own thoughts, like hearing a recording I'd made, of which I had no memory at all. So bizarre, I lost all ability to concentrate.

A rumor? *What* rumor?

Someone had left that phone for me at the reception desk, it hadn't been posted. Could it be that

Maxim was close, or at least *had* been? Had Maxim himself passed on information about me? The circle of people who knew I was a one-dub was tiny: Maxim, Sacha and Atlanta.

And also Madge, apparently, I reminded myself. Unfortunately, it seemed that I had few secrets from my friendly-neighborhood CIA officer.

If I had to bet, my money would be on Maxim himself dropping the rumor. Maybe he'd disguised himself again, swept through the lobby of the hotel like a brand-new twister, stirring the dust, shaking things up on a micro level before suddenly vanishing, like smoke.

By the time I tuned back into my surroundings, all the guys around me, including Kenzie were staring at me in bewilderment.

"What's wrong?" Hao Li's question was blunt, insistent.

"I'm sorry," I mumbled. "It was a dumb mistake."

"She hates to be wrong," Kenzie chimed in. He gave Hao Li and the North Koreans a friendly smile. I saw the edge of alarm in his eyes, though. He had no clue what had happened, but he was doing a pretty good job of covering for me. "Such a perfectionist." He pointed at the nearest boy's lapel pin. "We probably should have noticed the Kim pins. He's your leader, right?"

Hao Li was still suspicious. "So?" he asked me, raising his chin. "What's up, what triggered you? You hate North Koreans so much?"

I was instantly, super apologetic. "God, no! Of course not! It's just that... I've heard you – they – get in trouble for talking to foreigners. I was worried I'd get them in trouble."

That was nicely played.

Hao Li's two Chinese team-mates said something to

him. He turned to face them for a moment, exchanging some words in Chinese.

Hao Li is translating for them. I'm sorry I shocked you.

Cautiously, I allowed my eyes to sweep the group, taking in all four members of the North Korean team and also the two Chinese boys with Hao Lin. Was Jang right here, broadcasting to me? I still couldn't work out how he was using my own voice. Would he give me a sign? Whichever of the four team members he was, Jang was managing to control his expression, perfectly mirroring the other boys, who continued to look on in bemusement.

Hao Li appeared to relax just a little. "In trouble? Just for *talking* to people? Wow, your Western propaganda is pretty mean. DPRK is a normal country. Why wouldn't they be allowed to speak to foreigners? They're talking to *us*, and we're Chinese."

At this, one of the four North Koreans broke ranks, bursting into raucous laughter. It was the boy who'd reacted to hearing me mention K-pop, the boy with the reversed name badge.

SIXTEEN

 FINDING JANG

"Very funny," the boy said, between guffaws. He spoke with a strong Korean accent, too, but at least had some English, which explained his reactions to things I'd said in his presence. This couldn't be Jang Saero-yi; Jang was raised in the Krylov Foundation, speaking English and Russian and presumably Korean and Mandarin too, if not more. Maxim himself spoke six languages fluently – an essential skill for any telepathic secret agent.

Immediately, I glanced at the name badges of the remaining three North Koreans, whose bland expressions revealed little about whether they understood why their team-mate was laughing. As my gaze moved swiftly from one to the other, the final boy casually flipped his badge so I couldn't see the identity details.

My pulse spiked. Was *this* Jang Saero-yi? I didn't dare to look at his eyes. Hao Li was watching me very closely, I'd noticed. Could he be somehow involved?

Hao is dangerous. Be very careful what you let him see.

"What's funny?" Kenzie asked the English-speaking North Korean.

"Chinese are brothers to us. Most friendly nation."

I took advantage of the distraction to study this calm-eyed boy with the accented English, who'd laughed so abruptly. He was quite handsome and his smile, glimpsed oh-so-briefly, lit up his face and revealed teeth with running-track metal braces. His hair was neatly buzz-cut with the most severe, straight-line fringe I'd ever seen.

Then something happened. The boy, grinning and joking in either Mandarin or Korean, allowed his gaze to rest on me for *just* longer than necessary. And when our eyes met, he blinked, slow and sure.

This was Jang. He'd broken cover, risked revealing that he spoke English yet covered it up by putting on an accent. Very smart. I reminded myself yet again that the Krylov Foundation kids had received training to work in the intelligence services. I glanced over at Kenzie. Had he also realized?

"Would you speak to us, then? If it's not forbidden."

The North Korean beamed, this time a polite, careful smile. He bowed his head. "Sorry, my English not good for interview."

Ask Hao Li to translate.

I swallowed my surprise and turned to the cute Chinese boy. "You speak good English though, right? Could you translate?"

Hao Li watched me for a moment, his expression still on the friendly side, but now I sniffed suspicion. He gave a quick nod. "Okay. But not Saero-yi. Since I can translate, you should talk to Kim Woo-sik, he's the captain." Here he indicated the boy who'd flipped his name badge the instant I'd tried to read it.

Woo-sik is captain because he's a Kim, his father is a cousin of the leader. He'll lie to you; he knows Hao Li can't be trusted. But you should accept anyway.

I put on my 'grateful' face. "Thank you, that'd be super."

Hao beamed. "Super," he echoed. "You want to do

it now?" He indicated the main ballroom, which was set for the opening session, hundreds of chairs facing the stage.

Before you go with them I need to know one thing, quickly. How much help do you need from me on a scale of one to ten? Say anything with a number.

"Would *nine* o'clock be too late?" I asked Hao, apologetically. "Kenzie and I have to record a live for our socials in a bit, we need to get ready. Then there's dinner, then..." With a shrug that implied studied helplessness, I trailed off. Hopefully Jang had gotten the message by now.

Nine, okay, I got you. Ask to meet in the bar.

Hao nodded, his expression now neutral. "Nine pm. We should..."

Interrupting again, I said, "In the bar?"

This seemed to throw Hao off, a little. "The bar? But none of us are old enough to order alcohol."

"The bar has *ambience*," Kenzie offered. He grinned at Hao and also the North Korean team captain Woo-sik, who hadn't even slightly relaxed his stern expression. "It's a better backdrop. For our socials, I mean. We're trying to show people that this isn't, y'know, a massive nerd-fest, that it's all about international cooperation, and all."

"Nerd-fest?" asked Jang, wide-eyed and innocent.

Hao said something, I guess translated 'nerd-fest' into Korean, and all the North Korean boys tittered with what was definitely polite laughter.

"All right then, see you in the bar at nine pm," Hao agreed. He sounded satisfied, at least, maybe because we'd given him an opportunity to push some North Korean-slash-Chinese propaganda over drinks; soft drinks at that, so no blunting of the experience, yay for that.

You should both come to interview Woo-sik. I'll be close, I'll give you the questions. After exactly nine minutes past nine, your boy goes to the nearest bathroom. I will meet him there. That's how you get a message to me. Do it quickly or they'll get suspicious.

I gave a friendly nod to each of the Asian guys, in turn, careful not to linger even briefly on Jang. Then, turning away, I reached for Kenzie – my 'boy' I needed to get up to speed on Jang's telepathic instructions. "Enjoy the dinner, see you later!"

Kenzie let me hold his hand until we'd put a few walls between us and the North Koreans. Then he demanded to know what was going on. He wasn't all that surprised when I told him.

"I figured it was something like that. Dude, you need to be more careful. I'm starting to be able to notice when you're using your psi powers – your eyes get wider. Not by a lot, but I see it. Does Hao Li know Jang is a two-dub?"

We agreed that if Hao was somehow policing Jang, then he probably did. Maybe Hao was telepathic, too. Even if he was, he wouldn't be able to 'eavesdrop' on a telepathic broadcast directed only at me. On the yacht with Sacha and Atlanta I'd come to realize that two-dubs seemed to have a lot of control over the width of their telepathic 'beam.'

It seemed like a good idea to go back to the room and take a time-out to plan our next move. I thought about calling Daniels for advice but couldn't bring myself to do it. The more I interacted with her, the more I'd feel obliged to let her recruit me. And I wasn't ready to go there, not even in my thoughts.

Maxim, on the other hand, might be useful. Also, Jang had offered to help us. He seemed to have been expecting us, information we figured had come from

Maxim. Was Maxim in San Francisco, right now? He or an associate had left a phone for us at the Westin – how had they known we'd be staying there?

"Maybe they didn't," Kenzie suggested. "They knew we'd be coming to this hotel, wherever we chose to stay, because of the math contest."

Maxim knew the CIA were following us. I doubted he'd risk getting anywhere close. When we'd spoken earlier, he'd seemed majorly ticked off that any CIA had managed to get their sticky paws on this operation. Ticked off yet also, resigned.

I decided to compromise. Margo Daniels had laid on a fancy room at the Westin, she'd clothed us. Listening devices could be anywhere in the room, but they wouldn't be able to monitor the phone Maxim had left for me. So, I texted him.

Meeting Jang briefly around 9pm. What should we tell him?

After thirty seconds, Maxim's reply came back.

Ask him for a precise time when he can get out of the hotel. There'll be a car waiting for you.

What type of car?

That's up to you. You and K will be sourcing it. You'll be the ones driving.

Okaaay if you say so. Where are we going?

I'll text you an address at 2110. In the meantime, find a car.

SEVENTEEN

LOGISTICS

We decided to take our discussion out onto Union Square, just outside the hotel. It was busy, crowded with office workers heading home and the evening crowd setting out to stroll and enjoy the local bars. The evening was warm and the air sticky with the aroma of hot asphalt. In the middle of all that urban jungle, the bright green foliage and grass of Union Square's tidy gardens stood out as peaceful havens, oases of calm.

Pointing there, I turned to Kenzie. "Let's hang for a bit."

I figured it would be difficult to pick out our conversation from all the others, and Kenzie agreed. "Difficult but not impossible. They did literally *exactly* that in *The Conversation*."

He was talking about some paranoid conspiracy thriller from the 1970s, a genre he'd become obsessed with in his early days of becoming a cyber-hacking crypto-bro. Tech these days made what the guy in that movie did seem trivial, he told me, very sure of himself. If we wanted to talk without being overheard, it'd be difficult in the city. Why hadn't we worked harder on our sign language? And so it went.

We had two problems. One: getting a car and two, not being overheard by CIA or Chekists, for that matter.

The moment when we had to pay over the odds to

rent a car, because we were so young and had limited funds – *that* would have been the time to call in help from our CIA benefactor, right?

Maybe. But that isn't what we did.

The hotel refused to book us a rental car at the highway robbery rate of several hundred dollars for two days, on account of us not having a credit card. A lot of 17-year-olds get a card from their parents, but that's not how Zara liked to roll. She'd been a tad conspiracy-curious, even before CIA had begun surveilling our house. She'd encouraged Kenzie's interest in cryptocurrency, she'd insisted on paying his pocket money in cash, he didn't have a credit card. On her vehement advice to Olga, my late guardian, neither did I. Although, a fat lot of good any of that did to protect their son from leaving a paper trail the state could follow. After he'd engaged in a plot to blow up a pipeline, Kenzie was under mad scrutiny. Off-the-grid and cash-only was looking like the only way he'd manage to achieve that. But Zara continued to do Zara.

Dealing with possible surveillance was simpler. Outside Saks Fifth Avenue, Union Square was being tidied by the city gardeners working on the hedges with power tools. The noise from those hedge trimmers would hopefully be enough to mask our voices, especially if we whispered directly into each other's ears. It took a few minutes to get into the rhythm of talking about our plans only when the gardeners buzzed those hedges, we ended up running two parallel conversations, one when they fired up the buzz saws and another one – pure gossip – when they didn't.

"We could buy a car for cash," Kenzie mused. "On Gumtree, or whatever."

Or ask CIA to supply one, or to drive him to a safe house: these options also crossed my mind. I ignored these thoughts, however, and listened to Kenzie. If I ended up joining forces with Margo Daniels, it would be my choice. After Alaska, I planned never again to allow myself to get extorted into doing something dangerous.

It was a quarter after six. Dinner would be at seven, our 'interview' with the North Korean at nine. So – we needed a car and we needed it by nine. Before that, we had to be able to tell Jang Saero-yi *what* car to get into, at least.

"We don't have to do that, not if one of us is there to flag him down," Kenzie said.

I thought it over. What if he only had time to get onto the sidewalk and climb into a waiting car? What about giving our identity away?

The car was the bigger problem. There was nothing available that we could have delivered or pick up in time, from any of the websites we tried.

I sighed. No choice but to ask Daniels, after all.

Another step closer to becoming her acolyte, then.

When I called her she seemed cautiously relieved to hear from me. "A car to drive y'all to the South Korean consulate? We can do that, sure. I'll have a driver pick you up. When?"

"No driver," I insisted, firmly. "A driver might spook Jang. Just the car. Nothing that stands out."

"It's not my first rodeo," Daniels interrupted, her tone bone-dry. "But you got it. If you reckon Jang might be thrown by seeing someone unexpected, I'll trust your judgment. You've met the boy, I haven't. So just tell me where and when. Keys will be in the glove compartment."

By the time we'd figured out the logistics of the car with Daniels, we'd missed the dinner for the mathletes, so we went out for burgers. By eight-forty we were back in the hotel room, I packed the few things we'd brought from Harrisburg into our backpacks and returned to the nearby street, where just as we'd agreed with Daniels, a white Volvo hatchback was waiting for us. Kenzie opened the door, slid into the driver seat and reached into the glove compartment. With a satisfied grin, he took out the key and started the car.

"I'm good to go when you are," he told me.

Tossing the bags into the trunk, I checked the time. Eight-fifty-eight. I sped back into the hotel to do the interview, already sweating a little, awkwardly conscious of my total lack of prep. On the way to the bar, I spotted Jang Saero-yi. He was with two teammates, at a table near the entrance. When Jang spotted me I saw confusion flash in his eyes, but he swiftly got that under control.

Where's your friend? It's just you?

Anxiety pulsed through me. I understood his confusion; I'd totally overlooked this part of the plan. He'd counted on Kenzie coming along for the interview. Now Kenzie was outside, in the car. Without him, the message would be harder to pass on. How were *me* and Jang supposed to meet privately in a public restroom? The entire team would see us leave at the same time.

Rounding the corner, I saw that Hao Li and Woo-sik were already sitting at the opposite end of the bar, a booth tucked right in the corner, next to a garish sculpture of a gorilla made entirely from wire coat hangers and sprayed with bronze metallic paint. Two tall glasses of ice and sweaty bottles of Coke Zero were on their way to them, carried on a tray held by a waiter wearing a crisp white shirt with sleeves rolled to three-quarters. I slid into the booth opposite the mathletes and nodded at the waiter's offer to bring me another Coke.

"We missed you at dinner," Hao began, ignoring my hello.

My hands shook very slightly as I placed my phone on the table. "Is it okay if I record the interview?"

Hao pulled a toothy but humorless grin. "Sure. So, what happened to you, why'd you miss the opening dinner?"

I tried to smile back but it probably came across kind of glassy. "To be honest, we had a thing about eating in Chinatown. It's not something we have in our hometowns."

"What'd you eat?" he countered, quick as a whip. "And where?"

Hao was one hundred percent suspicious. I tried to calm my fears, told myself that any handler of a team at threat of defecting to the USA would be equally wary.

I thought of the Chinatown in D.C., which I knew quite well and answered simply, "Something with duck. And I have no clue what the place was called. The name and the menu were only in Chinese. We just asked them to serve us something tasty."

"Something tasty," Hao repeated, as if sounding out the concept. "Duck dishes can be very good. You probably had Cantonese food. Szechuan is better."

I smiled at Woo-sik. "Should we begin?"

Ignoring Woo-sik Hao asked me, bluntly, "Where's your friend?"

I tweaked my smile a notch and turned to Hao. "We decided I can manage this alone."

Hao gave a curt nod. He was all about the business, now. "All right. Begin."

I started recording, scrabbling around in my head for some questions to ask.

Get your head in the game, Chica Curiosa. I told myself. *Time to get your investigative journalist on.*

EIGHTEEN

GETTING JANG

Maybe I don't always think things through properly. I blame the lack of time. From 'Remember the Lost Village?' through 'Find Unicorns,' 'Go to Alaska, or else!' and now 'Get Jang,' it often feels like I'm pushed from pillar to post without being allowed to sit and adequately chew on my options.

Then again, I remember hearing about a theory once, that all our decisions are made in the blink of an eye – what we consider to be the 'thinking it through' phase is just our brains trying to justify to ourselves, a decision we've already made. If that's true then I guess I must have some deeply reckless, self-destructive tendencies. After all, I keep putting me and Kenzie in danger, ever since I started investigating what happened to the Santiagos.

Maybe that's part of why I'm telling you all this – perhaps I'll figure out why I did what I did, reach some perfect understanding of the *me* that put me in all those situations.

Hao had just finished translating Woo-sik's response to the first question they'd agreed he could answer, which was 'What do you hope to achieve for your country here at the International Math Olympiad?' I glanced at my phone screen – eight after nine. I hit pause, stood up and gave an apologetic shrug. "Gotta use the ladies room," and then, when they obviously hadn't understood, explained, "The restroom. I need to pee."

The restrooms were through the lobby. The instant I hit his field of vision, I saw Jang leap to his feet and head off in advance. Now I understood why he'd picked a table so near the bar's exit. When I arrived at the restroom, I didn't hesitate. Maxim had already demonstrated this play when we'd first met at Mocambo in Harrisburg. Jang would be waiting inside, hidden in one of the stalls.

But this time, just as I touched the handle on the door to the women's room, I felt a firm hand grip my wrist. When I turned I saw Jang staring, wordlessly. He tugged, pulling me towards the men's room. Seconds later we were inside, the only people there. Throughout this, Jang remained totally calm, his expression even, unchanging.

"Better if we talk in the men's room," he said. The Korean accent was gone, he now spoke in perfect English, with a general American accent. "No-one cares if a girl steps in. We need to be quick. What do you have for me?"

A little breathlessly, I told him. "We need to leave right away. We have a car waiting to take you to a safe house. I'll go first so they don't see us leave together. You follow. It's a white Volvo, last three numbers of the license plate are seven, six, three."

Jang blinked and gave a quick shake of his head. His eyes were still calm; lovely, long-lashed honey-brown eyes, I just happened to notice.

"Unacceptable. The others will see you leave. They have a direct line of sight of the lobby." He blinked twice more, as if each blink performed hundreds of calculations. "This is what we'll do. I'll go. You wait.

Count thirty seconds. Then walk out. I'll distract them. Then I'll follow. Have the car pick me up in front of the hotel."

"Wait, I'm not sure the car can stop there, it might be a red zone."

He gripped my arm again, this time even harder, although his calm expression didn't change. "Make sure that you do."

The skin on my face tightened as I watched him walk casually back to his table. I'd counted to twenty-six by the time he reached his teammates. At which point he began to wave his hands in some kind of pantomime. Their laughter reached me when I hit thirty. I began to walk, smooth and swift as I made directly for the front doors. Once through them, I didn't look back, just jogged to the side road where Kenzie was waiting with the car.

Kenzie rolled down the window, looking confused and gave me the 'what gives?' sign. I jumped into the passenger seat. "Go round the front. Right in front of the hotel!"

He started the car. It stalled. Cursing the car and its provenance, he turned the key again. I held my breath. It faltered. He turned the key, took a deep breath and looked at me. "Then where?"

"What?"

"After we pick him up? Where to then?"

"Who cares?" I yelled. "Just start this car! You want me to get out and push?"

Kenzie's jaw muscles clenched tight. He turned the key. The engine fired.

"Go go go!"

We joined the stream of traffic and rounded the block. Kenzie tried to slide into the inside lane but the car behind wouldn't budge. He let two cars by, now holding up the second lane. Behind us, a horn blared. In my jeans pocket I felt the burner phone buzz. The car rolled forward, slowly. I took out the phone. Finally, a gap opened, and we jumped into it. A moment later we were crawling along Powell Street, towards the hotel's front entrance. We were in luck, there were few cars in the white zone. It was easy enough to find a spot. Breathing a little easier now, I glanced at the phone.

24th and Hampshire. Puma will be waiting.

Puma. *Puma.* The name was familiar, but it took me a few seconds to remember the girl from the Krylov Foundation, the one that Atlanta had a crush on.

Kenzie had more of an instant recall. "Oof. Yeah, I remember her. You think Maxim brought a team with him? Or just Puma?"

I took out my smartphone, opened the mapping app and began directing him to 24th and Hampshire. "Should get there in fifteen minutes, there's some traffic."

Another two minutes went by and still no sign of Jang. A parking attendant approached. Kenzie told her we were waiting for someone, and she responded, deadpan, "Shocker. Don't wait too long, this is a restricted zone." When she returned three minutes later, we were still there. This time, her tone was sharper. "At least take a spin around the block."

Kenzie didn't budge, just faced her down. My gaze was fixed on the Powell Street entrance to the hotel, so when the rear passenger door opened, I was surprised enough to cry out. Then there he was – Jang Saero-yi, strapping himself into the back of the car easy as you please, like we were his parents picking him up after school.

The parking attendant seemed satisfied and slapped the side of the car as Kenzie pulled out.

"Go faster, please," Jang said, leaning forward. "I left from the side exit. They won't be far behind. Drive." Then he stopped talking but peered over my shoulder at my phone screen.

Our car disappeared into traffic. We took a route via Howard Street, which seemed to have the least congestion. I could sense myself relaxing, the mission almost accomplished, as straightforward as we'd been promised. It was a warm, sunny day, cooler than we'd been used to back east, altogether pleasant. For a minute or two I allowed myself to watch the California people wandering along the sidewalk, relishing their walkable city and its shady, tree-lined streets. When Kenzie suddenly asked, "That white Chevy, two cars back. Anyone else remember it from outside the Westin?" I was as clueless as a duck.

Jang looked around, watched for a steady minute and then turned back. "It was."

I almost choked on my saliva. "Already? They've already found us?"

It made sense, now I stopped to think. If the North Koreans were such an escape risk, it would be smart to post a car outside their hotel. Jang, however, obviously hadn't considered the possibility – a serious oversight of his, not our fault at all.

"What now?" Kenzie asked. His fingers tightened on the steering wheel, his eyes flicked back and forth, from the rear-view mirror to the road ahead.

I spun around and glared at Jang. "Any ideas? You're the one who trained for these types of shenanigans."

"Yes." He gave me a quick nod then took a moment to assess the situation, carefully examining the car's surroundings. "Kenzie must get away from the tail. You should turn off your phones. They may be using them to track you. You memorized the route, yes?" He eyed me steadily, awaiting confirmation.

"Well, no," I blurted. "But now I will."

Kenzie had already tossed his phone onto my lap. "Turn it off. I'm going to race ahead, put more distance between us, and then I'm gonna stop. You and Jang hop out. You'll have to walk the rest."

I couldn't answer, my hands slippery and damp as I clutched my phone for a few more precious seconds, street names blurring as I struggled to fix them in my memory.

"Switch it off," Jang instructed. He placed a warm, dry hand on top of mine. Voice barely raised, he said, "Time to go."

NINETEEN

DEFECTOR

The route I'd memorized was the simplest – Potrero all the way from Costco and then right onto 24th. Kenzie drove into the indoor Costco parking, screeched to a halt beside the store entrance, where Jang and I leapt out. I grabbed my backpack from the trunk, threw my two cell phones inside and still looping the straps over my shoulder, I raced into the store, Jang right beside me. We began scanning the corridors for another exit. I was looking to exit onto 10th and from there to Potrero.

"It's twelve blocks, a thirty-minute walk," I told him as we jogged. "Faster like this, obviously."

He just nodded. The distance was well within my wheelhouse, but if we had to start sprinting, I knew I'd rapidly tire. Jang barely needed to jog, his long legs loping beneath him. I'd be the one holding us back, not him. We found the exit at 10th and Potrero, switched to the shady side of the street and settled into a steady pace. Fourteen blocks to go.

When we hit the junction with 22nd I spied a white Chevy on its way down towards Potrero. I grabbed Jang's hand and swung us both into the driveaway of an apartment block on the corner. Diving into the garden, I ducked behind some tall bushes and took a quick breather. Through the foliage, I watched the white

Chevy slow to a crawl as it approached the corner with Potrero.

Your fingernails are digging into my hand.

Hearing Jang's voice in my head was startling on *two* levels.

Firstly, that he'd stopped talking aloud and secondly, that I no longer 'heard' his broadcast thoughts in my own voice, but in his. Apparently, I needed to know a two-dub's voice to receive a broadcast that I'd 'hear' internally in anything but the default, which appeared to be my own voice. He was definitely sending me telepathic messages intentionally – I wasn't reading his thoughts. Not unless he only had one thought in his head.

I let go his hand. "Shh. I think they're getting out of the car... Dang it, they are! We have to go!"

We sidled through the garden until we found another exit on 22nd, hurried across the street and into the driveway of the San Francisco General Hospital, still heading south. We hit the exit on 23rd and I allowed myself a little shout of triumph. "In your face, fascists!"

24th was in sight now, Hampshire just one block away. I prepared to look out for Puma, ready to hand Jang over to her. But as we crossed 23rd the white Chevy slammed on its brakes. The car drew up to the curb, catching up to us by the time we reached the corner with Potrero. I prepared to sprint. But then, the driver's door sprung open. Out jumped a purple-faced Margo Daniels.

"In the car, both of you. *Now*, goddammit, or you'll see me get real angry, real fast." she hissed, glaring at me with such heat that I felt myself wilting.

We can still make it, Jang urged me.

"She's CIA," I told him, flatly. "We have to go with her."

Daniels appeared suddenly to relax. Now she was flexing friendly, smiling, all very disconcerting. She took a step closer and patted me on the shoulder. "You get it, I like that." With Jang she took a sterner tone. "Inside, now. They're waiting for you at the South Korean consulate." Opening the rear passenger door, she gave him a light shove toward it.

Jang resisted. "I don't want to defect to South Korea."

Daniels gave a cheerful shrug. "That's a shame, honey. Because that's the way we do these things."

"Better get in," I told him. There was no obvious way out of this – I didn't have the tools to evade the CIA and evidently neither did Jang.

This is why you keep your phone switched off. Have you any idea what you've just done?

Even inside my head, I could hear his frustration. My conscience was clear, however. I'd done what I could and probably more than I should.

Thirty-some minutes later, I watched a rather self-satisfied Targeting Officer Daniels deliver Jang Saero-yi, certified math genius and suspected North Korean cyber warrior, to the South Korean consulate. His initial anger at being forced to defect to his southern countrymen was nowhere to be seen. Either Jang had done a total 180 in the past half-hour, or he was a terrific actor. As we both stood by, watching his oh-so-polite exchanges with the sworn enemies of his country's leader, I asked Daniels if she understood what they were saying.

She turned to me with a neutral smile. "Not a word, dear. It's not my area."

"Why'd it have to go down like this?"

"South Koreans are our allies. When it comes to one of theirs, they set the rules."

"He's North Korean, though."

Her smile thinned out. "According to South Koreans, there's no such thing. Just part of Korea that was grabbed by pro-Soviet gangsters in a proxy war."

"But Maxim needs Jang," I objected.

She nodded at first, as if with compassion but then her eyes narrowed. "Needs him for what?"

"Money. He owes someone. Owes a lot. If you want Maxim to owe Langley a favor, you should let Jang go."

"Like I said, that's not my call."

Closing my eyes, I tried to gather my wits. This was no good. It wasn't yet up there with being inclined to dance to the tune of another two-dub, like some kind of flesh-and-blood-puppet, but it still sucked to be manipulated. "You're going to follow my every move from now, is that how things are?"

Daniels broke off from watching Jang with the South Koreans. "Yes, that's how. You should thank me."

I scoffed. This was the limit.

"I mean it," she insisted. "We got sigint two days ago that a Chekist has been assigned to you, full time."

I paled but pushed through with bravado. "So what? There's been a Chekist on me since Mexico. Earlier, maybe."

Daniels looked doubtful. "If you say so. But it's the first time we've seen your name in sigint. Specifically, you, I mean. Not generic, like."

"Wait, when you say 'sigint' you mean...?"

"Means we heard your name on a wire, sugar. Signals Intelligence. We've been monitoring the Internet for your name and also Maxim Santiago's. Bad news is – someone is trying to locate you. Don't take it wrong that we've been monitoring you, it's nothing against you or your buddy, or any skills or aptitude you feel you may have shown for this job. Just means you've tripped some kind of wire. Next, your Chekist shadow is likely gonna want to talk to you. Well, I can't allow that, obviously."

I didn't bother to hide my alarm. "I don't want to talk to any Chekist."

"That's good, cos those boys and girls, they can get kinda rough. Especially if they've figured you for one of mine."

"Are you trying to tell me you're protecting me?"

Daniels chortled. "This girl! Talk about ungrateful. Yes, like I said, I consider you an asset. Protecting an asset is pretty much the number one job of a CIA case officer."

She'd muscled in on my operation to deliver Jang to Maxim and now she wanted gratitude? That rankled. I didn't much like being described as a CIA 'asset,' either. A favor for an old buddy had been turned into an international incident. Now yet again, a Chekist was hunting for me. I could already see my future, this time maybe months of hiding out in the boonies, while I put my life on hold.

I needed to put some space between me and Margo Daniels, so I pretended to be studying the noticeboard in the lobby of the consulate. Almost everything was in Korean. Little wonder all the Korean kids I'd ever known spent their Saturday mornings in Korean school – if they didn't keep up the language they'd wind up strangers in their own land, unable even to read a simple notice.

Eventually, Jang's conversation with the South Korean official seemed to be over. He paced across the room and indicated two seats beside a snack machine. To my relief, Daniels seemed relaxed about giving us a moment alone.

You did great. Better than I hoped. But they do know about you, Daniels is right about that. They know you're a one-dub.

"Serious? But how?"

Doctor Susie Jang. You met her in Alaska. She got word out to the Reconnaissance General Bureau, the DPRK foreign intelligence. Susie is one of four RGB operatives from the Krylov, including me. She's my sister.

I could only shake my head in frustrated, furious silence.

TWENTY

THE DOUBLE

Reconnaissance General Bureau – a.k.a. RGB, a.k.a. North Korean foreign intelligence – had colluded with Cheka, according to Saero-yi. By now I'd figured out this was his first name, not 'Jang.' They have the order reversed in Korean. His sister, Dr. Susie, or more accurately Dr. Jang So-hyun, was back with the RGB after her arrest in Alaska. These days she worked as a 'double' i.e. she'd been offered a deal: work as an undercover CIA asset or go to a US prison for espionage. She picked the first option.

The team captain, Woo-sik, was Saero-yi's RGB controller. Hearing all this, I realized that it was probably Woo-sik that'd given Saero-yi the heads-up that a CIA asset with telepathic skills would be reaching out to him in San Francisco. Not Maxim, as I'd previously assumed. In fact, the more I learned about Saero-yi, the more I understood that Maxim most likely hadn't even made direct contact with his fellow two-dub. Maybe he wasn't even in town. There was a lot of CCTV in San Francisco, which made it a risky place for someone trying to stay off the grid.

Someone had left the envelope containing the phone from Maxim at the hotel for us, however, that someone must have found out about our last-minute change of hotel. Which meant that even if Maxim was staying out of reach, he had someone else following us. Was that person also a two-dub? And if so, had they reached out to Saero-yi? There was still a bunch of intel I was lacking. My bet was that Saero-yi probably had a few more answers, if only I could press him.

I asked, "So – all that about your sister and Woo-sik being Reconnaissance General Bureau – does Hao Li know?"

Saero-yi's usually serene expression was instantly transformed into pure scorn and contempt. "That crazy bastard? He has not a single clue. His father is some big shot in the Chinese Communist Party, so obviously, he likes to lord it over the other Chinese boys. And also, over our team, because he's *that* much of an idiot."

Margo Daniels joined us again. It was clear she'd at least had some clue about what we'd discussed. Everything Saero-yi had shared was super, highly classified, she reminded me. I'd pretty much guessed it was, but even so my heart sank when Daniels made *quite* sure I understood this to be the case. They wouldn't clue me in on something so secret, unless they expected something from me.

"You told me Hao is dangerous," I pointed out to Saero-yi. "I assumed you meant he was another spy or whatever."

Saero-yi gave a lofty sniff. "Hao Li is a snitch; he likes to go blabbing to the Communist Party of China, the CPC. But so far as I know, he's not working for Chinese intelligence."

"That's also our intel," confirmed Daniels. She tapped neatly manicured, clear-lacquered fingernails on the surface of the wooden table, before picking up the paper cup that held her coffee. She took a sip then immediately replaced it on the table, her face twisted in disappointment.

"Look," explained Saero-yi, very earnest. "The Chinese team are *real* mathematicians. Even the dumbass, Hao Li. Not like the North Korean team."

"What are you, if not real mathematicians?"

He answered this question with a noticeable puff of his chest. "There are no real mathematicians in DPRK. Anyone who excels in math gets recruited to study computer programming. Me and Woo-sik are cyber warriors, part of the Phoenix Protocol. The other two make nuclear weapons for the Kim. But still, the Kim wants us to win medals at the math Olympiad. It makes the country look good, which makes him look good."

Oh yeah, Saero-yi was proud of this, whatever it meant. And he wasn't the only one to find him impressive; Margo Daniels was gazing at him like he was her long-lost son. "The *Phoenix Protocol*, really? Darn it all if we haven't hit the jackpot with you, Saero-yi."

I huffed a sigh. "What's the Phoenix Protocol, when it isn't picking up drycleaning for your mom?"

"Cy-ber-war-rior," he repeated, forming the syllables carefully with his rather perfect, soft lips. The braces on his teeth didn't detract even a bit from his attractiveness. On the contrary, they were a single point of imperfection that added to his boyish cuteness, like a beauty spot. For a moment I lost focus, captivated by the expressive movements of his eyes and mouth in this new, animated mood he'd struck. As handsome as he'd been in unflappable, understated mode, it was surpassed by this confident, self-assured and slightly arrogant mode. "We take, we disrupt. Banks. Hospitals. Communications. Power infrastructure."

"Mind telling us what you're working on right now?" Daniels asked. She flashed him a grin, baring a row of white, even front teeth. The contrast with Saero-yi's was briefly distracting, I wondered whether she'd gone through a whole orthodontal ordeal to get them looking that way or was she just lucky? "Man, I'd just love to know. Think of it like a token of trust."

He pulled himself upright, cleared his throat and faced her squarely. "Mostly we're working on disrupting comms in Ukraine."

I gasped as the implications hit me. "You're working for the *Russians*?"

There was a definite hint of queasiness in his reply. "We don't get to pick and choose. The team either takes money from banks, or we work for hire. Lately we've been hired out."

"I *knew* it," crooned Daniels. She oozed triumph. "No way those Russkiy hackers are good enough to be causing all that ruckus in Ukraine. Shuttin' down satellites and whatnot, you know, we've estimated that maybe ten thousand people have gotten killed directly because of failed comms to the front line."

The sober content of her statement took down everyone's mood. Saero-yi's queasiness overtook him, all that prior confidence now deflated.

She kept talking. I wondered if she'd enjoyed shaming him like that. Or maybe it was a test – did he care that his work had gotten people killed?

"Looks like I snagged myself a Phoenix Protocol kid. Hoo-boy, Saero-yi, I think you may be just *too* valuable to defect." Before I could ask her to explain what the alternative might look like, Daniels once again turned her attention to me. "Veronica, you really are the gift that keeps giving. Bringing me a peach like this, it 'hits different' as you kids like to say."

It was impossible to resist sarcasm. "'Hits different?' Is that supposed to make it okay that the spy agencies for the world's most evil tyrants know about me now, that I have telepathic powers?"

Daniels frowned. "What makes you think Ilyin, or the Kim give a rat's ass about you? Prolly don't even know you exist."

The aircon was set too high, it made goosebumps prickle the bare skin of my arms. I took a moment to look around the tiny interview room into which we'd been put along with Officer Daniels and three cups of watery coffee from the drinks machine. No noticeboard to distract me, just bare, light gray walls and a dark gray carpet. At one end of the room a South Korean flag hung from a standing pole. It wasn't a flag I was familiar with, and I found myself wondering what the various symbols on it meant. When I'd tired of staring at the flag, I dragged my attention back to Margo Daniels, who was watching me with a wry expression playing about her face, like she'd heard me start a promising-sounding joke but doubted my ability to hit the punchline. Saero-yi, on the other hand, was now more alert than I'd yet seen him. He seemed to listen carefully to everything either of us said and reply only after he'd weighed our words.

"Because of what Saero-yi just told us! His sister, Susie Jang, told Cheka that I'm a one-dub. So, I'm asking you: do RGB, Cheka and your colleagues in Langley all know about me? Am I on their radar?"

I put my head on one-side, waiting for Daniels to reply. High-up on the wall opposite was a high window. Through it I could just glimpse the leaves of a cherry tree. I imagined myself sitting in that tree looking down into this room, watching myself. People every day took decisions that fundamentally altered the course of their lives. I was doing it from inside the air-conditioned chill of an anonymous office on land legally administered by a country I'd never visited.

Daniels pursed her lips. "*Someone* in each of those

orgs knows, yes. I highly doubt it's widely shared. These are very closed people, Roni. Secrets are life and death. In DPRK, probably only Doctor Susie, because well, like I said, she's working for us now. But all of this just goes to reinforce what I told you. It's why you should join us. You're *already in the game*. You're a player."

Bitterly, I laughed. "If I am, I'm what, a pawn?"

"Pawn can take the king," Saero-yi replied, softly. "Just like any piece on the board. You only need to be on the board and to stay in play."

"Maxim needs you," I told Saero-yi, looking him directly in the eye. I turned to Daniels. "I don't like to let my friends down. Please don't make me do that."

A tiny dimple formed in her rosy left cheek as a slow smile crept across her face. "I do declare, is that a threat, darlin'?"

My scoff barely touched the level of contempt I felt. Everything seemed to be a joke with this woman. It made me uncomfortable – I preferred things when I was the one hiding my fear with jokes. Was Margo Daniels actually worried that I might refuse to work for her unless she let me make good on my promise to Maxim, or was she just a psycho who found unsettling things funny? I consoled myself with the fact that at least I'd finally figured out what Maxim wanted from Saero-yi.

'We take from banks.'

Margo Daniels was practically salivating at the prestige and power she would earn from bringing a North Korean-trained cyber warrior, telepathic intelligence agent to her new unit in the CIA. She'd set her mind to military ops, to saving lives on the battlefield, to learning the secrets of the Phoenix Protocol. Maxim, on the other hand, wanted something a lot simpler: cash. With cash he'd be free from the threats of the Carillo family. That made a lot of sense to me – you definitely don't want to be in hock to a narco.

"I told Maxim I'd get Saero-yi so that he could help him get money," I said, addressing them both. "I don't know how you do things, but if I tell a friend I'm doing a thing..." I shrugged. "Then I'm doing it. So, whatever your plans for Saero-yi, Officer Daniels, first you have to let him do a thing. Something that hopefully gets Max a lot of money." I leaned my forearms on the table, resting my chin on my right palm. "There's pretty much zero way I can even *think* of doing anything else in the 'spy' category. Not until Saero-yi has done that."

TWENTY-ONE

GAMJATANG AND OTHER DELICACIES

Daniels left us again, this time heading off with two serious-looking men in suits, white shirts and neck ties. A ridiculously slim woman approached. She had on her own, tailored version of the suit and glossy black, patent leather high heels. She carried a generous-sized patterned cloth tied at the top with a big knot. Setting it down, she untied the knot and took out at least ten cardboard takeout boxes, along with plastic bowls and spoons. She left with a polite bow and some words in Korean. Saero-yi responded with a broad smile and his own bow. Then his expression became immediately feral and determined as he sat at the table and one by one, opened the boxes.

The air filled with delicious aromas, meaty and spicy. As he opened each box, he let out a happy groan and began spooning rice and then chunks of stew into his bowl. He took a bite, closed his eyes in rapture and then urged me to join him.

"Oh my gosh, *gamjatang*. They gave me this, my first day in Pyongyang. First real Korean food I ever tasted."

"You didn't have Korean food as part of your training?"

He spared exactly one second from his enjoyment of the food to utter a derisory snort. "At the Krylov? They *tried*. But they had no clue."

I watched Saero-yi lose the will to do anything but taste more of that food. Tentatively, I took a bite. It was good – a pork stew with beans and potatoes. Very spicy. As we ate, through careful questions I began to learn more about Saero-yi's life since he'd left the Krylov Foundation.

Like all the K-Foundation kids, his early education had been focused around languages. As well as the English and Russian they all learned, he'd also been trained to speak Korean, Mandarin and Cantonese. He'd mastered the North Korean and also two South Korean accents. His excellence in math had emerged when he was around twelve years old and from then on his training had been oriented towards it almost to the exclusion of everything else. He'd learned about the food and culture, too, albeit a tepid version of the real deal. Aged eighteen, he'd finally been delivered to the North Korean capital, Pyongyang.

I asked him if he'd been happy at the Krylov camp. The only two-dubs I'd known had hated it, but then again, I'd only met the kids who'd wanted to escape badly enough to make it a reality. So far, Saero-yi had shown little sign of having been unhappy there. Even now, he seemed bemused by the question.

"I liked doing math. It's good to do what you're good at."

I asked if he'd been close with Maxim. He shook his head, wiping sauce from his lips with a careful press of one of the napkins in the bag. "Jaguar? I was scared of him. Most of us were."

"Scared? Why?"

"Even the sentinels were scared of Jaguar. When he escaped, I was glad."

I pushed him a bit on this. Turns out that Maxim had vanished when he was around thirteen years old.

Saero-yi knew nothing about what'd happened to him. "He wanted to follow some kid called 'Rabbit,' a kid who supposedly escaped." Doubt filled his eyes, and he spooned more rice into his mouth. When he'd chewed and swallowed it, he continued. His table manners, I have to say, were impeccable.

"Then you haven't been in contact with Maxim, not at all?"

Firmly, he shook his head. "Haven't seen him for six years."

"Can you even do what he wants you to do?"

He chuckled. "Steal money for him? Yes. That's a lot of what we train to do – we're not as focused on it as the Lazarus Group, but the Phoenix Protocol has boosted major crypto in its time."

"How would you do it?"

Saero-yi shrugged, then turned his attention to the remaining unopened box. When he saw its contents, he laughed out loud. "Kimchi, yes!" Filling a spoon, he offered to add it to my bowl. "This you have to try. Fermented cabbage with radishes, ginger and garlic. A real taste of Korea." I tried some. Zesty with a lot of umami.

The food was evidently making a good impression on him. The South Koreans were learning who he was, no doubt. A guy with his talents was definitely a 'unicorn' for any of the intelligence services.

"Your dance card is going to get busy," I remarked.

"Huh?"

"You saw how Officer Daniels was drooling over you. A telepath who's also a cyber warrior! Makes me wonder how the North Koreans let you go."

"They didn't 'let me.' You took them by surprise. It was a good plan."

"Maxim's plan, with help from the CIA," I admitted.

"You did your part, too. To be honest, it's the first operation I've been part of that goes so well. In the past, well, we've had a few hiccups."

When I looked up from my bowl, Saero-yi was gazing at me as though I'd told a really skeezy joke. I scowled. "What?"

"This operation isn't over."

"Duh, I realize that dummy. You have to do your cyber warrior thingy for Maxim. But you can do that from anywhere, right?"

"Not from the South Korean consulate. They almost certainly won't let me do something illegal on their territory in a foreign land. And even if they did... that's not the problem."

"Oh?"

"The problem is – how do I get out of here? Woo-sik won't be the only RGB agent here in San Francisco. The second they figured out I was missing; they knew the score. Things like this happen for one reason only – an agent plans to defect. The South Korean consulate is the obvious place to take me. They'll know where to catch me."

"They Julian Assange-d your ass," I breathed, astonished. Then I had to explain that Julian Assange was a guy wanted for crimes relating to leaking CIA and other secrets, who'd taken refuge for years in an Ecuadorean consulate. Turned out that Saero-yi had many substantial gaps in his knowledge of the world. Now, apparently, he was trapped in a place where even his unique skills might be no use to him – or to anyone else. "It was too bad we didn't make it to Maxim's safe house."

Saero-yi took a long moment to reflect on what I'd said, meantime serving himself a second helping of the *gamjatang*, rice and kimchi. He began once again to eat, a contented expression settling over his features. "It's not all bad news. In another few hours the morphorium will wear off. Then my full powers will return. Maybe we'll think of a way."

"You're on morphorium? Then how were you managing to broadcast to me?"

"Broadcasting is so fundamental, the dose of morpho you'd need to inhibit it makes us ineffective for any higher brain processing. For example, I'd barely be able to code."

"Exactly *what* gets inhibited by morpho, then?" This seemed like an ideal chance to learn more about what two-dubs could do. I knew a little about the Gen 6 psi powers, which only Sacha and Maxim seemed to have mastered. I didn't, however, know what psi powers were shared with Gen 5 telepaths.

"Reading, empathy, blocking and clouding. All of those are dampened so hard by morpho, they barely work."

"'Reading?'"

He blinked a couple of times, then looked at me with earnest eyes. "You don't actually know what our powers are?"

"I know about clouding and blocking. And inclination, inception, somatization, derangement. The other two things didn't really come up."

Saero-yi continued to stare at me, his expression unchanging for a few seconds until finally he let go a tight, uncertain laugh. "What?"

"Clouding, blocking, inclination," I began.

"What the heck is 'inclination.' And all those other things."

Slowly, my mouth formed a small 'o.' "Do you know about Generation Six?"

Reader, he did not.

TWENTY-TWO

ARE YOU IN LOVE WITH HIM?

A lot happened over the next two hours. It began
with me explaining to Saero-yi the little I knew about
Gen 6 telepath powers – a surreal experience, since I'm
just a humble one-dub and pretty clueless at that. He
listened with absolute and intense concentration, which
over time softened into a dawning realization. My
explanation unlocked something, apparently; an
explanation for some of the odd things he'd observed,
in the months before Maxim-slash-Jaguar escaped the
Krylov camp.

"Jaguar would freak out before the skills evaluation.
It was the only time I ever saw him really anxious."
Saero-yi explained to me then that the more usual
response to the evaluation was a kind of hopeful
anticipation, not the drawn, pinch-faced silence that had
fallen over Maxim at least 24 hours before each
evaluation. "You wanted to impress the panel, for them
to see all the potential you had. We believed that the
best assignments would go to the most powerful
telepaths. Everyone knew that was Jaguar. It didn't make
sense that he would get so weird about the evals." He
began to nod with increasing earnestness. "But if he
didn't *want* them to know about those new powers?
Yeah. That's got to be the reason."

I thought about it for a few seconds, reflecting on

what Sacha had told me about their upbringing in the Krylov foundation. "If Krylov had known about those powers, perhaps he'd have made sure Maxim could never escape?"

Grimly, Saero-yi agreed. "Jaguar is a lot smarter than me. I was a cocky little math genius, and I didn't care who knew it. Therefore, I have never had the benefit of being underestimated."

He was more right than he knew. Even as we chatted, in some office within the consulate, a phone call was being placed from the office of the Kim. In the understated yet unmistakably blood-curdling language of diplomacy, the North Korean dictator issued his ultimatum. *Return my property immediately or suffer the consequences.*

Meantime, I took a call from Kenzie. He was raging about how things had played out. Why hadn't we stuck to the plan? What was he supposed to do, on his own, out in San Francisco? I reminded him that his moms were arriving in town any minute, he could hang out with them. For some reason, this ticked him off even more. "The point is, Roni, what about you? I'm supposed to just leave you here, in the clutches of the CIA?"

I chewed down on my lower lip, suppressing my instinct to snap back. Oh-so-many ways to snap back at a guy telling me I don't know what's best for me. But I knew he meant well, as hugely irritating as it was to have to let that one by. That's when I understood that in the game of love (if love is a game), Kenzie had in fact pulled ahead by telling me how he felt. Now I had to be nice to him, because *congenial* was all I could offer and only a total B is mean to her best friend, whose love she cannot return.

Kenzie's ragged sigh landed in the silence between

us. Then in a voice that sounded exhausted, resigned, he asked, "Are you in love with him? With Maxim? Is this why you're doing all of this?"

His question was like a lazy slap with a damp towel – heavy and slow but not painful. A blow I'd seen coming a mile away, because I'd asked myself that question a few times by now, even if I hadn't phrased it so obviously. A thing you hide from yourself can only be exposed if you sidle up to it, catch it unawares. Which somehow, is what Kenzie managed to do, even with his plain language, because the last place I expected to be talking about my feelings for Maxim was in the South Korean consulate, and the last person I expected to be giving any pause to my answer, was a Korean boy I'd met only hours before.

How could I possibly be in love with Maxim, or with Kenzie for that matter, if a hottie like Saero-yi had so swiftly caught my eye? Don't get me wrong – this came as a surprise to me, something I was glad to discover about myself. I've known for ages that love isn't for me – not yet anyhow. Love ties you down and I didn't want that. Not in mystery podcaster mode nor in this new possibility – spy!Roni. Maybe I was turning out to have what my mom used to call a 'roving eye.' One boy just might not be enough.

"Maxim asked me to do this, and I said I would," I replied, side-stepping Kenzie's question. "He owes money to a narco. Saero-yi can help him get the cash to pay him back."

"Not your fault, not our problem."

"Oh yeah? Maxim's money paid for us to get out of Cuba, it's paying our hotel bill here."

"Places we only had to be on account of doing something for him."

"I'd do the same for you, Kenzie. I keep my word."

He inhaled slowly, obviously vexed. I could have explained myself further, but right then I was annoyed with him for not understanding the obvious reasons, things that required nothing except respect for the firm bond of friendship we'd once had with Maxim, a bond we'd rekindled, at least in my view. The door opened then, and two consulate officers stepped into the room. The temperature seemed instantly to drop. One look at their faces was enough to tell me that the news was bad.

I was right – they were about to drop the news about the Kim ultimatum.

"I'll call you back," I whispered into the phone. "Something's up."

After a quiet word with one of the South Koreans, Margo Daniels cleared her throat slightly then turned to me, her features composed in a calm, serious mask. When she spoke, however, there was a catch to her voice that I'd begun to recognize. She was nervous.

"Well, I *can* tell y'all that a scenario is playing out, one we'd anticipated." Her eyebrows lifted a little before she returned her expression to its previous neutral demeanor. "The North Koreans figured that you're here, Saero-yi. They're not shilly-shallying, they know we want you. Well, Kim wants you back. Now there's a deal on the table."

Saero-yi wrapped both arms around himself and began to chuckle. "Sucks for him that he can't threaten to send my family to the labor camp, I guess. Krylov made sure I don't even know whether I *have* family."

Daniels shut her eyes briefly, then nodded. "I'll hand it to you; you're in the ballpark. If you don't go back they'll send the rest of your math team to the work camps."

Saero-yi burst out laughing. "Oh *really*? And tomorrow it'll rain lemon popsicles."

"Why not just deny it?" I asked, directing my question at the South Koreans. "Do they have any actual proof?"

One of them bowed a little before replying in smooth American English, barely a hint of accent; "They claim to have CCTV. It's plausible. The Phoenix Protocol could have hacked the city traffic cameras, unfortunately."

Saero-yi shook his head in disbelief and amusement. "Phoenix Protocol? You have one of them right here. Just give me access to the server. I'll find out where they broke in and delete whatever they took, from wherever they've stored it."

Daniels stared at him in wonder. "You can do that?"

Blinking slowly, he smiled. "Can I do that? Oh, yeah."

TWENTY-THREE

THE PLAN

You'd think there would be some guardrails around letting a trained North Korean cyber warrior loose on San Francisco's traffic server. Seems like Margo Daniels had enough reach to be able to authorize a thing like that, because within the hour, the South Koreans had installed Saero-yi in an office with a desk, laptop and three giant computer screens. After a few minutes, word got out and others left their own desks, gradually crowding into the office to watch in awed silence as Saero-yi waved his coding magic, flipping from screen to screen, typing in windows scrolling neon green text on black background, barely stopping to think for more than a second at a time.

I watched too, the whole time understanding basically nothing – just enough to know that maybe it was a good thing Kenzie had gotten trapped outside the consulate. Because – who knew how he'd take observing a master like Saero-yi? Maybe he'd be in awe too, maybe he'd turn into a total fanboy.

I suspected it wouldn't go that way, however. Kenzie had a fiercely competitive streak. When we were kids, Maxim had always been the talented one, the best at everything, so good that it was pointless to feel any sense of competition. There was none – he was literally in another league. So, it'd been cool years later for

Kenzie to discover he'd grown up to be good at something Maxim couldn't do. Now it turned out Maxim all along had a friend who showed up Kenzie as the amateur he really was.

No, Kenzie will not think it's copacetic.

Before the packed audience of South Korean consulate nerds, Saero-yi did just as he'd promised. There were hushed mutterings – all in Korean, so don't ask me what they said – and a senior dude was hauled in to coo over Saero-yi's findings. Unlike the other staff, he didn't wear a suit but walked round in rolled up shirtsleeves, no necktie and a light blue hoodie hanging around his shoulders. After a little while watching Margo Daniels, I realized that she understood Korean because she was occasionally nodding and smiling as the senior guy made a little speech, after which a burst of polite applause brought a huge grin to Saero-yi's face.

"He did it?" I whispered to Daniels.

"Oh lordy, did he ever."

After that, they gathered us back into the room we'd first been taken to. It felt like I was pretty much an after-thought by then, tagging along like it was Bring Your Daughter To Work Day. Unobserved, I watched everyone else. The senior dude, who I caught Daniels referring to as 'Park,' the two guys in sharp suits and ties, who'd been involved from the start, Daniels and Saero-yi. All spoke in quick-fire Korean, the discussion veering toward sounding punchy. Until Daniels poured oil over the troubled waters, or whatever it is they pour to calm everyone down. After she'd spoken in Korean she immediately switched to English. I guessed she was translating for my benefit.

"Saero-yi got rid of the evidence. Which is good, helps to avoid a diplomatic incident. He is legally of age, so he can officially request asylum. However, the

North Koreans are alleging that we took him against his will." She held a hand up then, silencing me before I could offer a suggestion. "Not much we can do would be convincing. They'll just up and cry 'coercion,' faster'n we can say 'crackerjacks.'"

"The boy needs to leave," said the be-suited consulate official who spoke great English. As though I'd just emerged on a dais from the ground, he seemed to notice me for the first time. "The girl, too. I suggest we use the BTS Plan."

The two other South Koreans nodded sagely, in complete agreement. Daniels nodded too, and then as if it were a mere afterthought added, "That's where y'all disguise someone as a pop star or some such shenanigans?"

I'd heard of 'BTS' – a one-time most-popular boyband, slingers of insanely adorable K-pop tunes, so I was just about able to intuit what a 'BTS Plan' might be. Not Saero-yi, though. We'd revealed a huge gap in his local knowledge – he'd never heard of this particular K-pop sensation.

"Of course he hasn't heard of BTS," said the consulate guy with the smooth English. He spoke in an aloof, slightly simpering way now, hands behind his back and nose ever-so-slightly tipped high into the air. "They give you years of hard labor for listening to K-pop in the North."

I flicked my head towards Saero-yi, waiting for his usual chortle of scorn. But no. Eyes solemn and round, he nodded. "It's true. Entertainment from the South is forbidden. A girl at Pyongyang university was taken away, and she wasn't even the one who did the crime. Her *sister* was caught distributing a popular TV show. Even its name was forbidden. They rounded up the whole family. No-one heard anything about them since then."

An involuntary gasp escaped my lips. "You're lying." I looked each person in the eyes, the two consulate officers in suits, Mister Park, Saero-yi and Margo Daniels. None flinched, each meeting my incredulous gaze with a sad nod or a resigned shrug.

They were serious. There was literally a place on Earth where you could get hard labor just because someone in your family watched the wrong TV show. And I'd led such a sheltered life that I didn't know anything about it, until that day in the South Korean consulate.

"So, we need a new plan," I said, trying to refocus. "Something less obvious than the BTS Plan. How about posing as a K-drama cast instead? I've watched some K-dramas, I might be able to help come up with some ideas. Saero-yi can be the lead in a new series. You two," I pointed to the consulate officials, "You could be his co-stars. The plot could be about a young, brooding hacker trying to escape his past."

Mr. Park, arms crossed and brow furrowed, shook his head. "Too on-the-nose, surely? The hacker trope is overdone, and it would raise too many questions. We need something with more depth, more nuance."

I blinked. Was Mr. Park seriously critiquing my (admittedly hastily-put-together) K-drama plot? "Alright, how about a time-travel romance with body-swapping Joseon princes?"

Saero-yi looked bemused. "Body-swapping princes?"

Mr. Park sighed; his tone exasperated. "That's been done too, and quite well, in fact. We need a fresh angle."

Saero-yi's confusion was almost tangible. "Wait, this is a thing? Time travel and body-swapping princes?"

"Yes," Mr. Park said solemnly. "It's called 'Rooftop Prince.' Hugely popular."

I glanced at Saero-yi, who was shaking his head in disbelief. "Alright, how about this: a small seaside village, shenanigans ensue when a visiting K-pop star gets stranded. We could say we're filming on location in San Francisco to capture the 'seaside' feel."

Mr. Park raised an eyebrow. "Seaside village shenanigans are classic, but we need something with a bit more gravitas. And a reason why a K-pop star would be at the South Korean consulate in San Francisco."

"Maybe a slow-burn romance in a garrison village," I suggested, getting into the swing of things. "Rich girl meets humble-yet-authentic boy. As for why they're at the consulate, well, surely they're here to get some documents sorted before filming starts?"

Saero-yi chuckled softly. "Rich girl meets humble-yet-authentic boy... in a garrison village? That sounds... like something that wouldn't happen in real life."

"Oh, you'd be surprised," Mr. Park said with a knowing smile. "There's a very famous drama called 'Descendants of the Sun' that's not too far off from that."

Saero-yi's eyes widened. "You're serious? These shows exist?"

Mr. Park nodded. "Indeed, they do. And they are beloved."

I rolled my eyes. "Okay, Mr. K-drama Expert, why don't you suggest something?"

Mr. Park leaned forward, fingers steepled. "What if we combine elements? Our cover story is this: a young, talented actor – played by Saero-yi – returns to South Korea after spending years abroad. He's back for a film project about a historical figure who time-travels to modern-day Seoul. Where he meets a parallel version of himself, who is an actor. The project is hush-hush, hence the need for tight security and minimal entourage."

Saero-yi looked thoughtful. "I'd play a historian? Interesting."

I grinned. "A historical *figure*, not historian. Although he could be an historian, why not? And you'd also play an actor."

"I like historian," Saero-yi replied, firmly. "Gives him a reason for the time-traveling. And he should be from the nineteen-twenties." He smiled broadly, showing off his tracks. "Gatsby era. Roaring Twenties, Prohibition, all of that. I love the clothes from that time."

I smiled back. It felt good to be creating something with him. "Sure, Jay, why not. Or are you more of a Nick? And our reason for being at the consulate is to handle the necessary paperwork for filming, ensuring everything is legit. After we're done, we head to LA for K-Wave Con, where we unveil a teaser for the show."

Margo Daniels finally spoke up. She'd watched our back and forth in silence, only the occasional arch of an eyebrow giving no clue to her reaction. "And who would be part of this Gatsby-esque entourage?"

"Saero-yi, me, and Mr. English Speaker over there," I said, pointing at the consulate official who had spoken perfect English earlier. "Maybe we can rope in another consulate officer to play another character from the nineteen-twenties." I thought suddenly of the sleek, elegant young woman who'd brought us *gamjatang*. "We need to keep it tight, keep it believable. How about that girl we spoke to before, the boujee one? If anyone's giving Flapper Girl, it's her."

Mr. Park nodded slowly. "Yoon Cha-young? Yes, she is most..." He suddenly blushed, became flustered. "An interesting suggestion. This could work. But we need a convincing backstory for each character, especially Saero-yi's."

"Easy," I said, feeling a surge of excitement. "Saero-yi is an up-and-coming actor, either he grew up or trained in the USA. You and Mr. Smooth English are his co-stars, and I'm the American publicist helping with the international launch."

"And what's our drama called?" Mr. Park asked, leaning back in his chair.

"How about 'Echoes of Time'?" I suggested thinking on the fly. "It's vague enough to encompass time travel and historical elements, but also modern intrigue."

Mr. Park considered this, then nodded. "Very well. We'll need to draft a detailed script and backstory to ensure consistency. And we must prepare Saero-yi for potential questions from fans and media."

Saero-yi looked at me, a mix of amusement and disbelief on his face. "I've never acted before."

I patted his shoulder. "You'll do fine. Just think of it as another form of hacking – except this time, you're hacking people's perceptions."

Margo Daniels chuckled. "Quite the analogy. Now, I wanna hear y'all flesh out this storyline."

We spent the next hour throwing ideas around, hammering out details. Saero-yi's character was a brilliant historian with a mysterious past in Sausalito, California, accidentally transported to Seoul in the future, where he meets his doppelgänger, a renowned modern-day actor. The plot thickened with romance, Gatsby-esque intrigue, and a dash of Prohibition era smuggling.

At one point, Saero-yi, who had been quiet for a

while, looked up. "This is all very elaborate. Are K-dramas really this intricate?"

Mr. Park gave a benevolent smile. "Some are even more so. You'd be amazed at the creativity and complexity involved. But this should be simple enough for us to execute convincingly."

As the meeting wrapped up, I couldn't shake the feeling that I was stepping further into a labyrinth, one where each twist and turn pulled me deeper into the shadows of a life I wasn't sure I was ready for. But as I met Daniel's approving gaze, I sensed there was no turning back from here.

"That was smart stuff, Roni," she said, her smile as fresh and honest as I'd ever seen from Daniels. "I had a feeling you'd have a knack for this. Good to see I was right."

I felt a strange mix of pride and unease. This world of espionage was surprisingly seductive, luring me deeper with each small victory. I glanced at Saero-yi, who was studying me intently. Could he sense my conflicting emotions? It wouldn't surprise me.

As we left the room, I realized that the line between reality and the fictional world we were creating was starting to blur. And that was both thrilling and terrifying.

TWENTY-FOUR

Alter Egos

"Beautiful young Korean actors exist in abundance in South Korea, that is true," observed Mr. Park, pensive as he gripped his chin with his left palm. He'd wrapped the hoodie around his waist by now, pushed his shirt sleeves up past his elbows as he got more intensely into the planning session. He struck me as a man accustomed to being listened to, maybe because he was a senior officer in the consulate, probably enjoyed it, too. There was another dimension to his enjoyment of *this* activity, however; I think he liked being the resident K-drama expert. "Beautiful young actors however, notwithstanding their abundance, simply do not materialize from a vacuum." He grinned then, baring his teeth as he spread both hands, like a flower opening. "Therefore, our 'actors' require backstories, screen credits."

"Not a problem," Daniels replied, with a smug nod first towards Saero-yi, then me, as if telling Mr. Park, 'Look at what I brought you!' "Roni's something of a journalist, she can create backstory, Saero-yi can hack into the Internet Movie Database, give them some of that sweet industry cred."

Park had a staffer bring in a laptop for me, while Cha-young, the stylish consulate staffer who'd given us *gamjatang,* arrived with a measuring tape that she used to size up both me and Saero-yi. When I asked if we could pick outfits for our alter egos, she replied with a serene half-smile. "Please, just trust me," was all she'd say, in her soft-spoken Korean accent.

Over the next hour, Margo Daniels wandered in and out of our office, perching on the edge of the desk and reading over my shoulder. She hummed with approval a couple times, snorted with satisfaction and then stepped out, already on a call by the time she'd reached the door.

Two hours later, we'd done enough to satisfy Mr. Park. He read over everything I'd written, passed it to Mr. Smooth English (whose name I never learned) to proofread, then suggested some TV dramas and stage productions suitable as early credits for our fake thespians. Saero-yi hacked IMDB easily enough and showed no hint that it was beneath his status as an elite cyber warrior. He inserted the fake names of our fake actors into existing TV show entries, giving them bit parts obscure enough that no-one but a total K-drama nerd would ever question the information. Then he created the entry for *Echoes of Time*, our fake show, listing it as 'In Production' and adding Sausalito, California and a few districts of Seoul as filming locations.

Park and Daniels finally let us get some rest, which was an opportunity to sip on the best green tea I'd ever had, feeling a queasy mixture of excitement and nervousness. We were led to yet another room in the consulate, which contained a pull-out couch that had been made up as a double bed. Saero-yi just about managed to kick off his sneakers and mathlete team polo shirt before hitting the pillow, where he fell instantly asleep. He had on a white sleeveless T-shirt that made him look kind of sweet and vulnerable, exposing his skinny frame and under-exercised upper body. I took off my sneakers and lay down next to Saero-yi with my back turned to him. Neither of us made a thing about sharing the sofa, and when we woke up in the early morning, neither of us made a thing about the fact that we were spooning.

In silence, I wriggled away from him, marveling at how completely natural and *easy* it was to be close to Saero-yi.

This is what it's like to be into someone who's not any kind of a brother to you.

By nine we were back in the planning office. Daniels arrived first, Mr. Park rolled up a moment later. She had on the usual pants suit, today it was dark blue, and her hair was back in CIA officer mode – a smooth pull-back and pony-tail. But Park now looked natty in the black jeans, black dress shirt and gray plaid sports coat that transformed him into our fictional director.

"Remember, Roni, you're his publicist, but maybe there's a will-they-won't-they tension going on between you? Hold hands once in a while. it adds authenticity – actors are such players. And Saero-yi, you need to be confident. Channel that same intensity we saw yesterday, when you were hacking the traffic server."

Daniels interrupted, casting her eyes over Mr. Park's outfit. "Uh-uh. Nope. Think I'm gonna let you walk out of here looking like that? You're too recognizable. Better get those snazzy clothes over to someone else; some gray-haired salaryman that showed up every day of his life in the same darn suit."

Park glared, eyes bulging for a few seconds before his shoulders crumpled in defeat. Daniels was right. I'd spent a whole day at the consulate and seen no-one else that remotely looked or presented himself like Mr. Park.

Cha-young had really outdone herself with all the costumes, which she'd had overnighted to the consulate.

Dressed in a simple, floral jersey wrap dress and knitted, powder-blue cardigan with crisp white Keds, a look that screamed, 'up-and-coming publicist,' I almost felt the part.

I waited for the usual widened eyes and 'Gee you look nice in a dress, why don't you wear them more often?' reaction from the guys present, which ironically made me want to wear them even less, but not this time, not even from Saero-yi.

Daniels seemed to pick up on my surprise because she approached discreetly and murmured, "Ain't it good to be appreciated for your accomplishments and not how good you look?" At first, I didn't follow her gist, but she continued; "Or maybe it's just because they don't know you well enough? Sugar, chill; I'm sure if Kenzie were here it would be different."

My cheeks flushed hot with confusion and embarrassment. Daniels acknowledged my response with a knowing nod. "I do my homework, Roni. Obviously that includes knowing which boys you like and which ones like you back."

Her trivialization injected some rage into the mix and the heat reached my eyes. With a merry chuckle, she sashayed out of the room, leaving me feeling like I'd had the rug pulled from beneath me. Was this how she treated an asset? It was either a ploy, which I didn't understand at all, or else Daniels could be a total dick.

I went with the latter, took a breath and made a decision to push it aside. "Okay, 'Choi Min-jun,'" I said to Saero-yi, using his new alias, as we checked out our reflections in the mirror. "Ready to take on the world?"

He glanced at me, a hint of a smile on his lips. "As ready as I'll ever be, Miss Delarosa."

As we moved to the consulate lobby, Daniels caught up with us again. "You two look the part," she said approvingly. "Roni, your age and inexperience actually work to our advantage here. Less suspicious."

I nodded, feeling a bit more confident. "Got it. Blend in, act natural."

Then came the rider from Park. "Oh, and Saero-yi, an orthodontist is waiting for you in room thirty-one. Cha-young will escort you." He pulled back his upper lip and with a fingernail, loudly tapped his own bared front teeth. "The tracks? They have to go. Let's hope your teeth are already beautiful enough underneath them."

While I was waiting for Saero-yi to get his braces removed, Kenzie checked in by phone. We both knew his phone was at risk of being monitored, so I could only tell him that I was okay and missing him. Before he hung up, Kenzie asked if I'd slept well. There was tension in his voice, knowing, brittle and also a little smug. As if he'd guessed that I might like Saero-yi, hinting slyly that he knew my type. I thought – *whatever, bro. I can like whoever I like.*

As we exited the consulate, a chunky black SUV stood waiting. Cha-young trotted up to join us. She'd changed too, out of the formal staffer clothes and into pale gray-and-white sneakers, cream-colored joggers with scooped white tee under a soft pink hoodie that dropped off one shoulder: 'Seo Hye-ko,' demure TV actress enjoying a rest day. I guessed she was relieved to be out of the high heels, for once. Beaming, she handed me a compact, stylish cross-body bag, whispering, "Everything you need is in there. Phone, documents, even some makeup for touch-ups."

As we drove through the streets of San Francisco, I gazed warily through the windows, scanning for any sign that we were being followed. The North Koreans had figured out that Saero-yi had gone to the consulate.

If the K-drama ruse had leaked already, this would be over pretty fast. The only question was – how? Would they attempt to kidnap Saero-yi? Or just assassinate him? I couldn't help but feel a thrill. We were really doing this. Our cover story was in place, and for the first time, I felt a strange sense of belonging in this world of espionage.

TWENTY-FIVE

I Spy

The first field test of our new identities came when we reached the boutique hotel where we'd be staying in Sausalito, a photogenic harborside town across from the Golden Gate Bridge. As we checked in, I played my part, chatting animatedly with Saero-yi about our fictional project, throwing in little details we'd rehearsed. The hotel staff seemed convinced, and I saw Saero-yi relax a little.

Arriving in the two-room apartment, he turned to me. "You're good at this."

"Guess all those drama club classes paid off."

"You studied acting? But the CIA woman said something about journalism...?"

I laughed softly. "I took those classes in the sixth grade. Daniels was talking about my podcast. I investigate cold cases, unsolved mysteries. At least, I did, until a few weeks ago. That's how all this got started. I was investigating Maxim – Jaguar's – disappearance. Feels like a lifetime ago."

Saero-yi absorbed this without further comment, just the same brief widening of his eyes I'd noticed each time he received some new information, as though he was swallowing a gobbet of data and digesting it.

We settled into our rooms, and as I unpacked, I noticed Saero-yi staring out the window, lost in thought.

"You okay?"

He glanced up and nodded. For just a second I caught a glimpse of the vulnerable boy I'd seen last night when he'd collapsed onto the bed, drained from what had been a very long day. "Just... trying to process all of this. It's a lot to take in."

"Do you feel bad about missing the math contest?"

Startled, he scoffed. "Do I care about denying the Kim my sweat and a medal? Hell, no. I knew this would be my chance to defect, I've been thinking about it for years, even in the Krylov camp. Jaguar promised he'd come for me, after he escaped. He never doubted that he'd find his way to freedom."

"Yeah, he's a confident guy, always was."

Saero-yi fixed me with a direct look. "Even so, I doubted him. He may be confident, but he alienates people. I didn't think anyone would help him."

"His brother did."

His eyebrows lifted high. "Jaguar has a brother?"

"You didn't know?"

With a shrug, he shook his head. "I didn't. He kept that pretty quiet."

"I don't think he found out until late in the day. Kenzie and I knew Max when he was a kid, until he was twelve. He never mentioned a brother then, either. Maybe he found out after you left the camp?"

"Possible. Anyway, when I found out from my sister, Susie, that this was on the cards..."

Interrupting I asked, "You felt bad about doubting Jaguar?"

A bashful smile flickered over his lips. "I didn't feel bad. I doubted him *all over again*."

"Yet here we are."

His smile became an awkward guffaw. "Here we are."

I walked over, placing a hand on his shoulder. "I get it. But we're in this together. And hey, if we pull this off, it'll make one heck of a story for my podcast. One day. If they ever let me tell my stories."

He smiled, a real one this time. "*If they ever let you*, yeah, it will."

In the living room of our hotel apartment, I set up my laptop, ready to act as the communication link between Saero-yi and Targeting Officer Daniels. On the burner, Maxim had sent me a link to a secure online location where he'd outlined our next steps. Most of it was in techie gobbledygook but I picked up enough to gather that he wanted Saero-yi to start probing some financial networks, subtly testing the waters.

Saero-yi read the message, frowning. "This is risky."

"I know," I said. "But Jaguar thinks it's necessary. And he trusts you."

He sighed but nodded. "Alright. Let's get to work."

As Saero-yi started his cyber operations, I watched his fingers fly over the keyboard, once again in awe at his skill. His fingers moved twice as fast as Kenzie's whenever I'd observed him, opening and shutting new coding windows at double the speed, too. This was a whole new world to me.

Kenzie called me around ten in the morning. He was ticked off that Daniels had ordered him right back to his moms and that he'd not been allowed to enjoy our room at the Westin even for one night. Miserably, he told me, "Didn't even get to the breakfast buffet. Daniels had some flunky pick up our stuff and deliver it to the B-and-B."

"Well, your moms do enjoy a cute B-and-B."

"It's literally adorable," he grumbled. "The rooms have handmade patchwork quilts with matching pillow shams. Home-made bread, eggs from their own chickens, all strutting about in the backyard. Peaches picked fresh from their own hothouse. My moms are in heaven."

Laughing, I tried to say goodbye, but he hesitated, hanging on the line until finally, he managed to say what he'd been holding back. "This feels wrong, only being able to talk by phone. I miss you."

"Miss you too," I said. It might have tripped out a little automatically.

Kenzie's voice dropped to a whisper. "I'm sorry. It's my fault Daniels got her hooks into you. I wish..." He fell silent for a moment, and I held my breath until he continued. "I wish you wouldn't do this. You don't have to."

"Kenzie," I reminded him, gently. "I'm doing this for Maxim. Not for Daniels."

A beat passed. I heard his breath catch. He started to say something and then stopped, switching to a croaky "Talk soon. Bye."

Hours passed, and as evening fell, Saero-yi and I took a break. I ordered room service; two turkey club sandwiches with a side of fries. We ate in companionable silence. I could see the strain in Saero-yi's eyes, the weight of the responsibility he carried. Just as we were finishing up, my phone buzzed. It was Maxim, checking in again.

"Padi, I need you to do me a favor," he said, his voice uncharacteristically serious. "Stick close to Saero-yi. Make him feel comfortable. I'm worried CIA are going to steal him from under our noses, so we're stepping up the hackery. We might need to move some cryptocurrency over the next few days, too."

I frowned. Sounded like Saero-yi had been on the right track. "Cryptocurrency? Why?"

"Let's just say it's a contingency plan," he replied, enigmatic.

There was obviously more to it than he was letting on, but now wasn't the time to press him. "Alright, I'll do what I can."

Apparently as an afterthought, he asked, "You're getting along okay, the two of you?"

I wasn't imagining it – there was a tightness in his voice as Maxim spoke these words. He sounded semi-strangled. In spite of myself, my stomach fluttered for a moment.

Is he actually jealous?

Max and Kenzie both vexed at the idea of me getting close to Saero-yi, alas, only made the boy more appealing.

After lunch I received a first message from the CIA. Daniels had forwarded detailed instructions for our activities for the day, outlining the fake filming schedule. Our cover was to film scenes near the iconic floating houses of Sausalito – a location that would draw minimal attention while providing a perfect backdrop for our fictional K-drama.

As I read through the message, I couldn't help but imagine the location. Sausalito was known for its colorful, quirky houseboats, bobbing gently on the water. The hues ranged from vibrant reds and yellows to soft pastels, creating a kaleidoscope of color that contrasted beautifully with the deep blue of the bay. The air would be filled with the scent of saltwater, mingling with the occasional whiff of seafood from nearby restaurants. Gulls would cry overhead, their calls blending with the gentle lapping of waves against the wooden docks.

I relayed the plan to Saero-yi as we prepared to

leave. He nodded, his expression serious. "Sounds good. We should be able to blend in."

As we sat in the back of the SUV, I hesitated before asking, "So, about what Maxim said... how exactly are you going to 'make cash appear out of thin air'? He said something about you moving crypto and transferring money, but it all sounded a bit... vague."

Saero-yi chuckled softly. "It's not exactly magic, Roni." Then, switching to telepathy he said, *What Maxim is planning is something called 'jackpotting.'*

I stared at him, bemused, and said nothing.

He nodded, leaning forward slightly. *A hacker gains control of an ATM, makes it dispense all the cash it has. In this case, I'll be hacking into a few ATMs in several Mexican towns. Maxim has a street team in place to collect the money from about a dozen machines. He recruited a bunch of people from one of those PA websites, young people mostly, gig economy types. We're looking at about two hundred and fifty thousand dollars in total.*

My eyes widened. "That's... a lot of cash."

He owes Carillo, replied Saero-yi with a shrug.

"And this street team... they're just going to collect the cash and get away without getting caught?"

"It's an easy gig," Saero-yi said, aloud. "Maxim knows what he's doing."

I absorbed this information, my mind racing. "What about the crypto part? Maxim mentioned something about that."

Saero-yi's tone became mysterious. *That's more complicated. Let's just say there's a larger plot at play. The crypto transactions are meant to cover our tracks, to make sure the authorities can't trace the money back to any of us.*

Slowly, I nodded, trying to wrap my head around the complexity of the operation. Here I was, right in the middle of something the details of which I was barely able to grasp. Yet I was beginning to understand why

Daniels had been so insistent on involving me. I wasn't there for my technical expertise; I was there because Maxim trusted me.

You couldn't say that about many people on this earth.

TWENTY-SIX

K-WAVE CON

Sausalito was all charm. The sun shone bold, casting a golden glow over the colorful boats. We set up near a particularly vibrant blue houseboat, its reflection shimmering in the clear water. The air was crisp and fresh, the salty snap of the bay mingling with the earthy scent of damp wood from the docks.

Our small crew consisted of consulate staff posing as camera operators, assistants and two more cast members played by Mr. Smooth English and Yoon Cha-young. They bustled about, setting up equipment like a genuine film set. Saero-yi and Cha-young took their positions, pretending to rehearse the handful of lines I'd written, purportedly from *Echoes of Time*. Mr. Park had helped out with this part – he'd pretty much insisted on it, as the resident expert. I could almost believe they were real actors, lost in the world of our fictional K-drama.

As we moved through the motions, I couldn't help but marvel at how smoothly everything was falling into place. The consulate staff were convincing in their roles, and the curious onlookers seemed to buy our story. It felt surreal, playing this part in such a beautiful and serene setting, all while knowing the high-stakes game in which we were truly involved.

During a break, I pulled Saero-yi aside. "This is

weird," I said, glancing around at the picturesque scene. "I mean, we're pretending to film a K-drama while you're planning a heist halfway across the continent. It's like living in two worlds at once."

Saero-yi smiled, a rare expression that softened his usually intense demeanor. "The money is just one piece of a much larger puzzle. Jaguar has big plans." He nodded to himself, silent for a moment, like there were aspects of this he couldn't share, and eventually concluded with, "Not many people are in a position to change the world."

I shivered slightly, not from the cold but from the dizzying implications he'd hinted at. I thought back to things Atlanta and Sacha had said about 'Jaguar' and his plans. What had seemed implausible when they'd shared their misgivings didn't seem quite so out-of-reach, not if he had access to serious wealth.

Just then the taciturn, be-suited consulate staffer appeared at my side. He'd been acting as the assistant director, taking orders directly from Mr. Park via an earpiece. It was the only time I remember him addressing me directly, for once speaking in English. "Problem," he said curtly. "Someone is taking pictures of the set. Might be nothing. Might be something. We need to go, quickly."

Tension rippled through the crew as everyone moved faster, packing up equipment and loading it into the van. I glanced at Saero-yi, who was already on his phone, fingers flying over the screen.

"What are you doing?" I whispered.

"Checking the area's network for any suspicious activity," he replied, his voice clipped in concentration. "If someone's tracking us, I'll find out."

I watched as his face remained impassive, the epitome of calm under pressure. Minutes later, he looked up, his expression a mix of relief and concern. "Nothing concrete, but better safe than sorry. We should move."

We piled into the van, the mood inside tense and silent. As we drove back to the hotel, I couldn't shake the feeling that we were being watched. Every car that followed us, every pedestrian we passed, seemed like a potential threat.

Back at the hotel, Daniels gathered us in the living room of the second apartment, where the other consulate staffers were staying. "Today was a success, but we can't afford any slip-ups. Tomorrow is the K-Wave convention. We need to be even more careful. Roni, Saero-yi, you two did great out there. I see y'all enjoying yourselves and that's good, it feels authentic. But keep in mind, this isn't a game. One wrong move, and this all gets a lot harder. North Koreans will use their own agents, and Ilyin will loan them Chekists, too. *Anyone* could be an adversary. Takes just a few seconds, one lapse in concentration, to whisk a person away. Don't give them the opportunity."

I nodded, the weight of her words sinking in. The line between reality and our cover was blurring, and the stakes were getting higher by the minute. As we dispersed, I caught Saero-yi's eye. There was a flicker of something there – determination, maybe, or resolve.

The morning of the K-Wave Con in Los Angeles dawned bright and clear. I was jittery, my nerves already frayed. This was a different ball game from the calm of Sausalito. As the self-appointed publicist for our fake K-drama *Echoes of Time*, I had to sell our little troupe to the throngs of K-drama and K-pop enthusiasts. Now in 'business' mode, I had on a smart, dark blue blazer, matching pencil skirt, and high heels, I felt like a clumsy impersonator in an ill-fitting role. My outfit, meant to project confidence and professionalism, instead felt like a prison.

From the moment I set foot inside the convention center I was hit by a wave of other people's energy and excitement. It felt like taking a soccer ball in the guts. For a full minute I struggled to breathe or even hear anyone else in our tiny group above the high-octane buzz of hundreds of gushing conversations. Everywhere I looked were loud marquees announcing the biggest shows, and behind them a couple dozen smaller booths for everything else.

It was overwhelming. I knew right away that I'd made a huge mistake agreeing to this. Gradually I tuned into Cha-young's voice, coming at me from my right.

"You must escort us to our booth and then complete the checklist of tasks." She tapped the clipboard that I'd been clinging to and had somehow forgotten all about. "Don't worry, 'Miss Delarosa,' I've planned many events like this."

In a small, strangled voice I replied, "Yeah. Thanks. Sorry, nerves. I don't do crowds. Classic introvert."

She closed her eyes and smiled discreetly. "I understand. Just work through the tasks. You will be okay."

The small booth for *Echoes of Time* was strategically located between more established stands, making our sudden appearance all the more conspicuous. Cha-young, posing as our glamorous lead actor, exuded effortless grace and poise. Saero-yi, meanwhile, looked intrigued and slightly amused by the whole spectacle.

A small crowd of fake fans, presumably briefed by Daniels or her minions, gathered around us, their enthusiasm loud but not infectious. Real fans glanced over curiously, their expressions ranging from confusion to mild interest. This was no BTS frenzy, and it showed.

My heart pounded as I fumbled with the event schedule. "So, we have a photo op at ten, then a Q&A at noon," I stammered, trying to sound in control.

Cha-young gave me a reassuring smile. "Great job, Miss Delarosa," she said in an accent surely exaggerated to sound adorable, then turned to a group of 'fans' and began signing autographs with what looked to me like practiced ease.

As the morning wore on, my nerves didn't settle. I tripped over my own feet in the heels, sweat dampening my blouse. I struggled to remember the fake backstories we'd created, getting timelines mixed up and blanking on details during conversations with curious attendees. Cha-young covered for me as best she could, seamlessly weaving together my faltering attempts with her charm and quick thinking. But it was clear I was out of my depth.

Saero-yi, as the 'quiet and brooding' actor playing a 'quiet and brooding' character, sailed through the whole thing, what with his natural tendency towards 'quiet and brooding.' At least, I thought so – until he broadcasted his thoughts at me:

This sucks. How do actors stand it? I've signed ten autographs, taken a ton of selfies and it's already enough.

I caught his eye over the fake fans, and we shared an uneasy smile. Some fans, not our tame crowd, caught the look between us and instantly began to whisper. Cell phones were raised and pointed at us both. I could see the headlines now – *Is romance blooming for up-and-coming K-drama actor and unknown Latina?*

Well, anyhow, engagement definitely seemed to rise after that. But it'd been careless of me – we should have orchestrated a moment like that between Saero-yi and his 'co-star,' who was way more beautiful than me.

A particularly enthusiastic fan asked me about the

filming locations for *Echoes of Time*. My mind went blank. "Uh, Sausalito and, um, Seoul," I managed to stammer.

The fan's face lit up. "Where in Seoul?"

"We're planning to film in several districts," I said evasively, and wished I'd bothered properly to read what I'd channeled from Mr. Park then hastily handed over to Saero-yi to post on IMDB. "Gangnam. Itaewon..."

That pretty much exhausted the names I could remember from the tiny handful of shows I'd ever watched, so I trailed off, casting my gaze about in search of a distraction.

From out of the corner of my eye, I spied a group of serious-looking men lingering near our booth. They didn't seem to be having fun, didn't fit the profile of TV show people, either. One in particular caught my attention; a man of Asian descent dressed in a tight-fitting black suit and plain white shirt. With a swift passing glance, I took note of his shoes: brown brogues.

Maxim had made sure Kenzie and I knew the importance of shoes in espionage. *'That's the most common mistake people make, not changing their shoes.'* As discreetly as I could, I brought my gaze back to his face: sharp, this time taking a moment to mentally record his angular features framed by neatly trimmed, bleached-blond hair and from under a knitted brow, a shrewd gaze. My paranoia spiked. Were they watching us? My heart raced. I scanned the crowd. Every glance felt scrutinizing, every murmur suspicious.

Cha-young noticed my unease and whispered, "You're doing fine."

But I wasn't. The weight of our mission bore down on me, and I felt like I was failing at every turn.

TWENTY-SEVEN

A COOKERY LESSON

The truth is, I struggled to keep up with the demands of being a publicist. Organizing the photo ops was a disaster. I forgot to arrange the backdrop and props, and the lighting was all wrong. The photos came out grainy and poorly composed, a stark contrast to the polished patina of the other booths.

At the Q&A, my nerves reached a breaking point. I fumbled the microphone, dropped it with a loud clatter that drew the crowd's attention. Embarrassment prickled my cheeks as I picked it up, hands shaking. Cha-young stepped in, took over with deft competence and answered questions with the grace of a seasoned actor. The fake fans cheered, but the real attendees looked more puzzled than ever.

As the day wore on, my paranoia deepened. Every camera flash felt like a laser pointer targeting our deception. Every murmur felt like a whisper of our exposure. I glanced around constantly, my eyes darting from face to face, looking for any sign that we'd been made.

Then it happened. During a break, I overheard a group of fans talking. "Have you heard of *Echoes of Time*?" one asked. "Before today, I mean."

"No," another replied. "And I follow all the news about the latest dramas. Weird, right?"

My stomach dropped. They were onto us. I hurried back to Cha-young and Saero-yi, trying to keep my voice steady. "We need to wrap this up," I whispered urgently. "People are getting suspicious."

Cha-young nodded, her expression calm but serious. "Alright, let's finish the signing session and then leave quietly."

But it wasn't that simple. As we made our way to the exit, I spotted one of the serious-looking men from earlier. He was on his phone, his eyes fixed on us. My heart pounded in my chest, my breath coming in shallow gasps. I glanced at Saero-yi, who looked equally tense. He nudged me, whispering, "Act natural."

Natural. Right. I forced a smile, trying to look like a calm, collected publicist rather than a panicked teenager in over her head. We moved through the crowd, trying not to draw attention, but it felt like every eye was on us.

Just as we reached the exit, a hand grabbed my arm. I spun around, jerkily. It was one of the fake fans, looking concerned. "Are you okay?" she asked. "You feeling dizzy, or something?"

I forced a laugh. "Yeah, just a bit wired. Thanks."

She gave me a wan smile and released my arm, but the damage was done. My nerves were jangling. We hurried out of the convention center, the cool evening air a welcome relief. As we climbed into the waiting car, I finally allowed myself to breathe. When the car swung into a driveway, I didn't even notice the name of the hotel.

Four hotel changes in three days. How do people live like this? The surroundings stay more or less the same, only the location changes.

Daniels was waiting for us in our suite, drinking from a beaded can of Diet Coke. She took one look at my pale face and quirked a grim smile. "That good, huh?"

"We might have been compromised." I sank into a chair, the adrenaline draining from my body. Saero-yi sat beside me, his expression unreadable. But in my head, his voice was clear as a bell. *Don't worry. You're an asset, a new one, at that. They don't expect you to be a pro.*

"Not gonna lie," I told them both, unsteadily. "That felt like a disaster."

He shook his head, very calm, no doubt whatsoever. "We got through it."

Daniels poured her Diet Coke into a glass of ice and something else, vodka or maybe tequila. She raised a glass to me and winked. "Not all adventure on the high seas, is it, Roni?"

I choked up a chuckle to hide a rush of nausea as I recalled hellish hours in the Bering Sea, on the yacht *Perseus.* "You won't hear me complain about that."

Her tone became brisk. "Let's reassess tomorrow. For now, you kids get some food, get some rest. We're on high alert until further notice."

We watched her leave, then caught each other's eye. Inexplicably, I began to laugh. Saero-yi's eyes lit up and after a moment, he joined in with a half-hearted chuckle.

"'High alert until further notice.' Omigod." I rolled my eyes. "FML, right?"

"I have no idea what that means."

I laughed harder. "We should eat."

He relaxed instantly. "Yes. I'll cook."

In the sun-dappled kitchen of the hotel apartment, I found myself navigating the uncharted territory of cooking with Saero-yi. It was a strangely comfortable moment, domesticity amidst chaos. A warm distraction. The kitchen was surprisingly well-stocked, and we had managed to gather enough ingredients for a simple Korean meal.

"You really can't cook at all?" Saero-yi asked, a hint of amusement in his voice as he watched me struggle with a knife.

I shook my head, embarrassed. "Nope. My dad was the cook in our house. Bobbie, Kenzie's mom, took over when I started spending more time at their place. I've never had to learn."

Saero-yi's eyes sparkled with amusement. "You were lucky. At the Krylov Foundation, they taught us to be self-sufficient in many ways, including cooking."

He began to chop vegetables with practiced ease, his movements swift and efficient. "I learned to make six dishes of very simple Korean food," he explained. "The irony was, neither I nor my teacher knew how they were supposed to taste."

"Who was your teacher?"

"A sentinel, an adult telepath who also grew up in the Krylov camp. She learned from recipes, but neither of us had ever visited Korea."

"Oh, I remember 'sentinels.'" I remarked. "I hid with a baby from them, when we were breaking kids out of the camp."

He nodded, as if I'd said something very normal. "Then you'll understand. She wasn't my friend," he said, simply. "But I've since learned how to improve the recipes."

"Now that you've tasted the real thing?"

He grinned, showing his newly brace-free, straight white teeth. "She wasn't a great cook."

We both laughed. I watched him work, captivated by the rhythm of his cooking. The scent of garlic and onions sizzling in the pan filled the kitchen, mingling with the fresh aroma of chopped vegetables. There was something calming about the way he moved, his focus entirely on the task at hand.

I peered over his shoulder. "What are we making?"

"Kimchi fried rice. It's simple but delicious. And some *pajeon*. They're Korean savory pancakes."

As he prepared the ingredients, I tried to help by handing him what he needed, but mostly I just enjoyed the atmosphere. The steady chop of the knife, the sizzle of the pan, and the fragrant scents wafting through the air created a sense of peace that I'd not had for days.

Soon, the table was set with two steaming plates of kimchi fried rice and a small stack of pajeon. We sat down to eat, and I took my first bite, savoring the explosion of flavors. The tangy kimchi, the slightly crispy rice, the savory pancake – it was all delicious.

"This is amazing," I murmured between mouthfuls.

Saero-yi smiled, though it didn't quite reach his eyes. "Cooking was an escape from the constant training and surveillance, in the camp. It gave me a sense of normalcy, something to hold onto."

I nodded. Small comforts matter even more in a place that seems devoid of them. "What else did you do to escape?"

He took a bite of his *pajeon*, chewing thoughtfully before answering. "We played softball, basketball. We went for hikes in the forest. I enjoyed the nature, very much. The camp is pretty isolated, the forest there is almost untouched. We had nicknames in the camp, most of us picked the name of our favorite animal from the area. Mine was 'Trogon,' after a beautiful bird, very colorful, red with blue or yellow."

I listened in fascination. Maxim, his brother Sacha and their friend Atlanta had all told me a little about their lives in the Krylov Foundation yet usually spoke with reluctance. But Saero-yi seemed to be more relaxed and forthcoming. Had his experience been different than theirs? Tentatively, I asked him.

He was silent for a few seconds, moving the food around on his plate, arranging the final three bites. "I lived in the North Wing, which was... less strict than the South Wing. That's where I knew Jaguar. He was in the North Wing, until he was moved to the South Wing as a punishment."

"What was he punished for?"

Saero-yi's eyes met mine. *I got used to not asking that.*

His sudden, telepathic reply surprised me. It'd been a while since he'd communicated in this way and I'd almost forgotten that before I'd heard him speak, when I'd first heard his thoughts, they'd been in my own voice. Weird.

"Why did you do that? There's no-one else here. Or do you think this room is bugged?"

Probably not. Daniels trusts you. At least I think so. And the CIA are guarding us well enough to keep Chekists away – for now.

"Then, why?"

Force of habit. In the Krylov, some thoughts were too dangerous to express, unless you were very good at blocking. I never was.

"But some were?"

"Yes."

I knew at once he was referring to 'Jaguar.' "Were you friends?" I asked, curious about their relationship.

Saero-yi considered this for a moment, his expression pensive. "We were friendly. Most of us were wary of becoming too close to Jaguar. Many feared him."

This landed heavily. I had heard it from others who knew Maxim in the Krylov, but somehow, it didn't match the boy I remembered from elementary school. "Feared him? Why?"

Saero-yi stared at me, his eyes reflecting a mixture of emotions. "He was different, even back then. Intense, focused, and capable of... things that most of us weren't. He had a drive that set him apart, but it also made him a target. People didn't know how to handle him, so they kept their distance."

I felt a pang of sadness for the friend I thought I knew. "It's hard to reconcile the Maxim I knew with this 'Jaguar' character."

Saero-yi shrugged. "The environment shapes you, molds you into something different. The Krylov would have been very, very different than growing up as a normie in the USA. That had to have affected him. But it doesn't mean that the person you remember is gone. He's just... layered."

"Thanks, Saero-yi. It helps to hear that." And I thought – *Sacha and Atlanta weren't as understanding.* After a moment, faltering a little, I managed to confess something that I'd never admitted out loud, even if I'd turned it over in my mind. "I... I helped Maxim. Kenzie and I, we helped him get almost all the kids out of the Krylov camp. I'd hate to think that we somehow put anyone in danger, by doing that."

"You're *still* helping him." He said it calmly but there was a brittleness to his tone. "And so am I. He can be very persuasive. That's his superpower."

"Kind of unfair to have an extra superpower, what with all the telepathy." I was mumbling now and too tired to continue such a heavy conversation. "Let's not talk about Maxim. It's getting late and we need to catch an early flight to Seoul. Anyhow, I want to know more about you." I checked the time on my phone. "For, like, a half hour. Then," I whistled and flipped my thumb towards the bedrooms. "Then I'm kicking you out. Gotta get my eight hours."

He smiled, and this time it reached his eyes. "Sure, Roni." He hesitated, then added, "Same for me. About you, I mean."

We continued eating and the conversation flowed easily between us. I found myself opening up to him in ways I hadn't expected, sharing stories about my life and listening to his experiences in the camp. Despite the hardships he'd faced, there was a resilience in him that I admired. As we finished our meal, I felt a sense of connection with Saero-yi that went beyond our shared mission. We cleaned up the kitchen together, our silence contented and companionable. For a little while, we were just two people finding solace in each other's company, a brief respite from the turmoil of our lives. And for that, I was grateful.

As I lay in bed that night, sleep eluded me. Every sound, every shadow seemed ominous. The line between our cover and reality had blurred; I couldn't shake the feeling that I'd almost blown our entire operation.

TWENTY-EIGHT

FAN SERVICE

Well, I managed to sleep about five hours, spread across the night. Our CIA-organized escort picked us up at six-thirty. The airport experience was bizarre, unlike anything I'd known at an airport. Did you know there are VIP routes through security? Me neither. It was *fast*. We kept up our cover of K-drama actors and their American publicist, me, gliding through the airport on the way back to South Korea. Daniels had taken a separate flight so we wouldn't be seen together; she'd arranged to meet us at a CIA safe house in Seoul. I checked my phone regularly, half-expecting her to stay in contact, but nothing. It seemed we were really alone.

The flight to Seoul was a blur of tension and exhaustion. My nerves jangled, every creak of the plane, every distant conversation set off my internal alarm. Saero-yi sat beside me, his face calm and composed, a stark contrast to me. He glanced over occasionally, offering a reassuring smile that did little to calm my fears. Cha-young and the minimally communicative male consulate staffer sat on the opposite side of the aisle, chatting softly in Korean.

We landed in Seoul late in the evening of the following day. Despite the late hour, the bustling airport was a cacophony of noise and activity, but we moved through it swiftly, our small entourage blending in with the sea of travelers.

As we rode through the city, I tried to watch for any signs of trouble, but pretty soon got distracted by the wildness of being somewhere so different than the USA. The streets of Seoul were vibrant and alive, a stark contrast to the dark, tense atmosphere in the car. Cha-young sat in the front, her eyes scanning the road ahead. Without Daniels physically present, it was up to us to ensure everything went smoothly. Not the greatest idea, since I don't speak Korean and neither me nor Saero-yi had ever visited the country. Nor did the consulate staffers appear to be all that interested in inducting us. I decided the best plan was never to take my eyes off Cha-young. Girl seemed relieved to be back in her city and *quite* eager to shake us off so she could get back to her life.

Too bad, sugar, I'm not leaving your side.

I caught myself then, found myself saying it to myself in Margo Daniel's voice. Then I realized how much it felt like hearing a telepathic message. Which made me wonder about the mechanism that telepathy uses: does it go via the imagination part of the brain? *Is there a part of the brain that does imagination?* I made a note to look into it. *La Chica* never stops being *curiosa*.

My phone buzzed in my lap, and I saw Kenzie's name flash on the screen. I hesitated before answering, not sure I could handle his disappointment and worry on top of everything else.

"Hey, Kenzie," I said, trying to keep my voice steady.

"Roni, where the hell are you?" His voice was a mix of frustration and concern. "You left without telling me."

"I'm sorry," I said, swallowing hard. "It was all last-minute, and... y'know, security reasons. Plus, I didn't want you to worry."

"Too late for that," he snapped. "You didn't have to totally exclude me. I could help, even from here."

"I know. But it's dangerous. I didn't want to put you at risk."

"I'm already at risk," he replied. "You think I don't know what's going on? Maxim filled me in on some of it, and now I'm just stuck here, powerless."

I said nothing, waiting for more, certain there *was* more.

"I know you don't feel about me the way I do about you." I heard him gulp. "And that's okay. It's my issue to deal with. But I got into this because I promised I'd have your back, remember? We did Cuba together; we did Alaska together. It's just a little hard to be on the outside this time. Y'know?"

Tears pricked at the corners of my eyes, sadness but also, frustration. What are you supposed to do when your best friend has a thing for you? Pushing him away wasn't an option, but hearing his unhappiness was no picnic, either.

"The more I think about it..." His voice grew more intense. "C'mon, you *know* what CIA do. They interfere in other countries, spread violence, and now they're recruiting you? You're smarter than that, Roni."

"Where's this coming from?" I reeled slightly at his growing vehemence. "Last time we talked you were just *sad* about it..."

"You went quiet for almost fifteen hours. I had no clue where you were."

"But you knew I'd be going to Korea."

"But not when!" he blurted, sounding more hurt than angered. "And while you were, I guess, flying over the ocean, I've had more time to think. Roni, you *can't* work for CIA. They're literally part of the problem, why everything's going to shit."

"I know all that," I said, suddenly defensive. "But it's not that simple. I gave Maxim my word. The only way to help him is to work with the CIA."

"I can't believe you of all people are buying into this. Daniels is using you."

"I'm not buying into anything," I insisted. "I'm trying to make a difference. Better that Saero-yi is on our side, not Ilyin's. In the end, isn't that what we've been fighting for ever since Cuba?"

"Fair," he admitted, his voice softening. Then with sullen reluctance he added, "Maybe that's why I don't like being here on the outside, watching you dive into this mess alone."

"I'm not alone, Saero-yi is here."

The silence that followed practically crackled. When he spoke again I heard suspicion and resentment. "It's 'Saero-yi,' now is it? Is he your latest replacement for Maxim, like Sacha was?"

I said nothing, shaken by how on-the-nose this was. Then anger surged within. "You want to control who I'm friends with, now?"

"Not at all." He sighed. "I'm sorry, that was a dick move. They're telepaths, you're kind of telepathic, too. There's an extra bond, I get it. Even if I don't like it. It's just... I worry. Just be careful," he said, his voice dropping, sweet and low. "I can't lose you, Padi, I can't."

"I will be careful," I promised. "And back before you know it."

He drew a long, shaky breath. "Okay. What's the plan?"

"I can't say, not over the phone."

"Sure, got it. Well, keep me updated, okay? If you need anything, I mean."

"I will. Thanks, Kenzie."

The call ended, leaving me feeling both reassured and more anxious than before. The fake cast of *Echoes of Time* and their fake publicist, a.k.a. me, were already in a car on our way to our next engagement – a party on the yacht belonging to the father of a K-drama superfan.

I stared out the window as we approached Seoul's marina, the water a glittering black mirror of the city's night lights. The yacht party was in full swing, music and laughter floating across the water. It seemed so normal, so carefree, but I knew better than to let my guard down.

We stepped onto the yacht, and I couldn't help but marvel at its opulence. The deck was filled with guests flexing fresh styles, champagne flutes in hand as they mingled, the laughter ringing a notch higher than was natural. To my surprise, even amidst such swanky display, Saero-yi slipped effortlessly into his role as taciturn, brooding actor, greeting the billionaire's son with a polite bow. Cha-young stayed close, her eyes scanning the crowd with practiced ease.

Our outfits were on point – Saero-yi had on a sleek, white tuxedo with pale blue silk bowtie, while I'd been dressed in a cute little electric-blue dress so tight-fitting, it felt sprayed on, under a black, tailored jacket and shiny, black court shoes. Given that she was supposed to be the show's female lead, Cha-young's outfit was relatively understated – a cream-colored pants suit and white sneakers. She wore her hair loose, straight and glossy, and light-touch make-up, all dozy pinks and subtle shades of beige that made her skin positively glow. In short, she looked amazing.

I tried to blend in, my nerves still tetchy. The yacht was bigger and a lot fancier than the ill-fated Perseus, which had been a hardworking expedition boat. This by contrast was a maze of luxury, with beautifully decorated state rooms and a sprawling deck overlooking the marina. I moved through the crowd, my eyes darting to every unfamiliar face, looking for any sign of danger. Daniels had warned us about the possibility of North Korean agents trying to infiltrate the party. Once again, I couldn't shake the feeling that we were being watched.

As the night wore on, I began to relax slightly, lulled by the music and the seemingly endless supply of champagne. (Yes, I drank an alcoholic beverage. No-one asked me for ID.) I found myself chatting with a group of fake fans who were excited about *Echoes of Time*, their enthusiasm so infectious, I wondered if they even knew it was a fake show. Maybe we'd done enough work by now to persuade fans it was real? On the other hand, the yacht was festooned with giant publicity photos of other K-drama stars from real shows and none for our fake show, so, who can tell? Either way, the word had gotten out and fans were curious and eager to meet Saero-yi and Cha-young. I found myself busy corralling a bunch of uber-friendly, delighted folk and marshalling their requests for selfies with our 'co-stars.'

For a little while there, I almost forgot the danger we were in.

TWENTY-NINE

GIRL TALK

Sashaying through the billionaire's yacht party, acting like I belonged, I did what I could to hide some low-key imposter syndrome. I felt like a goldfish tossed into a shark tank; everywhere I looked, predatory competitors masquerading as gorgeous people. Every last one of them looked like they stepped out of a magazine. I didn't recognize any of the faces, but I could tell they were celebrities just by the way their skin and teeth seemed to glow beneath the chandeliers. I might have been glowing too, but it was mostly due to stress sweat.

I needed to reboot, stat. So, I headed in search of the head, which is boat-speak for bathroom. As I navigated through the decks and stairways, my ears perked up at a familiar voice: Cha-young. She was speaking Korean, quick and sharp. I sidled behind a nearby wall, took out my phone, selected a translation app and turned on the mic. Korean writing appeared on the screen, translated below into scrolling English.

"Saero-yi's location is confirmed. Make sure you are ready when we dock," Cha-young said. The urgency was clear from her tone.

Why was Cha-young discussing Saero-yi's location like it was some covert operation? Alarm bells went off in my head. My brain was still processing that nugget of paranoia when my phone buzzed. Great timing. I rushed to the aft deck, trying to find a quiet spot, where I could actually hear myself think.

I glanced at the phone number, which I didn't recognize. "Who's this?" I answered, hoping my voice didn't betray the fact that I was teetering towards panic.

"Just checking in," I heard Margo Daniels say, cool as a cucumber in an ice storm. "I'm calling from a new burner, so make a note of the number. Everything's going according to plan. The South Korean National Intelligence Service did a sweep of the yacht and ran security checks on everyone on the invitation list, so I'm feeling pretty relaxed, for now. Go boss your cast members around a little, get them to press the flesh some, especially with fans. Then at midnight you should make some excuses and herd them off the boat. We'll have a car waiting for you in the marina, same car and driver as picked you up from the airport."

She got me to confirm the name of the driver, the model and license plate of the car.

"All righty, then. We'll meet at the safe house later, but it looks like your operation is pretty much accomplished. Jang Saero-yi has effectively defected!"

I nodded, even though she couldn't see me. "Got it. Thanks, Officer Daniels."

I heard a sharp intake of breath, like she was surprised that for once I used her name. "You can call me 'Margo,' darlin'. There are some other names I know the boys in the office like to call me... But for you, 'Margo' will do just fine. I just wanted you to know, Roni, you've done well."

She paused then, perhaps waiting for my reaction. Her praise felt like a cozy blanket, but it was quickly followed by a cold dose of reality. Was the operation really over? What about Saero-yi's work for Maxim? From what I understood, Saero-yi could hack from pretty much any computer that wasn't in a location monitored by the intelligence services. Would the South Koreans release him as a free citizen, or would they be watching him for months, years or longer, in case he was a double? It'd been a while since I'd heard from Maxim.

Then there was Cha-young and her strange phone conversation, only minutes earlier. A lot to think about, all things considered.

One thing at a time, Padi. That's what Maxim would say, if he were here, probably. I shook my head in irritation, as though the gesture might toss out a guy who seemed to live there, rent-free.

"Thanks, Margo," I replied, trying to keep my voice steady. "But... Y'know what? Something feels off."

Daniels sighed, a sound that conveyed both patience and mild annoyance. "Look, it's natural to feel on edge. Ops like this are complex. I need you to trust the process. But if it helps..." She paused and I got the distinct impression that her next words came straight out of a human resources guidance manual. "If it helps, I'm happy to hear your concerns. Top-line it for me though. If you can."

For a moment I hesitated, then words tumbled out before I could stop them. "It's just... Well, about the whole potential recruitment thing. Kenzie. He doesn't trust the CIA. He thinks you guys get too involved in other countries' politics, that you're too quick to spread violence. And now *I'm* being recruited, and he's not. It's just... complicated."

There was a pause, and I could almost hear Daniels thinking. "Kenzie's concerns are valid, obviously. But he's your friend. Not your romantic partner. Unless I'm out of date? Anything you need to tell me?"

Sullenly, I confirmed that she wasn't misinformed.

She replied briskly, sounding relieved. "Lookit, you need to focus on your own path. The Agency isn't perfect, but we have a job to do. You're good at this. And as I may have mentioned, you're in a somewhat unique position to help us."

"I know," I said, my voice barely a whisper. "But it's not just that. There's Maxim. I'm worried about him. Like, what happened to him at the Krylov Foundation? He's not a kid anymore, I get that. But the way people talk about him, Sacha, Atlanta, even Saero-yi, I sometimes wonder if they're talking about the boy I grew up with."

"Maxim has been through a whole heap of trouble, from what I understand. The kind of things that change a person. You can't dwell on the past."

I swallowed hard, feeling a blockage in my throat. "And then there's Saero-yi. He's... different than I expected, than he seemed to be, at first. He reminds me of Maxim, but also not. I think... I might have feelings for him. And if I'm totally honest, I had a similar thing going on about Sacha, too. Both of which things are, like, *bonkers*, because I only just met Saero-yi and as for Sacha? He's younger than me and he's Max's brother. Argh! It's a mess."

Daniels's voice lowered to a growl. "Honey, no. *Girl talk*? At a time like this? Now you're disappointing me. I took you for a tougher nut than this! C'mon, you need to get on top of all that stuff. This line of work requires focus and detachment. You cannot afford to be ruled by emotions."

Her words hit me like a slap in the face. What had I been thinking? Daniels was *not* my friend, not my mother, not my sister. She was my CIA *handler*. I was her 'Joe.' Was it possible that I'd confessed all these things to her because I needed someone to play that role in my life?

Dammit, Padi, get a grip.

"You're right," I said, forcing myself to sound more composed. "Yeah, feelings are *the worst*. I'll be more careful."

"Good," Daniels replied, her voice simmering down. "Stay sharp, Roni. We'll talk more at the safe house."

I hung up, the phone feeling heavy in my hand. I gripped the gunwale and stared across the dark water towards the dazzling night-lit city of Seoul. A part of me wanted to cry, to scream, to let go all the pent-up frustration and fear. But I couldn't. Not here, not now. I had to stay focused, controlled, strong. I made a silent promise to myself to figure this out, to balance my emotions with the demands of this job. Because if I didn't, I knew it would consume me.

THIRTY

TRAPPED

Standing on the aft deck, I sucked in a deep breath, trying to shake off the unsettling conversation with Daniels. The balmy night air and easy sway of the yacht helped to ground me back in the present moment. I let my eyes wander, soaking in small details of our surroundings. The mega-yacht's main deck was a study in polished teak and gleaming stainless steel. As I reached the side deck, my gaze fell on a white, cylindrical container mounted near the railing. Life raft, check. We'd used a similar piece of kit to evacuate the Perseus. The casing was covered in safety instructions and diagrams that not long ago, would have looked like hieroglyphics to me. Now I had a fair idea of how to use it, not that it was likely to be necessary right now, with the yacht still moored.

Nearby, I spotted a large crate secured to the deck with sturdy straps. It was labeled 'SCUBA' in bold, black letters. I felt a tiny thrill of recognition. Our scuba training course in the murky diving lakes of Pennsylvania had been a lot of fun. I'd learned to assemble and disassemble gear, check air tanks, and handle various underwater situations. Inside, I could make out the shapes of tanks, fins, masks, and wetsuits. The distinct scent of neoprene and the faint metallic tang of the tanks brought back vivid memories of my first dive. Pretty cool that specialist technology which had been utterly foreign to me a couple months ago, was now part of my everyday vocabulary.

I headed back to the party, running my fingers along the railing. The moonlight reflected off gentle waves, creating a shimmering path that stretched to the horizon. Briefly, I let myself enjoy the peace. The night was calm, the stars twinkling above like distant diamonds.

This operation was going way easier than I'd imagined. Maybe this was what happened, when you actually worked closely with the professionals? In Alaska, Kenzie and I had been pretty much thrown into a lion's den, at least it felt that way. Being on another operation so soon afterward triggered uncertainty and a heightened sense of danger. I had to admit, however, it was also exhilarating. Right now, for example, I felt like a character in some classic spy novel, caught in a web of espionage and intrigue, but with a more casual wardrobe.

Daniels's praise rang faintly in my ears, but my skepticism was louder. However straightforward this operation was turning out to be, I knew how hair-raising things could get. And that was before you factored in the human element – capture and interrogation. If anything like that happened, I was fairly certain I'd sing like a canary.

As I got closer to the DJ's sound system, the thump-thump of techno-pop shuddered through the soles of my feet and fingers, when they touched the railing. I scanned the deck for Saero-yi and Cha-young. One last feint and we'd be out of here.

At the thought of Cha-young, the back of my neck tingled. Why did her phone conversation seem so ominous? I wanted to trust my instincts, but what if they were just the product of an overactive imagination? Worming my way back into the heart of the party, I tried to shake off the unease. Daniels was a pro. If she said everything was peachy, it should be. Right? Yet that little voice in my head wouldn't shut up. Cha-young's words kept replaying in my mind like a broken record. Was I being paranoid, or was something seriously off?

And then, as I approached the staircase on the way down to the main deck, I spotted him: the fair-haired, angular-faced man from the convention. He was on the yacht, a guest at the party, judging by the confident way he entered the room. His outfit here had a totally different vibe than the black suit and white shirt he'd worn to the K-Wave con. Black-and-white streetwear; tight black jeans, chunky white sneakers and an oversized, baggy hoodie, black with white pocket-trim and a white hood. He even had on a brushed steel neck chain. A beautiful Korean woman dressed in a little black dress hung off his arm, pouting so fiercely, I thought she might slap him. Dressed like this, he could pass for ten years younger, and his cheekbones looked sharp enough to draw blood. Yet I was sure it was the same guy. When he caught my eye and held my gaze for a fraction of a second too long before turning away, I knew it was him.

My heart hammered against my ribs as I followed them, trying to stay inconspicuous. He led the woman towards a plush lounge area near the bow and I moved faster, although with not a clue what I'd do if I caught up. Before I could reach him, Cha-young seemed to materialize out of nowhere, blocking my path.

"Roni, we need to talk," she said, her voice strident, one hand gripping my wrist.

"Can it wait?"

Cha-young's eyes were intense, faintly threatening. "Not really."

Those internal alarm bells were now a full-blown fire drill. I tried to pull away, but her hold became like a vice. "Cha-young, what's going on?"

Her eyes darted around the room. "We need to leave. *Now.*"

My mind was racing like a caffeinated squirrel on a sugar high. I had to warn Saero-yi, but could I trust Cha-young? Every instinct screamed *no.*

"Daniels said we should do some more meet-and-greet."

With surprising intensity she replied, "No."

"All right, if you're sure," I said, forcing a calm I didn't feel. "After you."

As we made our way through the yacht, I prepared myself mentally to bolt at the first sign of trouble. Then I remembered Saero-yi and my promise to Maxim. Surely I'd done enough for him, just getting him away from the North Koreans and into Seoul?

A sinking feeling gripped me as I faced up to it: whatever Daniels claimed, this wasn't over until we got back to the safe house. I reminded myself why I was here; the West's so-called "Mind Game" against the Russian Czar, an existential battle to control information and a struggle over the finite and often unwilling resource of talented telepaths. Weirdest of all, I had a part to play in all this – me. So surreal.

As Cha-young led me through the crowd, I couldn't help but notice how seamlessly she moved, her expressions carefully controlled, her interactions natural and effortless. This definitely wasn't her first rodeo. That alone was sus as heck. If she was a mole then she'd had us dancing to her tune for some time.

She walked me back to the aft deck, where the

music and laughter were a distant hum. Then Cha-young finally let go of my arm.

"Seriously, what the hell?" I hissed.

Her eyes narrowed. "I'm trying to protect Jang Saero-yi. There are things you don't understand, Roni."

"Like what? Why were you talking about his location? Who were you talking to?"

For a second her nostrils flared, the only sign that she was surprised. Then she let out a weary sigh, like she was having to deal with an annoying child. "Look, there's things you don't know. We're not safe here. The North Koreans are closer than you think."

My heart sank. Again with the North Koreans? This was bad. Really bad. And yet, something in her tone made me question everything.

"How do I know I can trust you?" I asked, stubbornly.

She didn't answer right away. Instead, she looked past me, her expression unreadable. "You don't," she finally admitted. "But right now, what choice do you have?"

And just like that, the last bit of my resolve crumbled. I had no idea what was going on, who I could trust, or how I was supposed to navigate this treacherous game of espionage. All I knew was that I had to keep Saero-yi safe, no matter what.

Taking a deep breath, I nodded. "Fine. Tell me the plan."

"I'll keep it simple: you follow me," she said, through gritted teeth.

We started moving again, the tension between us was palpable. *Here we go, back to the lions – again.* But I had to see this through, for Saero-yi, for Maxim, and for myself. As we neared the central side deck and the exit to the dock, I caught sight of Saero-yi. He stood about fifteen yards away at the opposite end of the side deck, a drink in one hand, surrounded by a small group of admirers. Then I spotted something that plunged an icicle into my heart. The boat was no longer moored. The exit ramp had been removed, and the jetty was more than ten meters away. The yacht was setting sail along the Han River, headed towards the ocean.

We were trapped on the yacht.

Surrounded by the loud music and chat, there was no point yelling. Instead, I widened my eyes until I looked like a person deranged, trying to get Saero-yi's attention.

Let's face it, at a time like this, one-way telepathy was turning out to be almost useless.

"Stay close," Cha-young whispered, her voice low and urgent.

This was it. The moment of truth: make a break for it or trust her? With one last, desperate look at Saero-yi, I couldn't help but wonder if we would make it out of this alive.

THIRTY-ONE

BRIG

It went against my instincts to go along, but as Cha-young had pointed out, I didn't have a lot of choice. Leaving behind the sight of Saero-yi basking in the fake attention of fake fans of a fake show in which he was a fake actor, I followed Cha-young's firm lead down the yacht's stairs and corridors. The laughter and music from the party above deck faded, replaced by the echo of our footsteps and the loud hum of the ship's engines. We descended, the yacht's lavish upper levels giving way to narrower, more utilitarian corridors with metallic walls and shiny, linoleum floors.

My suspicion about Cha-young had been bubbling inside me, but as we got further from Saero-yi, one thought rose uncomfortably to the surface, like a burp just before you vomit.

Was she a traitor, a North Korean mole?

We stopped outside a metal door that looked more like it belonged in a prison than a luxury vessel.

Finally, I turned to Cha-young and said, simply, "What have you done?"

In that moment, I swear she actually looked sorry. Her eyes narrowed and she gave a small shake of her head. "Only what's necessary."

Close to despair, I glanced up and down the corridor, searching for a way out. Further up the corridor, I saw Jang approaching and I froze. Behind him strode Mr. Cheekbones, one hand on Saero-yi's shoulder, another holding a chunky black pistol to his jaw.

Curtains seemed to be descending in front of my eyes, a red filter that cast everything in dark light, unlocking a new quality of fear. I called out Saero-yi's name, or at least I tried to. What actually came out of my mouth sounded more like a dry croak. Part of me logged the detail as if from afar, another hideous entry in the catalog of my available terror.

Cha-young took a key from the pocket of her tailored jacket, slotted it into the solid-looking door. She turned the key and the door swung open to reveal a small cabin, dimly lit, with barred windows that offered a tantalizing glimpse of freedom we couldn't reach. Two cots, a small table, and a dim light bulb hanging from the ceiling made up the sparse furnishings. My nostrils filled with the smell of brackish saltwater and my own sweat.

"Inside."

My muscles must have stopped obeying me because I stepped into the cabin as she'd ordered. *Meek. Lamb to the slaughter.* Everything you tell yourself you will never do.

Within the minute, Saero-yi appeared in the doorway, Mr. Cheekbones right behind him, his expression a mix of boredom and menace. Again, I tried to catch Saero-yi's eye. Why wasn't he broadcasting to me? If I could, I'd have been furiously plotting some way out of this, but all I saw in his eyes was shock and confusion. Cheekbones shoved Saero-yi inside with a force that made him stumble, then wrestled him to the ground and snapped plastic zip ties around his wrists and ankles. When he was done with Saero-yi, he did the same to me, leaving me on one of the cots, trussed up like a Thanksgiving turkey.

Briskly, Cha-young frisked me, found my cell phone and held it up. "For me? Don't mind if I do. Officer Daniels won't be calling you for some time, I fear." She backed up until she was standing in the doorway, one eyebrow slightly arched as she dangled a keychain from her index finger. "That was gratifyingly straightforward," she remarked. "Thank you for not fighting back. You'd have risked serious injury, and we have no desire for that. Therefore, it is good that you understand this is nothing personal. We merely wish to talk to you. Hopefully a frank, open discussion."

She sounded sincere but beside her, Mr. Cheekbones smiled a thin, watery smile, his eyes glinting with predatory eagerness. "Wait here," he said, after a moment. "We brought a surprise."

Cha-young closed the door. I turned to Saero-yi. He was breathing steadily, very controlled and focused. When he eventually returned my gaze, he seemed slowly to emerge as if from a trance. In my mind, I heard his voice. *This is not good.*

I wanted to hit back with snark, but the words wouldn't flow.

He brought both hands to his face, as if it was only now dawning on him, the bad trouble we were in. To distract myself from his mounting fear, I turned my attention to our surroundings. Maybe there was a way out?

My eyes were still adjusting to the dim lighting of our prison when the door swung open. I saw Cha-young enter the room, followed by Mr. Cheekbones carrying a toolbox. My heart sank as he placed the toolbox on the table and opened it with a slow, deliberate creak.

Mr. Cheekbones began laying out its contents: pliers, a small blowtorch, syringes filled with clear liquids, a gleaming scalpel, and long, thin needles. Each item was a new jolt of fear, my mind flashing through a montage of horror movies, each scene grislier than the last. Like some frosty ice-queen, Cha-young watched my reaction, deadpan.

I couldn't keep the betrayal out of my voice. "So, you're working for the Kim, after all. I knew it."

She pounced on this. "Really? Then why didn't you fight me?"

"I should have."

"I might have hurt you."

I said nothing. She was probably going to do it anyway, now, but I was trying not to think about that.

"What do you want from us?" Saero-yi asked. I saw fear in his eyes, but his voice was steady.

"We want you back, Saero-yi," Cha-young said, stepping closer. "And for Roni here to understand the consequences of meddling in matters far above her pay scale." She stopped then and fixed me with a beady glare. "Assuming you *are* getting paid?"

When I didn't reply, she let out a snide chuckle. "Honestly, I'm surprised. You're just a kid, but I didn't take you for a fool." Then, bringing her face close enough to mine that I could smell the clean, powdery vanilla scent of her make-up, she whispered, "Don't wait too long to figure out that the only worthwhile reason for doing this – is *money*."

Mr. Cheekbones picked up a syringe, tapping it lightly as if expecting to hear it ring like a bell. The liquid inside seemed to shimmer with a malevolent glow. "This should help you remember your place," he said as he approached me, his tone chillingly calm.

Saero-yi's protest was immediate and loud. "No!

You can't do this!" he yelled, straining against the zip ties and managing to rise from a cross-legged position to his feet before Cha-young cuffed his ear and knocked him back to the floor. His eyes were wide with desperation as they approached me with the syringe, and I was just about the same. But just as the needle was about to pierce my skin, Mr. Cheekbones suddenly shifted his focus to Saero-yi.

"First up, the telepathic wonder-kid," he said, turning to Saero-yi with a cold smirk. When Saero-yi cried out in protest, Mr. Cheekbones gave him a hard slap across the face. The sound was like a gunshot in the small cabin. He reeled, but before he could recover, Mr. Cheekbones punched him in the shoulder, making him cry out in pain.

"Maybe you should take this to the other room?" Cha-young said. "Things could get rather unlovely. Don't forget to take your... *toys*." Her attention flicked back to me, coldly observing my reaction to her sadistic quips.

It wasn't easy, but for brief seconds, I blanked her, gazed straight back into her robot eyes with no emotion at all, zero, nothing.

"What, why, hey, seriously, guys, stop, stop!" Saero-yi's protests became a stream of panicked words as Mr. Cheekbones dragged him by the collar toward an adjacent cabin. His voice grew fainter, more desperate, until it was once again muffled. The door closed behind them with a final, resounding thud, leaving Cha-young and me alone, my ears straining to hear any sounds coming from next door. Taut as a wire, the quiet stretched on for a minute, then another. I turned to Cha-young, glaring. "What are they...?" I began. Then I stopped as the first scream shattered the momentary peace.

"My apologies, we only have these two cabins," she said. Her eyes were fixed on me, icy, calculating, silent as she watched me with an intensity that made my skin crawl.

Saero-yi's scream was raw and primal, a sound that pierced through the walls and burrowed into my brain. My pulse spiked, a frantic rhythm that matched the rising tide of panic inside me. My breathing became shallow, each inhaled breath a struggle against the weight pressing down on my chest.

I tried to block out the sound, but it was impossible. Each scream was a blade, slicing through my resolve. My hands shook uncontrollably, the hard plastic biting into my skin. The room seemed to close in on me, but Cha-young's gaze never wavered. She was studying me, measuring my reaction with a clinical detachment that made the horror of the situation even more pronounced. I could taste fear rising up my throat, sharp and bitter.

What were they doing to Saero-yi, to force such terrible screams from him? And would I be next?

The screams continued, each one more harrowing than the last. My vision blurred with unshed tears, my mind conjured images of what they might be doing to him. The pliers, the blowtorch, the needles – all instruments of agony that I could almost feel myself.

I pressed both hands to my ears, wrists straining as I tried frantically to muffle the sound. Saero-yi's screams echoed in my mind, a relentless assault that drove me closer to the edge of panic.

"Stop it," I whispered. "Please, make it stop."

But Cha-young remained silent, her expression unreadable. She was waiting, watching, taking in every flicker that crossed my face. I was trapped in a nightmare, each second stretching into an eternity of terror.

When the screams finally stopped, the silence was almost worse. It was heavy, oppressive, filled with the ghostly echoes of Saero-yi's suffering. I stared at the door, half-expecting it to open and reveal some new horror. But it remained closed, the barrier between me and whatever lay beyond it.

Cha-young finally spoke, her voice a soft murmur that cut into the silence. "Now do you understand, Roni? This is what happens when you interfere."

I couldn't respond, my throat locked with fear and grief. I could only nod, my mind a chaotic swirl of panic and despair. I was trapped, powerless, with no way to help Saero-yi or myself. The horror of our situation settled over me like a shroud, heavy, suffocating, inescapable.

THIRTY-TWO

QUESTIONS

The muffled sounds from the adjacent cabin grew sharper, more defined. Saero-yi's anguished cries cut through the walls, each one like a needle into my heart. I pressed myself into the cold metal of the cot, dizzier by the second as panic whirled through my mind. Cha-young leaned against the table, her eyes boring into mine, inspecting me like I was a frog pinned out on a lab bench. Tightly, I screwed my eyes shut.

Mr. Cheekbones's voice came through the room's meager partition. He spoke in a low voice, steady and calm, a stark contrast with Saero-yi's sobs and shrieks. "Let's start small, shall we? Pressure points are a good beginning."

Saero-yi's scream of agony followed, gut-wrenching, raw. I clenched my fists until fingernails dug into my palms, pushing back the urge to imagine what was happening next door.

"My colleague is quite skilled," Cha-young commented, lightly, as if discussing what she'd binge-watched over the weekend. "He's adept at many methods. Pressure points, twisting fingers, even the ancient art of nerve pinching. He knows how to inflict maximum pain without causing permanent damage."

My breaths began to falter and fell into a pattern of short, panicked gasps. The dizziness was getting worse.

I felt sick. I forced myself to focus on anything but the sounds of his suffering.

An extended groan turned into a high-pitched wail as another method was applied. My thoughts spun out of control, spiraling toward full-blown panic.

Breathe. Breathe, Roni. Don't forget.

Incredibly, Saero-yi's voice jarred in my head. How was he managing to sound so steady? Had he somehow dissociated his mind from the pain in his body? Were the hideous sounds of his suffering being wrenched from his body, while he took his mind somewhere else?

Maybe I could do that, too, I thought.

What was it Sacha told me about shielding his thoughts from another telepath? He constructed a block, a mental image crafted with such loving detail, anyone trying to pry would be lost in it, unable to peek behind at the private thought.

Maybe I could try that, too?

I began to force myself to disassociate, to steer my thoughts from the reality of the torture. I latched onto an idea of an image I could re-create, a place where I'd been happy; the ice-cream parlor in Tapachula. I'd been reunited with Maxim, there, after so many years. The creamy, peach-orange color of his mamey ice-cream. What had I ordered? Vanilla? Strawberry? A sob stalled in my throat – I'd forgotten. The mental image began to unravel, like film peeling away at the edges.

Doesn't matter, I told myself, firmly. *Let's say it was strawberry.* Two soft scoops of pink ice cream. The combination of cold, tart fruit and cream on my tongue. The stripey awning that shaded us outside on the sidewalk. The white metal tables and our two sundae dishes there. *Mango sorbet – that's what I had.*

The image changed, solidified. Two dishes of ice cream, two shades of orange. Maxim's face came into view. Dark brown eyes searching mine. Light brown hair that touched his shoulders. The tension in his jaw. The flutter of my pulse at the sight of him grown tall and broad-shouldered, familiar and strange, all at once.

"Do you hear that, Roni?" Cha-young's voice buzzed at the edges of my consciousness. She sounded far away. "That could be you. It *will* be you if you don't cooperate. Tell me, what has Saero-yi promised to do for Maxim Santiago?"

Maxim. His name in her voice. It jolted me back to the present. Maxim, with his slick charm and dangerous connections. My mind raced, trying to latch onto a story, a lie that would satisfy her without giving anything away. Maxim needed the money from the 'jackpotting' they'd planned, to free himself from the narcotrafficking Carillo family. I couldn't jeopardize that, couldn't betray Saero-yi or Maxim.

"Maxim?" I forced a confused look onto my face. "Why would he tell me? It's between them. I'm just doing him a favor. Margo Daniels asked me to help bring Saero-yi to South Korea. Don't you know that?"

Cha-young blinked quickly. "Don't play dumb with me, Veronica. Maxim's plans go beyond just helping a friend. He has bigger ambitions. Has he ever discussed his plans with you? His *real* plans, I mean."

Saero-yi's agonized cries were now punctuated by sharp gasps and muffled groans. The horror of it made my stomach churn, but I knew I had to resist, somehow. I couldn't let her break me. "Max... he talks a big game," I stammered, trying to buy time. "Like... like, he talks about getting his group out of wherever they are now and into somewhere safer. But it's never anything specific."

Cha-young leaned in closer, her face inches from mine. "I think we both know that's not what I meant.

He's a Generation Six telepath. What do you *think* Maxim's endgame is?"

I swallowed hard, my mind racing. Maxim always had a plan, always scheming ten steps ahead. But what was he after, really? "He wants out of the cartel's grip," I told her. That wasn't a major secret, surely? "He wants enough cash to disappear, to hide."

Her eyes bulged very slightly, yet even this minor expression of threat was enough to transform her face. "You expect me to believe this is just about money?"

Enough money to have to answer to no-one, just like the Atlas Group. He wants to be another Artem Atlas – a boss of his own telepath 'family.' Every general needs an army, like Atlanta said. The army that gives him a seat at the table, playing the 'Mind Game' against Czar Ilyin, CIA and all the rest.

But all I said was, "Power *and* money, probably." I flashed her a cynical glare. "Doesn't it always boil down to that?"

Saero-yi's cries suddenly stopped, leaving an eerie silence in their wake. The absence of sound was almost worse than the screams. My heart thudded as I waited for the next wave of terror.

Cha-young straightened, a satisfied smirk on her face. "Very interesting, yes. Power and money. Perhaps. I wonder if that includes a crypto heist. Ever hear him mention a casino in Ecuador or a bank in Turkmenistan?"

A shiver trickled down my spine. A crypto heist? Maxim had most definitely mentioned cryptocurrency. My heart began to plummet as I remembered – Saero-yi and I *had* talked about a plan of Maxim's that involved crypto. *Is that how Cha-young knew? Had the North Koreans bugged our apartment in the hotel, overheard our conversation?*

With a groan, I realized that if so, then all this was almost certainly my fault. Saero-yi had used telepathy when we'd discussed it. Like an idiot, I'd probably repeated some of it aloud. Yet again, I had to ask myself if being a one-dub was all that. But this wasn't the time, I reminded myself. Right now, I needed laser focus. No more getting wrong-footed by Cha-young.

Casinos and banks in far-off countries? Maxim's crypto plan sounded more substantial than I'd imagined. This was how he was going to do it: buy his freedom, protection and a future. And I'd put all of that in jeopardy, because now Saero-yi was back where he'd started – property of the North Korean dictator, the 'Kim.'

Cha-young's phone buzzed, and she glanced at it, her expression hardening further. "Ponder that a little while, would you? Think about what Maxim and Saero-yi might have been planning. We'll talk again soon."

She exited the cabin, closing the door behind her. I waited, perfectly still until I couldn't hear their voices. Silence settled over me. My thoughts were a chaotic mess, but one thing was becoming crystal clear: I had to get us out of here.

With Cha-young gone, I allowed myself a moment to breathe, tried to let go some of the tears I'd been holding back. But nothing. I couldn't afford to break down. Saero-yi needed me, I had to be strong for him. After a moment I pulled back my hair tight at the temples, focused on the sensation of stretching my scalp.

First job – get out of the zip ties. For the second time, Bobbie's training for evading capture was coming into its own. When Cheekbones had shackled my wrists, I'd put my hands together with thumbs tightly locked, just as we'd learned. Now I rotated my palms to face each other and began working with the extra space, sliding palms and wrists against each other until one hand slipped free, then the other.

The dim light in the cabin seemed to grow brighter as my eyes adjusted. I scanned the room again, this time more closely. There had to be something, something I could use to undo the zip ties around my ankles. A tool, a screw, anything I could use as a shim. That's when I noticed it: lurking low in the corner behind the second cot; a small vent. Hope sparked within me. It might just be wide enough for me to crawl through.

It wasn't much, but it was something. I crawled over to the vent, carefully studied it. The screws were old and rusted, the metal grate brittle. With enough force, I could probably pry it off. And bonus – I'd get a screw that I could use to undo the ankle ties.

Using the edge of the cot, I managed to leverage the screws, loosening them one by one. I pressed the tip of the screw against the zip tie's locking mechanism, the small locking bar that did all the work. It was gradual and painstaking, but the thought of escaping and rescuing Saero-yi drove me on. After a creakingly slow two minutes, I freed my legs.

Great, now to get out of here.

When I removed the final screw in the grate, it came free with a faint metallic groan. I squeezed through the narrow opening. The vent was dark and cramped, but it led somewhere. That was enough. I crawled forward, heart pounding in my ears. The air was close and stifling, each breath a struggle, but I kept moving.

The only way now was forwards. Forwards to hope, backwards to despair.

THIRTY-THREE

WAKE UP

The whole time I'd been figuring out how to escape, there had been no sounds from outside the door to my cell. Wherever our captors were, they probably weren't right outside, because I'd certainly made enough noise to alert them, moving the cot around, and whatnot.

All of which made me think Cha-young and Cheekbones assumed we were trapped, until they decided to release us.

Well, we'd see about that.

Squirming on my belly, I dragged myself through the vent, mind focused on two actions I had to take: Get the key, unlock the door to the neighboring room, where they were holding Saero-yi.

After ten yards or so, the vent opened into a tiny storage closet filled with cleaning supplies and tools. The space was barely two yards deep. I scanned the area, and my eyes landed on a set of five keys that hung from a hook by the door. I grabbed them, my hands trembling with a mix of fear and adrenaline.

Guided by the direction of the vent, I headed for the corridor outside the two cabins that were acting as the ship's brig. When I got close, I heard a door open, footsteps just behind the door that separated me from the nearby corridor. Pressing myself against the wall, I held my breath. If whoever it was opened one more door, I'd be discovered. Running now would draw attention, too. I might get away in time, but then I'd lose all hope of returning to free Saero-yi.

Unless...

An idea occurred to me. Taking tiny, backward steps, I returned to the closet from which I'd emerged minutes before. Closing the door behind me, gently, I turned my attention to the cleaning supplies. Bleach, floor cleaning fluid, disinfectant spray. A mop and a broom. I unscrewed the plastic handle from the broom, picked up the floor cleaner and the disinfectant spray, stashed the broom handle under my arm, then tiptoed back to the corridor outside Saero-yi's prison. With my ear to the door that separated that area from the main corridor on the deck, I listened. Nothing. I waited a little longer. Then I heard something that sent a jolt through my entire body.

Footsteps were approaching – from somewhere behind me. I gulped down a breath and then turned the first door handle I could reach, pushing myself through. Inside, I leaned against the door, in case whoever was on their way to Saero-yi might have spotted the door close. I waited, heart pounding so hard, I felt it in my throat. A few seconds later, I heard the corridor door click twice: open, shut.

I took three more breaths and tried to visualize the space outside and thought *Dammit, Saero-yi, why don't you send me a message, let me know how you're doing?*

He was probably thinking that I can't get back to him, so what's the point?

Selfish two-dub, only reaching out when there's something in it for him.

Okay, it was all on me, for now. I glanced down at the yellow plastic bottle of cleaning fluid in my left hand, aerosol can of disinfectant in the other.

Let the chemical warfare begin.

I cracked the door to the nearby enclosure containing the brig, then poured out all the sticky, green cleaning fluid, poured it slowly, trying not to attract attention. But within seconds, whoever was guarding the brig must have noticed the approaching slick of green liquid, because they barked out a warning. In my left hand, I readied the disinfectant spray to use like mace and prepared to swing the broom handle with my right hand. Beyond, I heard a door open and then Cha-young's voice crying out in alarm. I guessed she was emerging from the cabin holding Saero-yi – a lucky break for me that she hadn't checked the other door first and noticed I'd gone.

One of them set off towards me and the first part of my plan slotted into place – the floor hazard. I heard Cha-young yell, then curse loudly as she crashed to the floor. I sped back to the cleaning closet and locked the door. I jammed the mop's stringy head under the door handle and stuck it into the head of the broom. Then I grabbed the mop bucket and did my best to brace it and the broom head against the opposite wall. It'd hold the door a little longer, at least. Holding onto the keys and the disinfectant spray, I went headfirst, back into the air vent and began slithering along towards the next opening, which was the cabin I'd escaped.

It was a gamble, but I'd counted on them not guessing that I'd choose to imprison myself, so soon after I'd broken out.

A couple minutes later, I'd wormed my way back to the brig. I listened at the door, waiting for a few seconds before slowly, silently as possible, I slid the first key into the lock. It wouldn't turn. Fumbling for the second key, I struggled to remain calm.

Cha-young had probably gone looking for whoever

had turned the floor outside into a sloppy slip hazard. Did she suspect it was me? That air vent had been fairly well hidden by the cot, the screws rusty, untouched. Was it possible she hadn't checked, didn't know it was there? Even in the midst of my rising panic, this struck me as weirdly lax. I pushed aside that thought, forced my attention back to the task at hand – escape.

A plan of sorts was coming together in my mind. Step one – free Jang Saero-yi. Holding my breath, I tried to turn the second key. It wouldn't move. Hand trembling, I tried the third key.

This one turned smoothly in the lock. I was getting out again, this time through the door. I opened it onto an empty corridor. Five yards over, the door to the main corridor now stood wide open. Cha-young and Cheekbones were nowhere to be seen. I moved swiftly to getting Saero-yi out of his locked cabin, testing first one key, then a second, which worked.

I braced myself for the sight of Saero-yi all beaten and bleeding, and pushed back the door.

Saero-yi lay on the cot, hands and ankles still fastened together with zip ties. He wore only a white shirt and trousers now, the white tuxedo jacket, bow-tie and shoes were nowhere to be seen. From where I stood, he seemed to be asleep. I moved closer, touched his shoulder. His face was a little red from the slap I'd seen him take, but other than that, he looked fine. Without touching him, I gave his hands, face and neck a quick once over. As peaceful as a sleeping baby.

Something was wrong.

I nudged his shoulder. When he didn't respond, I shoved him a little harder, fearing the worst. What had they done to him? Was he in a coma? I crossed the room to the table. The toolbox lay there, unopened. I searched inside and quickly found a scalpel. A minute later I had sliced through all our zip ties. Saero-yi could walk out of here, drama-free, if he'd only wake up.

Spotting an aluminum bottle behind the toolbox, I checked the contents. No smell, clear liquid. Looked like water, felt like water, a little cold to the touch. I emptied the bottle over his head. That did the trick.

Saero-yi stirred awake, sputtering. I grabbed both his hands, hauled him to his feet.

"Wake up, Sleeping Beauty. Time to get off this boat."

He peered at me through bleary eyes. "Padi," he said, with a lazy grin. "You're here. That's great." He sounded drunk and swayed a fair bit. I propped him up against my shoulder. What had they given him? There had to be an antidote. I led him to the door, leaned him against the nearby wall and went back to the toolbox. Inside were three syringes labeled BZD, flumanazil and morphorium. The BZD syringe was empty. I picked up the remaining two.

"Okay, Alice, help me out. which one makes you sleepy and which one wakes you up?"

He raised a trembling finger and pointed at the morphorium syringe in my left hand. "Keep that. Use the other."

I held up the flumanazil syringe. "Use this?"

He nodded.

I got close to him, looked into his eyes.

"They already used morpho," he said, haltingly. "Can't use telepathy. Not for hours. You can't leave it. Hurry with the other. I'm falling asleep."

He sagged to the floor, collapsing slowly, like the Straw Man from Wizard of Oz, when the Wicked Witch does her thing. I lifted the edge of his shirt and injected the milliliter of flumanazil into the thin layer of fat around his belly. Waiting for it to take effect, I gripped his left wrist until I could feel his pulse. It was good, strong. Whatever 'BZD' was, I guessed they'd used it to put him to sleep. Hopefully the flumanazil would wake him soon.

Carefully, I pocketed the capped syringe of morphorium. Then, my eyes went to the door. Any second now, Cha-young and Mr. Cheekbones could be back. I doubted we'd get another chance if that happened.

"Wake up," I urged Saero-yi, touching a finger to his cheek. We had to leave, fast, and move onto the second stage of my escape plan. With no functional phone, no way to call for help, no psi powers from Saero-yi, our goose was pretty far cooked if we didn't get out.

THIRTY-FOUR

DARK EXPANSE

So – they'd shot Saero-yi full of telepath-kryptonite, a.k.a. morphorium. I guessed they'd used a dose high enough not only to inhibit his telepathy, but also to prevent him from thinking straight. At least, that's what he'd told me soon after we'd first met: '*Broadcasting is so fundamental, the dose of morpho you'd need to inhibit it makes us pretty useless at any higher brain processing.*'

The *why* of it all niggled at me, like a piece of grit in my eye. I didn't have time to think about that, though. How was I going to get him off this yacht, if he didn't wake up? My plan was rough, with few details, no contingency. *Not my style*, I thought. Then I caught myself. Since when did I have a particular style, when it came to escaping capture? Maybe I was confusing myself with Maxim? He was the great planner, the details guy. But maybe improvisation was going to work better for me? After all, it'd been my idea at the last minute, to switch up the plan for getting the telepathic kids out of the Krylov camp. Maxim had struggled with that, at first, but I'd talked him around.

Beside me, Saero-yi stirred. Then he sat bolt upright, wild-eyed, one hand shooting out to clutch my shoulder. He sucked in a huge breath, as if he'd been underwater, then, glancing around, his eyes widened and he glared at me. "*Joj-Dwaesseo.*" he groaned, which is

Korean for a sweary version of 'I'm royally screwed.' "We're still here? We have to go."

He tried to stand, tottering unsteadily for a moment until I stabilized him. Saero-yi and I slipped out of the cabin, moving as one unit, our movements synchronized by necessity and desperation. Every sound felt magnified, every shadow a potential threat. The dimly lit corridors of the yacht seemed to stretch endlessly before us. The sounds of the party above were a strange juxtaposition to our perilous situation, creating an eerie soundscape.

We crept along the corridor walls, our footsteps barely more than whispers against the polished wood floors. Our captors were still dealing with the slippery mess we'd left earlier, their frustrated curses echoing through the halls. We paused at each corner, holding our breath and listening intently before moving forward.

A sudden noise – a bottle tipping over and rolling – froze us in place. My heart pounded, felt loud enough that I was sure Saero-yi could hear it. We pressed ourselves flat against the wall as someone slipped past us, too preoccupied with their own problems to notice us.

"Tell me you have a plan," Saero-yi managed to grind out.

"I have one," I replied, keeping my eyes peeled for any movement. The crate of scuba equipment I had seen on the aft deck was our best chance. "You swim, right?"

Saero-yi hesitated. Anxiety flickered in his eyes. "Not well. Only in a pool. I've never swum in the ocean."

"And your psi powers...?" It was a slim hope, but I knew it'd make all the difference.

He looked despondent. "Not a drop. Morpho lasts too long."

My heart sank. The water was our best escape route, but his admission added a new layer of difficulty. "We don't have much of a choice," I told him gently. "Yacht's unmoored, we have to swim for it. But I found some scuba gear. It'll keep us afloat, and I'll be with you the whole time."

Saero-yi's face lapsed into a mix of fear and resignation and he was quiet for a while. "Okay," he said, eventually. "But if I drown, I'm haunting you and you'll have to be my ghost bride."

When I responded with blank confusion, he explained, "Like the famous K-drama. The stars of it are here, at the party."

I liked that; humor, even in this dire situation. "Ghost-married, deal."

We continued our cautious trek toward the aft deck, away from the party and the lower deck that housed the billionaire's creepy dungeon. When we reached the aft section, I headed straight to where I'd seen the crate of scuba equipment. It was still there, untouched.

I grabbed a scuba tank, two masks, and two sets of flippers. "Put these on," I instructed, helping Saero-yi remove his shoes and fit the flippers onto his feet. I adjusted the scuba tank on my back and secured the mask over my face. "Stay close and follow my lead," I told him, voice steady despite my racing pulse.

Saero-yi looked at the equipment, then back at me, his eyes wide with apprehension. "You're sure about this?"

"I literally just learned how," I said, firmly. "Trust me, it's all fresh in my mind."

Just then, we heard footsteps approaching. There was no time to second-guess. "Now!" I hissed, urgently.

Without hesitation, we moved to the edge of the railing. The sea below glistened in the moonlight, a dark expanse. I took a deep breath and, clutching Saero-yi's hand, we tumbled backward over the railing.

As we fell, I'm sure I heard Cha-young's voice call out, her voice rising desperately above the wind and waves. "Roni, no, no! You don't know what you've done!"

The initial plunge was a shock to my system. The cool water swallowed us. But after a minute it began to grow comfortable, a summer ocean. *Small mercies*. The water buoyed us up, the scuba gear doing its job. I turned to Saero-yi, who was thrashing in panic.

"Relax," I instructed through the mask, my voice steady and commanding. "Breathe slowly. I've got you."

He looked at me, his eyes wide with fear but slowly nodding in understanding. I stayed close, guiding him with steady hands. The scuba gear was a lifeline; it kept us afloat and helped Saero-yi stay calm.

We began to get some distance from the yacht, our movements slow and deliberate. The sounds of the party faded into the distance, replaced by the rhythmic pulse of my breathing and the soft hiss of bubbles. Each stroke took us further from the danger, each breath a small victory.

Saero-yi struggled at first, with uncoordinated, jerky movements. But he soon adapted, stayed close and followed my lead. His initial panic subsided, replaced by a determined focus. We swam in unison, moving through the water with purpose.

Then, from behind, a speedboat appeared. Sensing that it was searching for us, I went immediately onto high alert. Its engine growled as it cruised slowly through the area. A torch beam sliced through the darkness, scanning the water's surface. My heart lurched, and I grabbed Saero-yi, signaling for him to dive.

We plunged deep into the gloom. I shared my regulator with Saero-yi, our breaths synchronized as we swam deeper. The torch beam passed over where we'd just been, missing us by mere seconds. Saero-yi's mood shifted sharply from reluctance to terror. He clung to me, eyes wide with fear. For the first time, I saw that he was truly willing to do whatever I said, even without the extra security of sharing his thoughts with me.

Once he'd accepted my protection, we began to make smooth progress underwater. We swam for maybe five minutes before I dared to surface. I'd been trying to keep the coast on our right-hand side but there was a chance I'd gotten turned around. I tried not to think about what might happen if I had. Was Seoul on a bay? How long before we'd hit land, if we swam further into the open sea? These were the kinds of details that ought to be factored into a plan like this, I reflected.

Waving a hand in front of Saero-yi's face, I signaled to surface. As we broke the surface of the water, gasping for air, I took a moment to look around. The lights of the yacht were behind us, the city lights even more distant. We'd evaded the speedboat, but we were a long way from shore. I removed my mask, taking deep breaths of the fresh night air. Saero-yi did the same, his breaths ragged but steady. Thankfully there was no wind, the water's surface was smooth as a lake.

Exhausted but relieved, we floated together, the sounds of the party now a distant memory. The night was quiet, the only sounds the gentle lapping of the water and our labored breathing. We had escaped the immediate danger, but we weren't safe yet.

In the starlight, I spotted the faint outline of trees ahead, maybe a few more minutes' swim away from the marina. "Look," I said, pointing. "The shore. We can make it."

Saero-yi could only nod. He looked totally exhausted.

We swam slowly but steadily. The journey was grueling, my muscles already ached, but I was spurred on by the thought of finally getting some rest. The shore grew closer, a deserted patch of land, judging from the silhouetted trees. Finally, we reached the shallow waters of a beach. We staggered out of the water onto tightly packed sand. I felt ten times heavier than usual, dragging myself up on the beach until I collapsed on the first bit of dry sand.

"We made it!" Saero-yi said as he slumped, one second behind me onto the powdery sand. Through his bone-weariness, I heard amazement. "I thought we'd be getting ghost married, for sure."

THIRTY-FIVE

CASTAWAYS

We ended up sleeping where we'd fallen – under the stars on soft sand dunes. When I opened my eyes some hours later it was to the pink skies of dawn. Waves rolled gently onto the sand, no more than a few yards away from our feet. Beside me, Saero-yi lay on his side, cheek nestled in the crook of an elbow.

I watched him for a moment. He looked so relaxed, rather sweet. It seemed a shame to wake him. All it had done for me was a dose of hard-faced reality: we were officially in a pickle, to put things very mildly.

I stood up, noticed that my clothes were still damp. The breeze carried a faint smell of rotting seaweed. A few yards to our left, the sandy beach was strewn with gray boulders. Seagulls were noisily foraging on seaweed that had collected between rocks.

Standing at the water's edge, I peered at the horizon. Was that the mainland, in the distance? Or open water? In the light of day, I just couldn't tell. Either way, it was too far to swim. The yacht must have sailed clear of the river and into the ocean.

I'd suspected it even last night, when we'd beached ourselves, but now I was certain: this wasn't some uninhabited corner of Seoul, or wherever the yacht had sailed to, while we'd been in the brig. This was an island, a rocky outcropping to our left and forest behind it, as far as I could see.

To our right, the beach ended, no more than fifty yards away. Behind us was a wooded area. No sign of any buildings, or telephone cables, no electricity pylons. No sign that the island was inhabited.

We were castaways.

My stomach gurgled and I tasted salt in my mouth. Hunger and thirst, swift reminders that we had no food or water, no way to call for help. The idyllic sense of being at peace flew out of my head at once, replaced by the first flash of existential dread I'd had since Alaska, when I had thought we would surely die at sea.

Capture and torture are bad, don't get me wrong. Terrifying, at times. But the thought of dying from thirst and starvation is a fear that operates on another level.

Find water. Food's less of a problem on an island – plenty of fish. But freshwater, on a tiny island? There might easily be none at all. Then we'd have precious little time to work on getting rescued before our bodies shut down from a lack of water.

Too bad the abduction training we'd taken, at Bobbie's insistence, hadn't included a section on how to survive if they abducted you to a deserted island.

Retracing my footprints in the sand, I returned to where Saero-yi lay, still enjoying his peaceful snooze. Yeah, his little rest was over – I needed an ally to figure out how not to die.

He woke up easily, blinking hard as he looked up at me. "Where are we?"

"Lost," I said. "On an island."

He sat up, sharply. "An island?"

"Yeah. Any idea how that's possible, so close to the city?"

He rubbed his eyes with the heels of his hands, then stared, eyes adjusting to the light. "We might be near Incheon. There are some islands off the coast there."

"Do they get visitors? Cause we're screwed if we can't get off this one."

Saero-yi stood up, brushed loose sand from his soggy black trousers. "I don't know," he admitted. "Everything I know about South Korea is from what I studied at the Krylov camp. I've never even visited the actual country." He pointed to the horizon. "The sun rose behind us. Ahead, that's west. That's North Korea."

Startled, I took a breath. "So – we don't want to go that way."

"We don't."

"We should hike to the other side of the island, then," I said. "And look for water on the way." I turned to face the woods behind the beach. "This way. More likely to find water in the interior."

Saero-yi caught up to me and we fell into a steady pace, walking between sparse trees. After a minute they thickened enough that we had to pick a careful route between their exposed roots. But after another ten minutes we could already see the opposite side of the island. And beyond that, across an expanse of sea, a rugged, coastline of forested hills, behind which the sun was rising.

Shielding our eyes, we stared across the water. "That could be the mainland. Or one of the bigger islands."

I struggled to stay optimistic. "We could swim that distance. Probably."

He turned to me and shook his head. "No. Not me."

"We swam for at least fifteen minutes last night."

"That coast looks further away," he said. "Thirty

minutes, at my speed. Maybe more. I was full of adrenaline last night." *Today, I'd drown and so might you.*

"Your psi powers are back – that's something."

Yes.

"If we could figure a way for me to communicate without talking, we'd be all set."

One-way is better than nothing. I'm going to explore in this direction. You go round the other – and we'll meet back where we started. He headed off, not even pausing to check that I'd agreed.

"Can't do that," I called after him. "There are rocks on the other side of the beach. Meet back here in an hour."

You don't have a watch.

"I have a really good sense of time," I shouted. "One hour. Back here!"

Over the next hour, I collected an armful of five empty plastic bottles that had washed up on the beach. If we could find some plastic sheeting or similar material, we could collect morning dew. My mind was already turning to thoughts of building a shelter. And to collect rocks to spell out SOS on the sand. I forced myself to ignore the rumbles of appetite that were becoming painful twinges. If we could make a fire, we could boil water and collect the condensed steam. I felt a splash of water on my nose, then another. Rain.

Dammit, no fire if the wood gets wet. A second later, the penny dropped. I stuck out my tongue and let a few drops hit it before I swallowed. Hastily, I sank to the ground and partially buried the empty plastic bottles in the sand, tops open to collect rainwater. Then, I lay on my back, mouth open, drinking as much as I could while the shower lasted. When it was over, each bottle had collected a few dribbles of water. Combined, it came to just over an inch. Carefully, I screwed the bottle cap tightly closed. From now on, every drop counted. Then I turned back. The rain shower had used up almost twenty minutes – no more time to explore.

"We need more," was all Saero-yi said, when I handed him the bottle of water I'd collected.

I bit back the urge to snap at him. We had to keep it together. Face up to what had happened and make a plan to get off the island. "Collect stones," I told him. "We need to make an SOS."

It took actually starting on that task to dissipate a low-grade panic that threatened to blow up and send me through the roof. Once that initial drive to survive began to ease off, I realized that I hadn't asked Saero-yi anything about how he was feeling, after the horrific ordeal he'd been through. It wasn't just that, though. If I could hardly face recalling the hideous screams I'd heard through the partition, was it smart to remind him? Maybe I should wait until he brought it up?

Pondering this kept me silent for another few minutes, as we wandered back and forth from the widest stretch of beach and the rocky shelf nearby, gathering chunky-sized rocks.

After a while, though, I remembered how when my parents had gotten arrested and jailed, almost nobody had said anything to me about it. No-one apart from Kenzie and his family, of course. Kids I considered my friends averted their eyes when I approached, or gave me a generic 'sorry' gesture, a shrug with a kind of semi-pout. The gesture reserved for when something seriously horrible has happened, because let's face it, no-one's afraid to be openly sympathetic when your cat has just died.

I couldn't be the kind of person who'd brush over or even ignore something terrible, like what had happened to Saero-yi. And that's just the *terrible* that I knew about, of course. For all I knew, he'd been through similarly bad stuff in the Krylov camp.

So, I asked him directly. His reaction was not at all what I'd expected. He laid down the rock, completing the 'O' in 'SOS,' then glanced at me, puzzled. "What are you talking about?"

"Before they put you to sleep, I mean." I hesitated briefly, then said, "You screamed pretty loud. It sounded bad."

"When I asked them not to inject me?"

I thought back. He'd said 'no, please don't' at first. Then he'd just screamed. I relayed this as gently as possible.

Now I had his full attention. "They injected me with the benzodiazepam. I don't remember much, after that. I couldn't move, or scream. Fell unconscious almost immediately."

I stared. "There was a lot of screaming," I said after a moment.

He nodded, thoughtfully. "For your benefit, probably." He leaned over, positioned another rock, starting the final 'S.'

My cheeks flushed with embarrassment. Realization flooded through me; I felt like an idiot. They'd interrogated *me,* not Saero-yi. I'd been the true target, forced to listen to terrifying screams and imagine gruesome tortures, while Cha-young asked me questions about him.

But why *not* him? I picked up two rocks and positioned them, trying to brush the whole thing off, the way he seemed to be doing. Then I stopped. No. This was too weird. Something was wrong with the whole picture. What was it?

For another minute, I did nothing but watch Saero-yi work diligently to complete our giant 'SOS' in the sand. Then I gazed out to sea, where in the distance boats of various types were criss-crossing, none of them close enough to hear us.

My mind turned facts over, moved dangling observations that had made little sense at the time into new positions, took apart my own version of what had happened and reassembled everything to form an entirely different picture.

With fresh eyes, I observed Saero-yi, this good-looking, put together, warm and witty alleged genius and wondered – how much of this persona was real? Had I been with 'Trogon' from the Krylov Foundation, the cyber warrior that Maxim was so eager to recruit to his cause? Or was he something entirely different: not a guy who happened to be in the right place at the right time to help whichever intelligence agency got to him first, but an active, willing agent of the CIA?

THIRTY-SIX

RONI FIGURES IT OUT

The sun had arced high above the horizon, but clouds now swept in from offshore, blotting out its dazzle behind a flat gray haze. On the hunt for something to eat, I trudged along the rocky shore of the tiny, nameless island. I'd picked beach over inland, leaving Saero-yi to forage in the forest. Edible seaweed was worth a shot and there was always a chance of snatching a sluggish crab off the sand, before it scuttled for cover under a rock.

I tried not to focus on the issue of drinking water. That loomed massively as the factor that'd decide how long we'd survive. Right now, though, it was too scary to face. Especially with my thoughts fixated on unraveling the mystery of *exactly* how Saero-yi and I had come to find ourselves in this situation.

As the sun rose and lit up the opposite coastline, North Korea lay ahead of us, beyond the deep blue of the open ocean. The sound of waves crashing against the rocks was a constant reminder of our isolation, punctuating the eerie silence that surrounded us. Salty air stung my nostrils, and my stomach growled. But something more than hunger gnawed at me. There was a question, a creeping suspicion that had been brewing since the moment we plunged into the sea.

No – even before that.

I kicked a stone into the water, watching it skitter across the surface before sinking. I was lucky that my bare feet were relatively unscathed, after hiking across the island. Shoes would have been nice, but we'd ditched them when we'd swapped them for flippers. Then again, Saero-yi had his trousers. Between us we had one whole warm-ish set of clothes, if not particularly dry.

Concentrating, I tried to remember when I'd first sensed that something was wrong. Cha-young's behavior, Mr. Cheekbones' obsessive pursuit, the fact that we were on that yacht in the first place – which had struck first?

Cha-young's outfit. Yes, that'd tripped the first, faint alarm. They were allegedly trying to present her as the gorgeous star of a glamorous new TV drama, romantically paired with Saero-yi. But while he'd been dressed to the nines, a hottie in a white tuxedo jacket, Cha-young had been dressed like a sensible office worker, right up to the white sneakers for a daily commute. She'd been dressed for action, unlike me. While I'd been pretending to be a secret agent, Cha-young was actually *being* one.

If our outfits had been part of a set-up, then the whole yacht party was implicated, including everyone involved. I corrected myself – *not everyone*. Just everyone that took orders from Margo Daniels. Unless Cha-young had gone rogue?

Yes, that had to be a possibility. It was a worrying one, for sure. It'd mean that Daniels had no idea where I was. Also that the CIA was so incompetent as to yet again let their operation be infiltrated by a North Korean spy.

If I get out of this, I should walk away from Daniels, the

CIA, the whole enchilada. If you can't rely on your colleagues, really, what's the point?

As I walked, I kept replaying the events of the past few hours in my head, trying to make sense of it all. I remembered the way Cha-young's eyes had narrowed when she looked at me, the way she seemed almost disappointed when I didn't break under her questioning. Then there was the moment just before we jumped overboard – what had she yelled at me? It was something that had struck me as odd, but in the chaos, I hadn't had time to think about it.

'You don't know what you've done!'

A strange thing to say. Not what you'd expect from someone whose orders were to capture and interrogate me. I'd heard a note of desperation, too. As if we'd taken her by surprise, by jumping overboard. As if she hadn't expected us to actually go through with it.

That thought made me pause. I stared out at the ocean, the pieces starting to come together in my mind. Okay, so why would the whole yacht party be a setup? What if it wasn't for Saero-yi, but for me? It was almost like Cha-young was waiting to see how I would react, how far I'd go. Testing my limits. But testing me for what?

Was this really about discovering Maxim's plans for Saero-yi, or was there something else going on? Maxim had been cagey about the details, sure, but this level of intensity didn't make sense unless there was something more at stake.

At this point, I really couldn't tell whether it was the CIA or North Koreans pulling the strings. Both were scary. My stomach twisted at the thought that Daniels could be behind something so sinister.

I crouched down to inspect a cluster of seaweed clinging to the rocks, trying to distract myself from the rising panic in my chest. I plucked a few strands, inspecting them for anything edible. My hands worked on autopilot while my mind raced.

Saero-yi's behavior had been odd, too. He'd panicked at the suggestion of escaping by jumping overboard. Had it been a lie that he couldn't swim well? Or an excuse; the first thing he'd thought of? Certainly, although he'd seemed genuinely terrified at first, after a while he'd settled into it and managed pretty well. Then again, the sea had been becalmed all night. Even now it was like a lake.

Uncomfortable as it was, I thought about Saero-yi's actions, his reactions. How he'd fought against being taken, how he'd panicked when we were cornered. How he had believably struggled to breathe, when we were underwater. Even his response, when I'd asked about his torture, the horrible screams of pain I'd heard. Had all that been real, or was he playing a part? I had to know, and that meant watching him closely.

I glanced back towards the trees where Saero-yi was foraging. If this was a test, if Cha-young was somehow working for the CIA or South Korean intelligence, then Saero-yi could be in on it. But it didn't add up. Or else he was an artist of deception, and I'd bought his act, was still buying it now.

A rustle in the bushes caught my attention, and I straightened up, breathless. A moment later, a small, dark bird flitted out, disappearing into the dense foliage. I exhaled slowly, shaken by my own jumpiness. I *had* to stay focused.

Walking a little further down the shoreline, I combed the beach for anything else we could eat. The rocks gave way to the small patch of sand on which we'd landed. Irritatingly close by, given the time I'd spent searching, I found a cluster of clam shells scattered across the ground. I crouched down and began to dig. I pulled out one clam after another; they weren't much food, but they were better than nothing. Probably better cooked than raw, too. If we could make a fire. We had no matches or lighter and I had no idea how to do the stick-rubbing method, which I'd heard was a lot harder than it sounded. But if I'd managed to find some washed up plastic bottles, maybe we could find glass and use it to start a fire?

I switched to scouting for a clear glass bottle. As I worked, I couldn't shake the feeling that I was missing something. If Cha-young was CIA – or worse, some sort of double agent – then what was the point of all this? Testing my loyalty? That didn't make sense either. I had no significant connections to any government, no deep ties that would make me a target for something like this. So why go to all this trouble?

With a handful of clams, I headed back inland, my thoughts still spinning. Maybe this was about Maxim after all, but in some roundabout way that I hadn't anticipated? What if they were testing me to see if I'd betray him? Or what if this was about something entirely different, something I wasn't even aware of?

When it came down to it, did I even know what I was up against?

In my head, I heard Saero-yi's voice.

I'm done. Found raspberries. And something else. Come and see.

By the time I reached the beach where we'd agreed to meet, my nerves were getting close to a breaking point. Saero-yi was already there, looking smug, one hand hiding something behind his back. I forced a smile, trying to act like everything was normal.

"Found some clams," I said, holding them up.

Saero-yi grinned widely. "Nice. I found some wild

raspberries." He pulled out the objects he'd been hiding. "And glass. And a sheet of plastic. We can make fire. Heat water, collect condensation."

"Thank goodness, we're saved," I said, deadpan. "We can live here happily for years." But my attempt at humor didn't land. Or maybe he was just being polite, pretending not to hear.

We gathered dry twigs, grass and driftwood, made a circle of rocks and did our best to construct a heap of kindling. But despite our best efforts, with the sky dense with cloud, there was no way to capture the sun's rays to ignite the kindling.

I was about to say something when Saero-yi suddenly stiffened, his eyes glazing over as if he were listening to something only he could hear. "Saero-yi?" I asked quietly, trying not to startle him.

He blinked and snapped back into the moment. His eyes were wide, filled with a new kind of fear. *It's my sister.*

I leaned closer, trying to make sense of it. "Your sister, Susie Jang? Double agent, Doctor Susie?"

She's been deployed by CIA. To find us. His thoughts tumbled out in a rush. *She's close, maybe just a few miles away. But she says North Korean agents are searching for us, too. That we have to hide until we're rescued.*

Saero-yi's broadcast settled on me like freezing snow. If his sister was nearby, it meant we had some hope of getting out of this alive. But it also meant the danger was even greater than I'd realized. The North Koreans were still hunting us, and they were close.

I kept my voice calm. "Did she say anything else?"

Saero-yi hesitated, glancing around as if expecting the enemy to materialize out of the shadows. "She gave me a password, something to identify us to whoever she sends to help us. But we have to stay hidden until then."

My mind raced, trying to process everything at once. So far I'd been right on both counts: whatever this was, CIA was involved, North Korean intelligence, too. The question was, who could we trust? And what were we really running from?

I looked at Saero-yi, his face pale and tense. He was scared, genuinely scared. That meant he wasn't in on it – whatever 'it' was. And if he wasn't, then we were both in the same boat, both trying to survive whatever game we'd been dragged into.

"All right," I said finally, my voice steady despite the turmoil inside me. "We need to stay low, find a place to hide until your sister, or whoever she sends gets here."

Saero-yi nodded and drew a breath. "Yeah," he agreed, aloud. "Okay."

THIRTY-SEVEN

You're Risking A Lot

We gathered up our clams and raspberries and talked through the next steps. Priority one: find a concealed spot that also gave us a good view of the island. As we moved through the underbrush, the reality of our situation hit me. We were being hunted, caught in the crossfire of something much bigger than us. Too bad for me, because I couldn't afford to trust anyone completely.

Honestly, I'd never missed Kenzie so badly. Was this how it'd be, if I agreed to become Margo Daniels's asset, her normie conduit to the young two-dubs of the world? Life as a solo artist was very different – and I was only now finding that out. Until last night, I'd assumed I could trust Saero-yi. But now, not so much, at least until I knew exactly what was up.

We found a small, secluded spot at the north-western tip of the island, hidden among the rocks but with a clear view of the island's only sandy beach, which faced out toward North Korea. Unfortunately, there was nowhere high enough to give us sight lines over the whole island, so the Incheon-facing side, where the forest went all the way to the edge of the sea, was out of sight. We settled in, our nerves pulled thin as we waited for whatever might come next.

After a few hours the clouds cleared in time for us

to watch the sun dip low and cast long shadows across the water. The air grew cooler, the sounds of the ocean filled the silence between us. We sat side by side, sharing the two dozen raspberries he'd picked, most of them only semi-ripe, meantime trying to keep our spirits up. Saero-yi ate his share of the clams raw – he didn't seem too worried about getting food poisoning. Then I offered him my share, too. There was no point wasting them.

I was dying to interrogate him, to be honest. Gently, of course. Because by this point, only a complete life history, no gaps, full reasoning behind every major decision that had brought him here, would persuade me. He might even have agreed to tell me everything, too. Who knows? I couldn't bring myself to ask. That's on me and it's a rookie mistake.

It's easy to say, 'if you don't want to know the answer, don't ask the question.' Right then, watching him gulp raw shellfish while we waited for rescue to arrive, I should have been able to face up to what I'd gotten myself into. Saero-yi didn't know me, didn't owe me anything, really. Not even the truth. If he was on the level, if he really was a cyber warrior, desperate to defect from North Korea, he'd be just as anxious as I was.

Probably more, since I might conceivably have some protection from international law, if we were captured. Although even then, I suspected spies got pretty short shrift, in good ol' DPRK. However, we both knew it'd be nothing compared to what they'd do to one of their own. Even if Saero-yi had only belonged to the Kim for a few months, his entire bloodline had been designed for one purpose, the purpose he'd begun to fulfil as a cyber warrior and mathlete. No chance whatsoever that he'd be let off the hook, in case it gave other enslaved two-dubs any ideas.

It wasn't like we could talk about my history, either. Over the past few days we'd spent together, he had at some stage asked about my parents. I'd done what I usually do when forced to be honest about them – made light of the fact that they were in prison and then shut down any attempt to go into it.

Neither of us, then, was in the mood for the kind of conversation that might trigger any of our underlying fears. Instead, we talked about Kenzie and Maxim.

"You didn't want to talk about Jaguar," Saero-yi reminded me. "Back in the hotel, I mean. Was that just bad timing? Or is there a special reason for that?"

"For that?"

"The avoidance," he explained, briefly drawing his attention away from the beach we were watching, and onto me. "I sense you're not comfortable talking about him."

His even gaze began to make me uneasy, and I glanced out towards the horizon.

He continued, talking slow and carefully. "I've been thinking… about what you're putting on the line for Jaguar." Then he went to telepathy. *You're risking a lot. I'd like to know why.*

Our eyes met once again. This time I couldn't look away.

He's your friend. Yes? More than a friend?

Instinctively, I shook my head. "Not more."

Ah. But you'd like it if he were?

It was excruciating. With Saero-yi's thoughts in my mind like that, I couldn't seem to lie. I felt the sting of tears in my eyes as I tried to deny it. Finally, I let go a sound like a strangled gasp.

"I… don't even know. That's how weird it is. I can't stop thinking about him. Not for more than a few minutes at a time. Haven't been able to for months. And even before that, I think on some level, it was rumbling away, deep down. Ever since what happened with my parents, I've thought of Maxim. Right from the start, I thought of him. He's the one I wanted to talk to about them. For some reason, I believed that he'd understand."

Abruptly, I stopped talking and exhaled, one long shaky breath. I held up my hand. It was trembling. "Oof." I glanced at him and tried to laugh. "Where did that come from?!"

"Poor Kenzie," Saero-yi said aloud, grimacing. Then he did something so unexpected that it quite literally left me breathless. He leaned in close until his face was only a couple inches from mine. His eyes were huge, inescapable. I saw him glance down at my lips, then back to my eyes. He lifted a hand, touched the tips of his fingers gently to my face. Then very slowly and gradually, giving me plenty of time to escape, push him away, slap him, anything at all, he tipped closer until I felt the first brush of his lips. It was a soft kiss, incredibly gentle and purposeful. I let him kiss me, kissed back a little, as much as I could, what with every cell of my body in shock.

With a shy smile, he pulled away. "Just so you know, you have other options. If you ever want help to forget Jaguar, that is."

"Th-thanks," I managed to say, staring at him in bewilderment. My heart was pounding, I felt faint. Just utterly confused.

Sometimes it's easy to ignore what's under your nose, he telepathed. *If Kenzie allowed you to ignore him, it's his mistake. Not one that I'll make.*

"Kenzie says he's in love with me," I blurted, and felt instantly that I'd betrayed a confidence. Once it was out there, however, it felt only fair to elaborate. "So he hasn't 'allowed' me to ignore anything."

Saero-yi's smile was guarded. "All right, then consider my application filed, too."

"Honestly, what is it with boys? You're like buses; wait for one and two others show up."

A dumb thing to say but I swear, that's what I said. Saero-yi's kiss was a major curveball, it took me a while to recover. It did, however, break the ice enough for me to dare to ask what I really wanted to know. For some reason, with that tension between us suddenly broken, I felt like I could risk hearing some bad news.

"Are you working with the CIA to haze me, or something?"

Saero-yi looked surprised. "No. But I agree with you. That's what's happened. If 'hazing' means that Daniels is testing you."

I groaned with relief. "Yes! Finally! Then, I'm right?"

Shrugging, Saero-yi said, "I meant that I agree with your theory. Like I said, I'm not part of it, not that I know, anyway. The theory fits the data, everything that happened. Right until we jumped overboard, anyhow. Then it gets weird."

"That wasn't part of the plan! I knew it! Wait – if you're not part of it, then how can you know?"

"That guy with the cheekbones, he didn't seem like a North Korean to me. His accent was off. Sounded like a South Korean putting on a North Korean accent but also trying to hide it."

"That's pretty specific… are you sure?"

He nodded. "Languages are the main thing we study at the Krylov. Korean regional accents are pretty distinctive. I learned to speak with a North Korean accent, but I had to master three South Korean accents, too. That guy seemed sketchy from the start, because of the way he talked."

"If Mister Cheekbones wasn't a North Korean agent, then neither was Cha-young."

"I don't think so," he agreed. "But she wanted us to think she was."

"Hazing me, then. Testing my loyalty to Maxim, or whatever?"

"Or just messing with you, to see how much you can take. If you actually trained as an officer, it'd get intense. They train you to resist torture."

"Daniels was behind it, then?" Even though the same thought had occurred to me, it was one of my least favorite explanations.

Once again, he shrugged. "I think so."

"But your sister said North Koreans are coming. You think that's part of the test?"

I didn't think that. And he concurred. "No, I'm afraid that is real."

"Then we're really in danger. All because I had the insane idea to grab the scuba and jump overboard."

With a nod, he said, "You took it too far."

"That's why Cha-young lost it, right at the end, when she said, *'You don't know what you've done!'*"

Ruefully, he said, "That'd do it."

I began to laugh, quietly at first, then borderline hysterical. He put an arm around me, pulling me close enough to share the heat of his body, reassuring me, until I wasn't sure if I was sobbing or chuckling. All that energy wasted on trying to get found!

"Guess we'd better get rid of the SOS sign."

THIRTY-EIGHT

ABALONE

I'd seen enough to know that it would be impossible to survive on this island for more than a few days, without a source of drinkable water. The place was just remote enough to be dangerous, no escape unless you were a seriously strong swimmer.

Just as well we wouldn't be staying long. The question was – would we be leaving by choice, or hustled away by force, Saero-yi to spend the rest of his days in a North Korean labor camp, me to be used as a bargaining chip for the US government in their dealings with the Kim?

A breeze bit through the thin fabric of my tight-fitting little jacket. I shivered. The sun had dipped below the horizon, leaving the sky streaked with purples and reds that bled into the darkening ocean. The water, once a shimmering blue, was now a menacing shade of indigo, the kind of color that made you think twice about what might be lurking beneath the surface.

Saero-yi stuck close to my side, his eyes scanning the coastline with a mixture of fear and determination. I liked his way of looking at things. He could see straight through to the heart of the problem, which I found both comforting and unnerving. I tried to ignore the tiny part of me that still wondered if I could trust him. Was it possible he was still loyal to the Kim of North

Korea, that his defection had been a ruse from the start?

I mean, almost anything has a small probability of being true. But you'll drive yourself mad if you consider everything. Mostly I trusted Saero-yi for reasons I could no longer articulate. That's how friendship works, that's why we're so vulnerable to betrayal by the people we love.

I whispered. "Did your sister say who might be picking us up?"

Saero-yi shook his head, his expression grim. "She didn't. We should be ready to move fast, though."

The words were barely out of his mouth when we both noticed it – just a dot on the horizon at first but growing larger every second. A speedboat, slicing through water, thundering straight for the small nearby beach, where we'd landed last night.

My stomach dropped. I picked up one of the bundles we'd made of the scuba gear. "Grab your stuff. We need to go. Now."

We scuttled further along the highest point of the rocks, moving away from the beach. The island wasn't big, but other than twenty yards of a rocky cliff edge, it grew dense with vegetation, gnarled trees and shrubs that had withstood years of wind and salt. I breathed the stink of dried, rotten seaweed, heard the rustling of leaves, the distant call of a seabird.

We darted through the veneer of forest and onto the other side of the island, the side facing the Incheon shore. I calculated that the speedboat would be on the beach by now. If they'd landed on this nothing-island, it's because they knew where to look for us. It'd take them five minutes to cross to our side of the island. The trees would provide only thin shelter, once they started walking.

I glanced back through the trees and caught a glimpse of three figures disembarking – two men and a woman, all pale and with dark hair, the woman's in a ponytail. They were dressed in black and in one man's hand, I'm pretty sure I glimpsed a pistol. Even from this distance, I could feel the dread settling in my bones.

North Koreans. It had to be.

Roni, Saero-yi telepathed, grabbing my arm. *We need to hide.*

But there was nowhere to go. The island's shoreline was exposed, the only cover being the thick brush that lined the edge. We could hear the distant chatter of the North Koreans as they moved inland, their voices carrying over the water.

I glanced at Saero-yi, my heart racing. We had to make a decision, and fast.

"The water," I said, unsteadily. "We'll swim out, towards the mainland. We'll lose them."

Saero-yi stalled, his whole body tense. *Not swimming, not again.*

"There's no choice!" I snapped, more out of fear than anger. "I'll help you, okay? Even if they see us, they have to get back to their boat, sail around the island. We'll be underwater by then. Out of sight."

He hesitated for a moment, then nodded, the fear in his eyes replaced by a steely determination. "All right," he said, softly. "I'll trust you, again."

I grabbed my scuba tank, mask, and flippers, my hands shaking as I fastened the gear. Equally unsteady, Saero-yi did the same. His expression was unreadable, but there was still tension in his posture. We were running out of time.

The ocean loomed in front of us, dark and mysterious, a lot less tempting than it had been a few hours earlier. I forced myself to breathe, to focus. There was no room for hesitation, no room for fear.

"We're doing this," I said, more to myself than to Saero-yi.

He nodded, swallowing hard. I could tell he was scared, but he was doing his best to keep it together. I wanted to say something comforting, something to ease the fear, but there wasn't time. Instead, I just grabbed his hand and dragged him into the water, which came straight up to the trees, thanks to the almost non-existent beach on this side of the island.

The chill of the water hit me first, the water seeping through my clothes until I was cold to the bone. Saero-yi's grip on my hand tightened as we moved further in. The ocean floor declined rapidly, and soon we were both swimming, fully submerged in the water.

I placed the regulator in my mouth and inhaled, allowing the compressed air to fill my lungs. Saero-yi quickly put on the second mask, his breath panicked. He followed me closely as we submerged.

The world below the surface was a blur of shadows and shifting deep blue light, the ocean's depths stretched out into an abyss. The current tugged at us, dragged us away from the island and out into the open water. I kicked my legs, trying to fight against it, but it was like swimming through molasses, every movement a struggle.

Saero-yi clung to my arm, his breathing fast and shallow. I could feel fear radiating off him, threatening to slip into me, too. The water was cold, dark. Images of what might lurk beneath sent a trickle of ice along my spine.

I pushed these thoughts away, forcing myself to concentrate on the task at hand. I kicked harder, pulling Saero-yi along with me as we swam further from the island. The sound of the North Koreans' voices faded into the distance, drowned out by the rush of water in my ears.

But then, just when I thought we might be safe, I saw it – a large shadow against the deepening blue of the sky. My heart stopped. They'd sent another boat after us, this one a lot bigger than the first.

I grabbed Saero-yi's hand and yanked him down with me as I dove deeper. The shadow passed overhead, but I could still feel its presence, like the eyes of some predatory beast hunting us. I held my breath and prayed they wouldn't see us. But then the regulator gave a sudden, sputtering cough. With a jolt of pure dread, followed by a wave of guilt, I realized that I hadn't checked the air gauge. It was too dark to read it now, but it was all too obvious – we'd run out of oxygen.

Pulling us both to the surface, I yanked the regulator from my mouth. Instantly, saltwater flooded my mouth and nose. Saero-yi's panic erupted as he broke the surface, mouth wide open in a desperate gasp. We were out of time.

It's over, I thought. We were sitting ducks.

The larger boat was approaching, fast. I trod water, one arm around Saero-yi's waist, urging him to relax, wishing for the nth time that I could speak directly to his mind. Even though I could only receive a broadcast, I knew that some empathy was also involved in the transfer. The same way that the timbre of a person's voice can soothe you, I knew there were thoughts that could be comforting, too. Well, not from me.

Poor Jang Saero-yi, I thought, *getting stuck in open water with a semi-useless one-dub.*

As the boat moved closer, standing on its foredeck I saw the figure of a man, waving his arms and shouting something I couldn't hear. He wore a cream-colored cable-knit sweater. More like a fisherman than a North Korean agent. My vision began to blur due to insufficient oxygen, causing dizziness. Strong hands then pulled me out of the water and into the boat.

I collapsed onto the deck, gasping for air while the world spun around me. The smell of salt and fish filled my nose, along with something else – something earthy and slightly sweet. I blinked up at the sky as my field of vision filled with the wondering faces of a group of Korean women.

Saero-yi was beside me, his face pale as he struggled to sit up, spluttering seawater. I reached out to him and squeezed his hand. We were alive.

The man in the sweater who'd pulled us aboard was speaking rapidly in Korean, his voice rough and gravelly. I turned my head and saw him clearly for the first time – a middle-aged man with a mop of jet-black hair, weather-beaten skin and shrewd eyes.

"I am *Captain* Hong," the man announced, switching to halting English as he tapped his chest.

Apart from the captain, the rest of the crew appeared to be women, all different ages, from two who looked to be in their twenties, through to women with gray hair, all tied back. They had on neoprene wetsuits, and some carried nets still dripping with water.

While they peered at us like we were some rare specimens dragged from the ocean, I studied one of their nets more closely. It held several flat, oval objects with rough, pitted surfaces, encrusted with patches of mud and algae. Their thick, hard shells were a mottled mix of gray and brown, with sharp, irregular edges. They appeared inert, but their texture suggested they were more than just weathered stones.

One of the women, younger than the rest, knelt down beside me, following my gaze. She had sharp eyes with a hint of mischief, her mouth set in a determined line. She touched a finger to one of the flat discs inside.

In an adorable Korean accent she pronounced, hesitantly, "Ab-a-lon-e. Shell-fish. We dive." She cupped her hands together and gestured, like a diver arcing into water. She grinned and tapped the net again. "We take."

I blinked, looking around at all the women. Not a single scuba between them. "Dive?" I asked, blankly. "How?"

She burst into merry Korean chatter, and I was lost. But after a moment, Saero-yi's eyes widened as if alarmed by her words.

I turned to him. "What did she say? Hey, are you okay?"

"They don't use oxygen. Free diving! That's how they do it." His grin turned into laughter, and he began to laugh so hard, I thought he'd lost it.

"Dude," I growled. "Keep it together. Ask them if they're from South Korea, at least."

He rocked with laughter, while I stared at him, utterly bewildered. "They're abalone divers!"

"Yeah. I got that, from the contents of the nets." With the back of my hand, I cuffed him. "What's so hilarious?"

Shaking his head, he blinked tears from his eyes. "The password, from my sister. It was 'abalone.'"

THIRTY-NINE

INCHEON NIGHT

The boat moved smoothly towards the dock. As the engines slowed, I heard the gentle sound of water slapping the hull. I trembled, not from the cool evening air, but from the confusion that had layered up inside me, ever since Saero-yi and I had been fished out of the ocean like a pair of half-drowned cats.

Incheon was nothing like what I'd imagined. To be fair, I hadn't had time to form much of a picture in my mind. As Captain Hong's boat nudged into the harbor, I took in the scenery. The fading light of the sun landed unevenly across narrow streets that wound through a neighborhood of traditional tile-roofed houses. Eaves curved gracefully upward as if in a permanent, stoic smile, lanterns flickered to life and cast golden light on cobblestone lanes. The air was thick with brine and the faint, lingering smell of seafood. It was both comforting and unsettling, like stepping into a postcard from a different time.

Hong rarely spoke anything but Korean, while Saero-yi seemed reluctant to translate the few quiet words that passed between them. That all left me pretty clueless about our destination. The captain was a tall man who carried himself with the authority of someone in his fifties. He had broad shoulders and a surprisingly youthful complexion. His eyes were constantly scanning the horizon like he expected something to come leaping out of the ocean at us. Despite the kind of diffident vibe he tried to project, I couldn't shake the feeling that he knew exactly who we were and what kind of mess we were in. There was something in the way he avoided looking directly at me, like he was trying not to give anything away. Classic guilty behavior.

The abalone divers, on the other hand, were downright cheerful, even bubbly. I was a little in awe of them, the easy confidence of their movement around the boat, their laughter ringing out like wind chimes in the evening air. You wouldn't guess, especially the older ladies, that they were such incredible free divers, except for the fact that they smelled like damp neoprene and raw fish. Not to be judgy, after all, I probably smelled like a wet dog.

All my communication went via the youngest diver, a girl who couldn't have been much older than me, after she'd sidled up with a bright smile and a towel. Her English might have been shaky, but at least she had some, unlike me with Korean. She toed the empty oxygen tank that I'd managed to wrestle off my back. "Scuba trip? You got lost?" Her brow furrowed in concern.

I glanced over at Saero-yi, who was wringing out his shirt with a sort of resigned determination. "Yeah," I hedged. "Something like that. We got separated."

Her eyes widened, and she nodded like we'd just solved a mystery. "Ah! Very dangerous! Lucky Captain Hong find you."

I managed a smile, though my brain was still reeling. Sure, the scuba story made sense – heck, it was probably the best cover story we could've asked for. But there was something off about Captain Hong's whole shtick. He was too calm, too conveniently positioned to just scoop us up and bring us back to shore. Almost as if he'd been expecting us. Either way, my niggling gut told me that he knew way more than he was letting on.

The van Captain Hong led us to was a clunker, it had seen better days maybe a decade ago. As we piled in, I caught a glimpse of the abalone divers waving us off with those wide smiles, their faces lit up with a kind of uncomplicated joy that felt completely alien to me right now. I couldn't remember the last time I felt like that. Sometime before my parents were caught and sent to prison, that's for sure.

Incheon's streets were a maze of winding lanes and narrow alleys, the houses packed together like sardines in a tin. The roofs, curved and tiled, were a deep slate gray, their edges lifted up like the wings of a bird mid-flight. It was a strange mix of old and new, traditional homes standing shoulder to shoulder with more modern buildings, the kind that boast practicality over charm. The occasional sound of laughter or a dog barking floated through the air, giving the place a sense of life that was almost normal.

Except nothing about this felt normal. Not the way Captain Hong kept his eyes glued to the road, not the tightness in my chest that wouldn't let up, and definitely not my nagging suspicion that Saero-yi and I were being herded somewhere we didn't want to go.

I caught myself. *Not we – me*. Saero-yi, frankly, seemed calmer than he'd been since yesterday, when Cha-young and Cheekbones hounded us into the brig. Did he know more than he was letting on?

The van finally rolled to a stop in front of a small house tucked away in one of those alleys. It was a modest place, with weathered wood and shabby stone walls, but it had a kind of quiet dignity about it, like it was proud to be still standing after all these years.

Inside, the air carried a faint scent of incense, mingled with the earthy smell of the tatami mats underfoot. It was a relief, honestly, to step into a place that felt solid and real after everything we'd been through. The hallway was short, leading us to a room at the back of the house where Captain Hong motioned for us to enter.

The room was simple, spartan, with a low table in the center and a small futon rolled up in the corner. The walls were lined with shelves cluttered with books and papers, and there were a few personal touches; a fountain pen, a half-empty bottle of ink, a pair of reading glasses that looked like they hadn't been touched in a while. But the real draw was the setup in the corner: a laptop connected to three monitors, cables sprawled across the floor like a digital octopus.

Saero-yi's eyes lit up when he saw it. His smile of spontaneous delight made my heart skip a beat, even though I knew better than to get all mushy in a situation like this – I could practically hear Margo Daniels berating me for it. He didn't waste any time, he practically sprinted across the room and plopped down in the chair in front of the screens, his fingers already flying across the keyboard like he was born to do this. And in his case, I reminded myself, he actually was.

Meanwhile, Captain Hong started setting out bowls of rice and a bunch of side dishes on the low table. The food was colorful and fresh, and my stomach growled embarrassingly loud at the sight of it. I hadn't realized how hungry I was until I saw the spread. There was kimchi, pickled radishes, seasoned spinach, and a small plate of grilled fish that smelled like umami heaven.

"Soju," Captain Hong said, pouring a clear liquid

from a small, brightly colored bottle into a tiny cup and pushing it toward me. "Infused with herbs. Good for calming the nerves."

I picked up the cup and took a small sip. It was strong, like wine, but smoother and more warming. Definitely a step up from the kegger beer our classmates served at house parties.

"I know that Doctor Jang sent you," I began, trying to keep my voice casual as I picked up a pair of chopsticks and grabbed some rice. "Where is she now?"

Captain Hong hesitated for a second, before he answered. "Doctor Jang is no longer in the vicinity," he said, carefully avoiding my gaze. So – he'd decided to be at least partially truthful. "She had to return."

"To North Korea?" I asked, my chopsticks hovering over the kimchi.

His eyes flicked up to meet mine for a brief moment before he went back to setting the table. "Her work is delicate. It requires her presence there."

I nodded, even though I had no idea what that really meant. But it did confirm one thing; Susie Jang was holding up her end of whatever deal she'd made with CIA. She was still tied up in whatever was going on in North Korea, and that meant she was still involved in Saero-yi's life in a big way.

Saero-yi, meanwhile, was completely absorbed in whatever he was doing on the laptop. The screens in front of him were filled with lines of code that meant absolutely nothing to me, but the way he was working, it was clear this was important. I tried to focus on the food in front of me, but my mind kept drifting back to Captain Hong. If Dr. Jang had instructed him to look after her brother, then he was more than just some helpful fisherman. The computer set-up suggested immediately that he was her asset. If so – did he even realize that he wasn't working for North Korea?

Keeping track of the allegiances of a double agent was no picnic. One slip, a word to the wrong person, I reflected, and the game could be up. Hong had to be her asset on the South Korean side – she couldn't risk either me or Saero-yi tripping her up, if he was undercover DPRK. Not North Korean and also, not CIA, I suspected. Daniels had to be looking for us, too. She wouldn't appreciate Hong letting Saero-yi loose on a computer system she couldn't control.

I picked at the grilled fish, chewing slowly as I tried to piece everything together. "So," I said, after a moment of silence, "you're here to protect Saero-yi. That's why Susie Jang sent you, right?"

Captain Hong didn't look up from the table, but I could see the tension in his shoulders. "I was asked to help, yes. But I'm not the only one who's been keeping an eye on things."

That caught my attention. I set down my chopsticks and leaned forward, trying to get a read on him. "What do you mean?"

He finally looked up, but I was no clearer about his feelings on the matter. "There are others who care about Saero-yi's safety. People who have been watching for a long time."

"Oka-ay," I said, slowly, trying to manage my growing confusion. Had I underestimated him? What did he mean? CIA? DPRK? I widened my horizons. Atlas Group? Maxim Santiago? There were competing interests, when it came to the 'unicorns.'

The truth was, I wasn't even sure where Saero-yi's own preference lay. Only that like me, he seemed to feel some obligation to help Maxim. As for his future, I knew almost nothing. Other than what he'd expressed, or begun to express, with that kiss. I shrugged off the flip of my stomach at the memory. Maybe it had been a thing of the moment, something he'd deny if I reminded him.

Suddenly, Saero-yi's chair scraped against the floor as he pushed back from the desk, a satisfied grin spreading across his face. "It's done," he said, his voice tinged with relief. "Maxim has his money."

I blinked, trying to catch up. "That's it? Just like that?"

He nodded, eyes bright as they met mine. "I'd already done most of the prep, in the embassy. Now we've transferred the funds and triggered the jackpotting on the cash machines. Maxim's street team in Mexico will pick it up, and that's the end of it."

I felt a huge wave of relief wash over me. It was over. Saero-yi had done what he promised, which meant that I'd done what I promised. I stood up, crossing the room to where he was sitting, and wrapped my arms around him in a tight hug. "You did it," I whispered, my voice thick with emotion.

He hugged me back, his grip strong and reassuring. "Yeah," he murmured. "It's over. We're both free."

But before we could even start to savor the victory, a loud hammering on the door shattered the moment. The sound echoed through the small house, and my heart lurched in my chest.

Captain Hong was on his feet in an instant, his eyes flashing with alarm as he moved toward the door. My pulse raced as a thousand possibilities flashed through my mind. We'd been found – but by who?

Hong cracked open the door and then leapt back as from outside, a determined palm shoved the door towards his face. On the doorstep stood Targeting

Officer Margo Daniels, her cheeks flushed, eyes blazing with a mix of outrage and frustration.

In the dim light of the porch, her eyes located mine, her gaze boring into them. "Oh, honeybun, think you can just slip away?" she crooned, her voice dripping with disdain. "You think you can outsmart me?"

FORTY

TIME TO COLLECT

My blood ran cold the instant Margo Daniels stepped into the room with a face like a storm cloud ready to unleash its fury. Saero-yi was already on his feet, his expression ambivalent. *Here comes one of those monologues*, I thought. Her eyes zeroed in on me, then Saero-yi, and before I could even brace myself, she started in on us.

"Jumping off a yacht into the open sea?" she spat. "What were you thinking? You know the risks, Veronica! You had a death wish, or maybe a capture wish. North Koreans don't play games, honey. You two are lucky you didn't end up as prizes on some North Korean intelligence officer's mantelpiece."

Well, I can get furious, too. "Oh, really? Like I didn't know. You're the one who made us believe we'd been captured by North Koreans. Wasn't that the whole point of the test, to see if I'd escape? This is on you, Margo."

To my amazement, a transformation came over Daniels's face. The thunderous expression vanished, replaced by a warm, beatific smile. She lifted a hand to her mouth and I swear, I heard something like a strangled sob. Now totally confused, I gaped. "What's wrong?"

There was a pause, then a quiet chuckle. "You're

right, of course. Nothing more important than escape. Not a single thing, not even your secrets. Any operative who returns to us after being captured is worth their weight in gold. More than that, even! Intelligence like that can't be bought." She gave me a grudging nod. "Just that, well, you put yourself in more danger than we expected."

I wasn't ready to back down so easily. "If it was a test, why did you leave scuba equipment there? You must know I'd recently trained to use it – you had a guy following us to the diving lakes, for chrissakes."

Daniels pursed her lips. "You may have a point. We should have vetted the yacht more carefully."

"You underestimated her," Saero-yi told Daniels. He shook his head in disappointment. "You failed to protect an asset."

"And it's not the first time," I added, accusingly. "What about Alaska?"

She drew herself up tall, shoulders thrown back, winding up to give us the full Targeting Officer Margo Daniels experience, when Cha-young appeared in the doorway. I don't know how she manages to appear out of nowhere like some kind of stealthy, impeccably dressed ghost, cool and detached.

Cha-young waited a beat, exuding cold determination as her eyes flicked between Daniels and Saero-yi. Then she said something in Korean, her voice smooth and authoritative. She could have spoken slowly, and I still wouldn't have understood a word, but in my head I sensed Saero-yi telepathically translating. *She says it's time to go. Now.*

"What?" I shot back at him. "Just like that?"

Saero-yi shifted on his feet, fingers twitching. *She means it. There's a car outside.* I could sense his reluctance radiating off him.

Daniels, meanwhile, was glaring at Cha-young. "And what exactly are you saying, Ms. Seoul Intelligence?" she drawled, folding her arms. She definitely got pricklier when someone threatened her authority.

Cha-young wasn't exactly one to back down either. Switching to English she said, "We don't have time for this, Officer Daniels. Jang Saero-yi needs to come with me. Not another moment can he be trusted in this... delicate situation." Her gaze landed briefly on me. "South Korea needs him."

The words 'not trusted' hit like a punch in the gut. What was she saying – that Saero-yi was some kind of loose cannon? A danger? I looked over at him, but he just stood there, his face a stony mask.

Daniels, to her credit, held her ground. "Hey, Langley funded half of this operation. He's not a pawn for you to just whisk away whenever you feel like it."

But Cha-young had already shifted gears, her voice lowering into something almost... soft. "Then I suggest you take it up with my superiors at the National Intelligence Service, Officer Daniels, because we're in my country now, and it's our time to collect. And quite seriously, we don't have time for this," she repeated, but the sharp edges had smoothed out. She stepped closer to Saero-yi, her face now open, earnest. "Listen, Saero-yi," she said, glancing at him, "I know this is hard. But this isn't about you anymore. It's about all of us. Millions of lives are at risk. South Koreans... North Koreans, too. You know the Kim doesn't care about his people. He sees them as his vassals, cogs in a machine that serves him. And you've seen the inside of that machine."

Saero-yi stayed silent, but I could feel his resistance crumbling.

Cha-young's voice dropped even lower, almost a

whisper. "We need you," she said. "And you owe us. We got you out of a bad situation. Away from your controller. But now... now you're never going to be safe without us. You have to face up to that. We can protect you, but only if you come with me. Right now."

Daniels sighed, rubbing a hand over her face like she was deciding whether to intervene or not. But I could tell even she couldn't deny what Cha-young was saying.

Cha-young stepped closer to Saero-yi, looking him dead in the eye. "This isn't just about hacking or cyberwarfare. You know that. They're watching for you. They look like us, they sound like us. Every CIA safe house in Incheon? North Korean intelligence, the RGB, they could eventually find them all. You're not safe here, not anywhere. Unless you leave with me. Now."

Saero-yi finally met her gaze, his eyes a mix of determination and something else. Fear? Resignation? Maybe a little of both.

"I need time to think," he said softly, but it was a weak protest, like even he knew he didn't have any time left.

Cha-young's demeanor shifted again, disarmingly warm now. "It's over," she said gently. "And now, you need to come with me."

I knew then that he was going. This was it. The whole room seemed to shrink around me, like I was watching it all from inside a tiny, fragile bubble that could pop at any second. Saero-yi turned to me, and our eyes locked.

I thought back to our kiss, that one moment of reckless, sweet insanity that now felt so far away, even though it had only been yesterday. I had just started to feel... connected. Like maybe, just maybe, this was something that could be real. That despite all the chaos,

I could allow myself to feel something other than fear and anxiety. But it was slipping away, just like Maxim and Sacha had before him. Every time I let myself begin to fall for a guy, the universe seemed hell-bent on yanking them away from me. Was this the price for living in this world of shadowy deals and constant danger? No possibility for love, just fleeting moments that were gone before you could even really grasp them?

My chest felt tight. I wanted to say something profound, or maybe even something faintly ridiculous, like, "Don't go," but the words stuck in my throat.

Saero-yi moved closer to me and his eyes softened. He reached out, hesitating for a second before pulling me into a hug. He was warm, solid, and for just a moment, I let myself sink into that. His chin rested on top of my head, and I could feel the steady rhythm of his breathing. I wanted to memorize that feeling, to keep it in some corner of my mind where I could pull it out whenever I felt like the ground was slipping away again.

Take care of yourself.

I nodded against his chest, swallowing the lump in my throat. I didn't trust myself to speak.

He pulled back, just enough to look me in the eyes. *The hardest part is over.*

He was trying to comfort me, like everything would be fine now that he was out of the immediate danger zone. But deep down, I knew this was just a pause. The danger never really went away, did it? It just changed forms, wore different faces.

Saero-yi took a deep breath and stepped back. The loss of his warmth was immediate and sharp, like a brisk chill slicing through the room.

I opened my mouth, ready to say something –

anything – but the moment passed, the quiet broken by the sound of Cha-young clearing her throat. "We need to go now," she said, her voice resolute.

Daniels watched all this with a mix of mild interest and impatience, like she was watching a tennis final, but needed to get away for a Teams meeting.

When Saero-yi turned to leave, my heart lurched in my chest. I wasn't ready for him to walk out of my life, not after everything we'd been through. But that seemed to have become normal in my world now, and I didn't get to decide when people left.

As Saero-yi and Cha-young headed for the door, Daniels raised an eyebrow and then, with a surprising amount of sincerity, said, "C'mon, sugar. I know a way to cheer you up."

Saero-yi glanced back at me, offering a small, almost rueful smile. I didn't know what Daniels had in mind, but for once, I wasn't in the mood for surprises. The knot in my stomach tightened as the door closed behind them.

And just like that, he was gone.

FORTY-ONE

GOODBYE PIE

The kitchen of Captain Hong's house was tiny, its single work bench busy with the blue-stripey plastic bags of groceries that Daniels had brought with her. In silence he watched from the doorway until with a motion of her hand she dismissed him. "Thanks, Cap. You did real good, leave this with me, now. We'll talk soon."

She gestured at me to join her, unpacking saltine crackers, a stick of cold butter, a carton of heavy cream and a half dozen bright yellow lemons. I glanced around the kitchen, cozy but cluttered and clean, chipped ceramic mixing bowls, metal skillets hanging from the wall, a heavy stock pot on the stove, and one high shelf lined with neatly arranged, colorful bottles of infused alcohol.

"You remember what we ate, when we first met?" she said, easing us out of the tension that had started to build.

A little suspiciously, I replied, "At the diner? Atlantic Beach pie, you mean?"

She beamed. "Knew you'd remember." Daniels stood at the counter, her hands moving with practiced ease as she crushed saltine crackers for the crust. Her motions were quick, confident, like someone who could make this pie in her sleep.

I leaned against the counter, arms crossed, trying to seem casual even though my mind was a whirl of thoughts. "So, this pie. It's supposed to make tough decisions easier?"

She passed me the butter and a small skillet from the wall. "Melt this, would you?"

I did as she asked. Daniels didn't look up from her task, just kept crushing the crackers into fine crumbs. "Maybe not easier, sugar, but it sure makes them taste better." She gave me a quick smile before dumping the crumbs into a bowl and adding the butter I'd melted. "When you're faced with big decisions, it helps to have something sweet to end the day with."

The aroma of the buttery, salty crackers mixed with the sharp scent of lemon, creating a blend that was as comforting as it was strange in this setting. I managed to smile, although the weight of what she'd just said wasn't lost on me. The truth was, I felt like I was standing on the edge of a cliff, and the only thing keeping me from falling was this absurd pie-making session.

As Daniels mixed the crumbs with the butter, I tried to focus on the task at hand, but my thoughts kept drifting back to Saero-yi. I felt my throat clench at the thought of him being moved somewhere even more secure, somewhere I'd never see him again. Just when we were starting to understand each other, maybe even more than that. He'd be the first two-dub I'd gotten close enough to say that about. Maxim and Sacha had their differences, yet they'd both succeeded at keeping me further away than I'd have liked.

But of course, I couldn't say any of this out loud. Not to Daniels. She'd see it as a weakness, a distraction. I could already imagine her telling me to get over it, to

249

compartmentalize. The thought made me grit my teeth. "So, where do we go from here?" I said.

"It's simple." She flashed me a grin. "Make me a podcast."

I tried to conceal my surprise – this wasn't what I'd expected. "What exactly do you want me to say?"

Daniels set the pie crust aside and began zesting a lemon, her movements deliberate. "I think you know what I'm about to ask. And before I do that, I want you to know that I need not just an honest response, but a considered one. Especially if your answer is 'yes.' So – what with you being a podcaster, I thought I'd ask you to express your answer that way."

Her words hit harder than I expected, and I struggled to keep my expression neutral. She was right, of course. I knew what she wanted to ask me. And it wasn't to join some after-school club – it was a risky proposition, with potential to seriously impact or even end my life.

I wasn't even sure that I *could* make any decision like that, not when my head was still spinning with everything that had happened. Saero-yi's face flashed in my mind, and my stomach did that idiotic fluttery thing again. I didn't even know when that had started, but now it seemed like every time I thought of him, my thoughts became this jumbled mess. Then there was Maxim – always in the background, always this complicated, unresolved thing between us. I still wasn't sure how I felt about him, but the idea of never figuring it out left a sour taste in my mouth.

And Kenzie, too. I couldn't leave him dangling forever.

"You're getting that look again," Daniels said, snapping me back to the present. "You've got too many damn thoughts runnin' around in that cute head of yours."

I sighed, trying to shove the thoughts away, but they lingered stubbornly. "It's not easy, you know? I keep thinking about all these people who've come into my life and then just… left. Or had to leave. And now you're telling me that Saero-yi's going to be moved somewhere secure, where I probably won't ever see him again. It really sucks."

Daniels's eyes narrowed, but not in the way I'd expected. "Roni, I've told you before, you can't let your heart lead you in this line of work. You've got to be smart, be in control. Emotional entanglements, especially in this business, are dangerous. They make you weak, and weakness gets you killed."

Her words stung, even though I knew she was right. But still, it felt like she was asking me to cut out a part of myself, the part that felt and cared. The part that was maybe just beginning to love.

I turned back to the counter, focusing on pressing the crust into the pie pan with my fingers. The buttery, salty crumbs stuck to my skin, and I had to concentrate to keep the layer even. "So, what are you saying? That I should just stop caring about people? Because I'm pretty sure that's not how it works."

Daniels's expression softened, just a little. "I'm not saying stop caring, sugar. I'm saying you need to learn how to separate what's important from what is not. Saero-yi, Maxim, Sacha – heck, I'm sure they're all fine young fellas in their own ways. But you can't let yourself get so wrapped up in them that you lose sight of the bigger picture. Have your fun, sure. Find yourself a nice boy outside of all this craziness, if that's what you need. But don't let it interfere with what you're capable of achieving with me, with the Agency."

I could feel the frustration bubbling up inside me, but I swallowed it down. She didn't get it. This wasn't just about 'having fun' or finding some random guy to distract myself with. These were people who'd walked in and out of my life, leaving marks that I wasn't ready to erase. But how could I explain that without sounding like a naive kid?

Daniels finished pouring the lemon custard into the pie crust, then slid the pan into the oven. She wiped her hands on a towel and turned to me, her expression unreadable. "Look, Roni. I wouldn't be offering this to you if I didn't think you had what it takes. But this life, it's not for everyone. You have to be ready to make sacrifices, to let go of things that are holding you back."

I stared at the closed oven door, watching the heat waves dance behind the glass. "But what if I don't want to let go?" The question slipped out before I could stop it.

Daniels's lips pressed into a thin line. "Then you'd better make sure that whatever you're holding onto is worth more than what you're letting go of."

Her words hung in the air, like smoke. I didn't have an answer for that. I wasn't sure what was worth more. But the thought of never seeing Saero-yi again, of him being whisked away to some secure bunker, where he'd be safe but completely out of reach – it made me feel like I was losing something important. Something I hadn't even had a chance to really understand.

"Listen," Daniels said, her tone softening slightly. "I know this is a lot to take in. No need to make up your mind right this second. But I do need you to think about it seriously. And I want you to make that podcast. Not for me, but for yourself. So that you can figure out what you really want."

I nodded slowly, the idea of sitting down in front of

a camera and spilling my thoughts out into a video both terrifying and strangely appealing. It was a chance to sort through everything – to figure out what the hell I was doing with my life. But at the same time, it felt like I was being forced into making a choice I wasn't ready to make.

"Alright," I said finally, my voice steady despite the turmoil inside me. "I'll do it."

Daniels gave me a small, approving nod, like I'd passed some kind of test I didn't even know I was taking. "Good. Now, I need to do some work while we wait for that pie. Then we'll see if we can't make the rest of the world disappear for a little while, huh?"

With that, she turned to her phone and proceeded to ignore me for the next twenty minutes, while I resorted to flicking through the small collection of well-thumbed paperbacks on the shelf. One of them was 'Jaws' by Peter Benchley. Huh. I didn't know that movie was based on a book.

The pie came out golden and perfect, the crust flaky and crisp, the filling set just right. Looking like a proud mamma, Daniels spooned whipped cream over the pie, practically cooing with satisfaction. It was the kind of pie that made you feel like everything might be okay, even when you knew it probably wasn't.

In the Incheon safe house's small living room, I knelt down beside the low table, where she was already helping herself to a slice of pie, gesturing for me to join her. No CIA, no telepaths, no impossible choices. Just me, Daniels, and a chunk of goodbye pie.

But as I took my first bite, the reality of what was happening came crashing back down. Saero-yi was going to be moved, and I was going to be left behind. The podcast I'd agreed to make loomed over me, and with it, the decision that would change everything.

Daniels watched me, her expression softer now, but there was still that edge of expectation, of judgment. "You know, Roni," she said, her voice low, "sometimes the hardest part of this job isn't the missions or the danger. It's the choices we have to make, the things we have to give up."

I met her gaze, feeling the weight of her words settling in my chest. "Yeah," I admitted. "I'm starting to get that."

FORTY-TWO

WHEN IDEALS CLASH

Daniels watched me, her gaze steady as we lingered in the quiet after Saero-yi's departure. Still assessing me again, the way she always did, like I was a piece on her chessboard, but not just any piece. Something valuable. Something she worried about losing control over.

"Now, sugar," she murmured, her southern accent softening the sharp edges of her words. "Before we get into the other thing, there's something else we need to talk about. Lord knows, I've been putting it off long enough."

I didn't like the way she leaned in, or the way her tone dropped to the level of seriousness I'd heard her use when she wanted to unload some ugly truth. It wasn't her 'you screwed up' voice, more her 'this is for your own good' voice, which somehow felt worse. I braced myself, already dreading whatever was coming next.

"I need you to rethink your attachment to Kenzie," she announced, dropping the words like lead weights.

I froze, fork midway to my mouth. The darn woman was steps ahead of me.

Daniels leaned back on her wrists, eyes on mine. "He's a security risk, Roni. And we both know it."

"Daniels, I mean Margo," I started, but she held up a hand, to silence me.

"I'm not saying he's done anything yet," she continued, "but let me say my piece. Kenzie is loyal to you. I don't doubt that. But loyalty only goes so far when you're asking someone to go against their core beliefs. And Kenzie? He's anti-CIA. Opposed to everything we stand for."

"Yeah, well, maybe that's because he's, you know, not a fan of the whole disrupting political situations in other countries thing," I throw back, more defensive than I intended.

"Which is exactly my point," she replied, calmly, making no attempt to deny the accusation. "You might trust him now, Roni, but what happens when push comes to shove? When his ideals clash with what you're involved in? When he's staring down a choice between protecting you and staying true to his own values?"

I stared at her, trying to force down the rising tide of anxiety in my chest. I wanted to argue, to tell her she had it wrong, that Kenzie would never betray me. But the truth was, I couldn't know that. I'd always suspected that Kenzie saw the world differently than me, when it came to this kind of stuff, that I wasn't as 'pure' as him. Maybe it's because I'd heard my parents justify their crimes with some of the same language. Like money laundering for enemies of the USA shouldn't be a crime, if those enemies had any valid criticisms of US policy. I don't fault him for it. He might even be right. But that didn't make any of this easier.

Daniels pushed aside her plate, on which remained only a smear of the creamy lemon pie. She leaned forward, her eyes narrowed just a fraction. "Look, I'm not asking you to cut him off completely. But you need to keep in mind that his beliefs make him a liability. You can't afford to have someone that close to you who's philosophically opposed to what you might be trying to accomplish."

Uncomfortably, I scooped up the last of my own dessert and chewed, while guilt thickened my throat. Kenzie had been my best friend for years. We'd shared everything, risked our lives together and for each other. He said he loved me, and even if I couldn't return those feelings I couldn't just push him out of my life. I don't know if I could even if I wanted to.

"He wouldn't betray me," I say, my voice quiet but firm. "Kenzie is my family."

Daniels sighed, her patience thinning, though she was still trying to keep her tone gentle. "Roni, hon, it's not about betrayal in the sense you're thinking. People don't always choose to hurt the ones they care about, but they do when their backs are up against the wall. You can love someone and still be fundamentally opposed to what they're doing. Kenzie's got a line in the sand, and sooner or later, he's gonna reach it."

I shook my head, trying to clear the tangled mess of emotions churning inside me. "I know Kenzie has feelings for me," I admitted, barely above a whisper. "And I don't feel the same way, not exactly. But that doesn't mean he'd turn on me."

Daniels didn't flinch, didn't offer any reassurance. She only watched me with that cold, pragmatic gaze, waiting for me to catch up. "Family is one thing, but…" she made a whirling gesture with her hands, over her heart. "The mushy stuff? You don't need to feel guilty about *that*," she said bluntly. "All that is a distraction, and you know it. If you're worried about what he wants from you, you've already lost focus. If you're keeping him around out of loyalty, or guilt, or whatever, you're only setting yourself up for trouble."

Frustrated, I ground my teeth some. Her words hit

way too close to home. I hated that she was right, that she saw through me, could pinpoint the exact fears I'd been pushing down for weeks. And I especially hated that she didn't seem to give a damn about how I felt.

But then again, I reminded myself, this was Targeting Officer Margo Daniels. Not my therapist, not my friend. As much as I might want to believe that there was a human being buried somewhere beneath her layers of Southern steel and CIA pragmatism, I knew better than to start expecting sympathy from her now.

"Look," I began, trying to keep my voice steady, "Kenzie's been there for me. He's always had my back."

"And I'm not sayin' he hasn't," she countered. "But what happens when what you're doing becomes more than he can stomach? When his principles get in the way of your work? Can you honestly say he'd put you first if it came to that?"

The question lingered in the air between us, a messy tangle. I had no answer. Not one that I was ready to admit, anyhow.

"I know this isn't easy," Daniels said, her tone softening just a little. "But you need to keep your eye on *your* future, sugar. You're not a kid anymore. This is no high school drama. If – and that's a big if – we do this, you'd be stepping into a world where people's lives are on the line, where secrets and alliances and who you trust can mean the difference between survival and failure. Dead weight is only gonna drag you down."

Her words cut deep; I sensed the sting of tears threatening to surface. I didn't want to believe that Kenzie could ever be 'dead weight.' He'd been my rock for so long, the one person I could always count on. But now? Now, with everything shifting beneath my feet, I didn't know what to believe anymore.

"Like I said, maybe you should find yourself a new beau," Daniels commented, and there was a flicker of amusement in her eyes as she added, "Someone that's not mixed up in all this. Go have some fun with a guy who has zero interest in politics. Keep it simple, sugar."

I rolled my eyes, more out of habit than anything else.

"Yeah, because that's totally easy. I'll just go find some random chud who works out, or spends all his time gaming and… what? Pretend I'm not wrapped up in this humungous international 'Mind Game?'"

Daniels grinned, but no humor there. "Girl, you're smarter than that. You know what I'm talkin' about. You have a lot of potential, but you need to clear your head. If you're gonna work for me, for Langley, you can't afford to be tangled up in your own feelings all the time. You need to be sharp, focused. Like you were in Cuba. Like you were in Alaska."

I didn't respond right away. What could I say? I'd been tangled up in my feelings since this whole mess started. *Maxim, Sacha, Saero-yi. All two-dubs*, I thought, ruefully. Maybe it was true that I had a thing for them because of their psi powers. And now Kenzie. It's like I couldn't escape the emotional quicksand I'd waded into, and the harder I tried to pull myself out, the deeper I sank.

Daniels didn't care about any of that. As if to hammer her point home, she reminded me: "C'mon. Don't act like I'm trying to recruit some total newbie here. *You* know what you did, what you're capable of. And you know what they're capable of, too. Your buddies, the unicorns."

Then she simply watched me, waiting for me to get it together, to make a decision. I wondered then how much she really knew about the telepathic powers that had appeared in Generation 6. Did she know they could use telepathy as an attack?

I sniffed, cleared my throat, blinked back my angry tears and looked her straight in the eye. "All right, then. Get on with it. You said you were about to ask me, properly. Let's hear it."

FORTY-THREE

MY APPLICATION

"Roni, I could begin by talking turkey – what's in this for you. Because obviously there's a deal on the table. Almost no-one can afford to work for nothing, even though for a lot of our assets, their motivation has nothing to do with money. So let me say from the outset – if you decide to work for me, I'm gonna see that you get a fantastic education, the best money can buy. No-one will ever know that it's funded by Langley, naturally. I'm talking top dollar – tuition, housing, travel, clothing allowance, full health coverage.

"But let's be real. You and me, we're not sitting here just because you're smart, though you sure are. I'm here because I see something in you that most folks wouldn't notice. You've got this instinct, this knack for keeping your head straight when things get intense. You know, when the pressure's on, it's like time slows down, almost like when people are on mushrooms, and suddenly, you're seeing everything more clearly, noticing details that others miss. That's a gift, sugar.

"And there's more to you than that. You've got this rare ability to communicate with psi-powered individuals, and not just communicate, but form real, deep attachments with them. That connection? It's something few people in this world have, and honey, it's going to take you places.

"Now, I know life's been hard for you. I know what happened with your parents, how they got caught up in money laundering and worked with some folks who'd even turned their backs on this country. That's not easy for any kid to carry. I see it in you, how it weighs on you, that guilt by association. You didn't choose their path, but I'm sensing that you feel responsible for it in some way, like you need to set things right. Look, I respect that. That drive to make up for what they did, to prove that you're better than the shadow they cast? That's powerful. It's something that can fuel you – if you allow it."

I felt tears prickle behind my eyes, tried to blink them away. Dammit if this woman hadn't found her way under my skin, knew just how to twist the knife.

She continued, perhaps sensing that she'd found my weak point and was finally homing in on her target.

"Being an intelligence operative isn't just about knowing what to do; it's about acting when the stakes couldn't be higher. Whether you're an officer or an asset, there are moments when the whole world seems to stop, and you've got to make choices that change lives. And I see you, Roni, thriving in those moments – not just because of your instincts, or even your abilities, but because you've got the heart to do this. You've got a purpose that runs deep. With the right training, you could channel all of that – the pain, the guilt, and the strength – into something extraordinary.

"Not everyone has that, Roni Padilla. But you do. And that's why I'm here, because I see the makings of one hell of an asset. And when you're old enough, if you should choose it, a case officer. You've got the potential to be one of the best. I'm here to help you realize it, to help you step out of that shadow and into the light. I'm not even asking you to lie to your friends, the telepaths. The horse bolted that stable, before you and I even met. They're welcome to approach me directly, my door is always open to them. In the meantime, however, I'm hoping they'll see you as a 'back channel' – a way to get messages to us without having to step into the open. Roni, you could help keep the line open, maintain the kind of communication that's kept the world from going 'kaboom' a couple times at least – and that's just the ones we know about."

Yeah, it was a classic motivational speech. And I have to admit, I *was* motivated. So, I began to work on a script for the podcast she'd requested – my 'application' to become what, let's be honest, I already was – Margo Daniels's asset. If she accepted, it would be official.

Margo Daniels. Madge. You know, there's a funny thing about working for 'Langley' as Madge likes to call the CIA. No one tells you that charisma is basically part of the job description. When you're the one getting pulled into this world, you don't really see it coming.

Take Margo Daniels, for example. My very own, slightly terrifying CIA handler. North Carolina's finest – she can disarm a room with a smile, win you over with a piece of pie, while she sets about recruiting you into a sketchy world of espionage with just a hint of promise – or was that a threat? – about my college future.

The truth is, I'm doing this podcast for her. Not for the CIA. No – this one's all for Madge. Officer Daniels, who thought it'd be cool to teach me to bake an Atlantic Beach pie while also convincing me to join her mission of keeping tabs on the psi-powered underground. If you're wondering what the hell that means, you're not alone. I'll need time to figure that part out. It's a process.

But before I dive into all that, let me just set the scene for you, the place where I'm recording this, at my handler's request. Imagine a kitchen that smells like butter and citrus, a countertop covered in crushed salty crackers, and me, sweating it out under the critical gaze of Targeting Officer Daniels, trying to hold onto some semblance of professionalism.

Why? Well, apparently, she believes I have 'potential.' Potential to bridge the gap between her world and the telepaths. Maxim, Atlanta, Sacha, Saero-yi – all of them are playing their own high-stakes games. And me? I'm the one who's supposed to 'keep the line open' while figuring out which side they're on, who they're secretly working for, and what exactly they plan to do next. No pressure or anything.

And hey, if I screw up, I guess there's always pie?

Truth is, it's not like I have too many other options. Daniels made that pretty clear. My college tuition is more or less hanging in the balance, not to mention the ugly cloud of shame which follows me about, thanks to my parents' crimes. Yes, I could walk away, turn my back on all this crazy, hope that a regular old scholarship comes through, brazen it out re Ma and Pa. Change my name, perhaps, so their shame won't stick too hard, when it comes to college funding and job applications.

But when you've seen the things I've seen, walking away is not so easy.

So, here it is: my podcast application to be on payroll as a CIA asset. Something to show future-me – or anyone else that might ask – that I did this of my own accord. Why I'm willing to be on the same side as Margo Daniels in the 'Mind Game.'

My reasons? Where to start? The world's on fire. Literally, in some places. Climate change, global inequality, a dash of nuclear brinkmanship, Czar Ilyin's imperial ambitions and, oh yeah, a candidate for US president who *backed an insurrection and now wants to totally upend our society, with one half of the country egging him on. Potentially a nightmare. And no, this isn't me quoting some dystopian movie script. This is real life.*

Somehow, telepaths are part of this salsa. Sacha Montecristo and Atlanta, two key players from the Atlas Group, a clandestine operation with roots in Russia and zero oversight. Then there's Maxim Santiago – Sacha's brother has been playing his own game for years. A game, by the way, that I have barely begun to untangle. And now, Saero-yi, a former North Korean cyber warrior who does favors for Maxim and is also connected to another telepath, his sister Susie, an undercover CIA asset working in North Korean intelligence.

Daniels thinks I can help her track these people, assess their loyalties, figure out who's pulling their strings. The 'unicorns' don't exactly come with user manuals, you know? They're complicated. Powerful, yes, but not invincible. Like any other humans, they will have weaknesses, they'll have vulnerabilities. Daniels wants to expose and exploit those. She thinks I can help her do it.

Am I qualified? Definitely not. But I know more about these guys than anyone else and now, I've got skin in the game. I've known Maxim since I was a kid. I've worked closely with Sacha, seen what he's capable of, even if he talks a less scary game than his brother Maxim. I've watched Atlanta, seen how they appear to be playing both sides, Maxim as well as the Atlas Group. Maybe one day Atlanta will let me in on the secret of which one they're really allied with. Then there's Saero-yi… well, that's complicated.

Even with hardly any training, I've seen enough to know that these telepaths – for all their powers – they aren't gods. They're just people, and people can be unpredictable. They can lie, cheat, and manipulate. But they can also be loyal. They can care. That's where I operate – a gray zone between 'normies' and 'unicorns.'

As much as I'd like to tell myself I'm doing this out of the goodness of my heart, that I'm some kind of selfless hero fighting for freedom and equality and justice for all, I'm not. There's more than one reason. One is that I'm doing this because I owe it to them. To Maxim, to Sacha, to Saero-yi. Even if they don't see it that way.

Daniels has a plan, naturally. She always has a plan. She wants me to help the West gain the upper hand in this 'Mind Game,' to keep tabs on the telepaths and prevent them from becoming tools for the bad guys. Whether that's the Third Russian Empire, North Korea, or some other shady organization lurking in the shadows, I don't know yet.

But Daniels is good at this. Like, really good. You don't realize how much she's got you until you're halfway through baking a pie and she's asking you to pledge your loyalty to her cause. For sure, there's some charisma involved. The kind of charisma that makes you believe that, yes, maybe you can make a difference. That maybe all of this is worth it. Even if part of you knows there's a darker side to it all, that maybe you're being played. I guess that's the price you pay when you get involved with the CIA.

Maybe I'm ready to step into the arena. To be Madge's girl on the inside, keeping tabs on the telepaths and making sure they don't get used by the wrong people. Hopefully at least I'll get a free college ride out of it.

As for what comes next, well, I'm still figuring that out. But for now, I've got my own pie in the oven, and a lot of questions that need answers.

And Officer Daniels? If you're listening – is this what you hoped to hear? That I'm doing this for you? Because in the end, the truth is that it's you I choose to work with.

Not the Agency. Not the cause. Just you. And that's my second reason for doing this, perhaps the most important one: to prove to everyone that my parents made a terrible mistake, but their values aren't mine. That by joining your team in the 'Mind Game,' I can finally make up for what they did.

A Message from the Author

Thank you so much for reading *Cyber Warrior*, book three of *The Mind Game: Volume One*.

If you have enjoyed this third installment of Roni Padilla's story, it'd be wonderful if you could post a review on Amazon and anywhere else you find your favorite reads, telling other readers what you liked about it. There's nothing like reader recommendations and word of mouth to get a book better known!

Please also sign up to my email newsletter to be the first to find out when new titles will be released, and to hear about special discounts and book giveaways – go to **TheMGHarris.com** and click on **Newsletter**.

I also post book-related content fairly regularly on TikTok: look for **mgharrisbooks.** My Instagram, which is also **mgharrisbooks**, has mostly holiday photos and recipes. You're welcome to stalk me there, too ;)

What's next for Roni Padilla? Well, that's what I'll be thinking about over the next few months. Our world seems to be changing faster than most people expected, and that means the fictional version of it featured in *The Mind Game* probably should, too.

So while I figure that out, in the next book to be published we're going back to where this all began – the Krylov Foundation and the story of how Maxim, Sacha and Atlanta escaped. Watch my newsletter and TikTok for updates about *Jaguar's Realm!*

Born in Mexico, Maria Guadalupe "MG" Harris grew up in Manchester, England. She's been a massive *Doctor Who* and *Blake's 7* fan since childhood.

Her writing addiction began with B7 fanfic. Before being published she was a molecular biologist followed by a stint as an Internet entrepreneur.

MG has authored three book series for young readers. *The Joshua Files* (Scholastic Children's Books UK), which was translated into 17 foreign languages, *Gemini Force One* (Orion Children's Books) and a young adult crime trilogy, *Emancipated* (Harper Teen, as M.G. Reyes), as well a novel for the Doctor Who universe – *Doctor Who - Doom's Day: Extraction Point* (Penguin RH).

Sacha Montecristo looked at the fence. He'd never seen it quite so clearly before, never with so much fear. Soon, his friend Flycatcher would be on the other side, in the outside world. Most likely, he'd never see her again.

Eva, not 'Flycatcher,' he reminded himself, enjoying the sound of her real name in his head. She'd given him permission to use that private name when they were alone. And she'd agreed to call him 'Sacha' but sometimes she forgot and called him by his camp name instead: 'Blackbird.'

He'd woken early that morning, two weeks after his twelfth birthday, his belly hard with knots. The day had arrived. Eva had been sold to a controller. Everyone left the Foundation when they reached eighteen; you got used to it. But no one he ever *really* cared about.

He was as far out as you could be from the campus, right on the perimeter, the shouts of kids circling the softball court on their bikes only just audible. He took another step towards the fence, closer now, beyond the line of giant mango trees. Their dense, dark foliage was laden with heavy fruits that hung from their long stems. Viewed from within the grounds of the Foundation, the trees obscured most of the fence's parallel wires. With the tip of his navy-blue cotton neckerchief he wiped a thin film of sweat from his upper lip. The sun was high now and the air was thick with heat, sweet with the scent of the pine forest beyond the perimeter.

There hadn't been enough food at breakfast, but Sacha hadn't dared to raid the pantry again. He'd sat with other kids, watching out of the corner of his eye. Across the room, Eva had been surrounded by friends close to her own age, five or six years older than him.

Quietly, without using the actual words, she was saying goodbye.

The tightness in his guts had worsened. He couldn't bear to watch. Hunger had driven him out to the edge of the grounds, to check if the mangoes were ready, licking his lips at the thought of that honey-sweet fruit. But although he looked hard he found nothing ripe enough to eat.

His stomach growling, he turned his gaze upon the electrified perimeter fence – the fence that loomed larger in his mind every time he heard one of those stories about escape.

He tried hard not to think about the kids that had died, trying to escape. He'd been to every funeral. Grim as the occasions were, they were compulsory. Six boxes he'd watched being put into the ground. Six teenagers – one of them only thirteen.

When kids ran, it was because they were close to reaching the age where they were put up for auction. Even though six were known to have died, rumors went round that escape was possible, that it had already been done. That in the end, it came down to the question of electricity.

How many seconds did the electrical current last?

Ten seconds and you were in with a chance, he figured. If the rumors could be believed, the current alternated: on and off for ten seconds at a time.

I could make it over in ten.

Blackbird, stop! What if you can't? Then you're toast. Well, pork crackling, more like.

Sacha managed to drag his stare away from the fence. He scanned the wooded area for the source of the voice in his head.

You're thinking about those escape stories, aren't you? The stories about the kid they call the Rabbit.

Flycatcher? Eva… Where are you?

She came into view then, strolling between two mango trees, her ash-blonde ponytail swinging behind her head. Like him and just over half of the young residents and *all* of the adults of the Krylov Foundation, Eva was white, her Slavic heritage obvious. It wasn't the only factor that made him wonder whether they were related, but it was probably one of the first that had triggered his curiosity.

One of the annoying things about not being told who your family were meant that everyone obsessed over details like that. But he already knew enough about how genetics worked to realize there was a chance that none of them were related. They were being bred for their talents but also and rather obviously, for their skin color and ethnic heritage.

Sacha had assumed it was so they'd blend in wherever they ended up. Yet Eva was heading to Singapore, an Asian country where white people were rare. So it couldn't just be about that – or they'd have picked one of the two-dubs with Asian heritage.

The early morning sun lit the trees behind her, framing the slender teenager in silhouette. Sacha held his breath for a second, startled by how grown-up she looked dressed in scarlet and black, the dress uniform of the Krylov Foundation.

Eva made him feel like a kid. Sometimes he liked that. But sometimes it made him feel irritated, uncomfortable. She was smiling but he didn't need to use his skills as an Empath to sense her true feelings. The sadness was all there in her eyes.

When Eva reached him, he glanced around, unsure where to look. He was tall for his almost-thirteen years, but she, at almost eighteen, was still a good two inches taller.

Don't get obsessed about the fence, Blackbird. I don't want to hear your name on that list of dead kids.

The one you called 'the Rabbit' didn't die.

The Rabbit! I wish I'd never even told you about him.
If it makes you feel better – I already knew.

"So – you're going," Sacha said aloud, his voice so tense that he almost had to whisper to keep it from cracking.

Eva nodded. "Coming to see me off?"

He glanced downwards, shook his head. He'd promised himself that he wouldn't cry.

Okay, we'll say goodbye here, just the two of us.

He nodded, still unable to look her in the eye.

Give me a hug then.

He didn't move. If she hugged him he'd cry, he was sure of that.

Eva hesitated for another second, then wrapped her arms around him. He stood awkwardly, unsure what to do with his own arms. She planted a light kiss on his forehead.

Bye, Sacha. Take care. Don't forget me.

He said nothing, trembling from the effort to control his emotions.

And don't cut your hair. It's cute like this – scruffy and blond.

Eva ruffled his hair with one hand, until it was scrunched high up on his head. He pushed her away, pretended to be crosser than he really was.

I'm gonna cut it. I look like a girl!

Eva pouted in mock disappointment. "And drop the obsession with Arabic! If you have to study an extra language in your spare time, make it Mandarin!"

His heart fluttered. There could only be one reason for her to say that. "They want me to learn Polish next."

"But try? At least *try.*"

If Sacha didn't speak at least one Chinese language then the odds were that he and Eva would never see each other again. Her controller was in a place called *Singapore* and they spoke Mandarin there. Sacha had run the atlas program on a computer, when he'd heard.

Singapore, he wondered. *What goes on there?*

"Watch out for Cayman," Eva said. She was fidgeting with the gray metal buttons on her jacket now. Soft, long-lashed eyes were on his, sad and serious. Sacha could feel her reluctance to leave. She was holding back something stronger than a few tears. "When you move up to the seniors, I mean. Cayman doesn't really like being a sentinel. What he really likes is to hurt you younger kids."

Sacha gave a brief nod. Eva had already given him the heads up about Cayman, twenty-four years old, real name 'Anton Trinidad.' Right now Cayman didn't pay much attention to him, thank goodness, but he'd heard all the stories. Once he turned thirteen he'd be moved into Cayman's group. Then he'd really have to be careful.

Sacha, listen. Never tell them all the things you can do with your mind. Never! Just let them carry on believing that you're a regular two-dub, like me.

Sacha didn't respond. A strange numbness was descending over him. It seemed so unreal that this was the last time they would speak for years – maybe forever. His mind, his feelings just didn't want to accept it.

Stay out of trouble. And study hard so they find you a good controller. Most of all, forget that you ever heard about the Rabbit.

Finally, he looked right at Eva. She stared back. He tried hard not to notice the film of tears in her eyes. With his right hand, he reached out, tentatively and touched her arm. Eva's eyes followed his movement, an instance of surprise. After a second, she smiled.

I'll miss you, little brother.

Sacha's breath stilled. If only it were literally true. Then he and Eva would be linked to each other for ever, joined by a shared, eternal ache; the parents they would never know.

I wish you weren't going.
Me too. Wish I could stay to watch out for you.

Sacha summoned all his nerve, steadied his gaze. *One day, it'll be me who watches out for you.*

Eva grinned suddenly, touched a finger to his cheek. "I believe you."

At that moment, so did he.

Which meant that one way or another, Sacha was going over that fence.

www.ingramcontent.com/pod-product-compliance
Lightning Source LLC
Chambersburg PA
CBHW030323200626
46816CB00006BA/1899